THE HOUDINI KILLER

ALSO BY P MOSS

fiction

VEGAS TABLOID
VEGAS KNOCKOUT
BLUE VEGAS

non-fiction

LIQUID VACATION

THE HOUDINI KILLER

P MOSS

Squidhat Press • Las Vegas, Nevada

Editor: Scott Dickensheets
Designer: Sue Campbell
Author Photo: Ginger Bruner

First Edition

ISBN: 978-1-64921-996-1 (print)
ISBN: 987-1-64921-781-3 (ebook)

Published by:

Squidhat Press
848 N. Rainbow Blvd. #889
Las Vegas, Nevada 89107

Printed in the United States of America

For Jay & Star

CHAPTER 1

The heavy guitar case made Evie lurch to one side as she walked out of the pawn shop and made her way through the East Village, fighting off the glare of a fierce summer sun as she cut over a couple blocks to Bowery, a boulevard of broken dreams where bums, dipsos and the hopelessly insane slept in doorways and fought over cigarette butts. Brown hair with a bit of natural curl hung halfway down Evie's back while oppressive humidity added weight to her jeans and sweat under the arms of a well-worn New York Dolls T-shirt. Two more blocks to go as she trudged past squalid flophouses and rescue missions in the direction of a condemned turn-of-the-century bottle factory that squatters had converted into artists' lofts. No water or electricity and the elevator had been out of service for years, so Evie lugged the guitar up six flights of stairs. Knocked on a door, then banged louder until her boyfriend, Ricky, opened up.

"Shit," he grumbled, hand shaking as he grabbed his guitar. "I thought you were Dee Dee."

"Where's the rest of the band? I got your guitar out of hock so you could practice for your show tomorrow night."

"Get off my ass!" Ricky snapped. Skinny with spiked hair and scratching himself with both hands under a T-shirt with the sleeves torn off as he kicked a pizza box toward a bunch of empty beer bottles. Leaned out a broken window beside a long extension cord used to rip off electricity from the building next door and anxiously looked down the street in both directions.

"I don't get it, Ricky. Why bother with the band at all if you're just going to sit around and get high?"

"Same reason as every guitar player. To get laid."

"And I was just next in line?"

"Did you think we were going to get serious?" He eyed her up and down. "I mean, you're not exactly a looker."

Evie threw a bottle at him.

"Don't sweat it, chicken," he laughed as the missile sailed wide. "None of this is serious. Not you and me, not the band, none of it. Do you think by the time the seventies are over that anybody will remember the Dolls? Or Blondie or the Ramones or any of them? Hell no. This whole downtown scene is nothing but empty rebellion."

"Rock and roll was born out of rebellion."

"Wrong. Early rock and roll was about fast cars, going steady and teenagers having a good time."

Point taken. But waiting for a connection and shooting dope was not Evie Eastway's idea of a good time. She picked up the guitar case, pulled open the door and hit the stairs.

"Hey!" Ricky yelled after her. "Where the hell you think you're going?"

CHAPTER 2

Having changed out of the sweaty T-shirt and jeans and into a comfortable sundress, Evie enjoyed a plate of cold sesame noodles as she gazed out the window of her eleventh floor sublet as dusk began to settle upon the East Village. Feeling good about getting her money back after re-pawning Ricky's guitar. Relieved that the misguided fling had flamed out so that thoughts of love could return to men who might actually be attracted by her looks and her talent, not men whose excuse for not showering was that they did not have indoor plumbing.

She flipped through the *Daily News*, perusing the latest scoop about the notorious serial killer Son of Sam, who had been running up the score in the outer boroughs. Thinking that even with some lunatic snuffing girls all over the city, the worst day in New York was still a damn sight better than the best day in Clifton, New Jersey. A suffocating little burg where the twenty-three-year old aspiring writer had come of age before migrating across the river to chase her dream. Getting a job at St. Mark's Bookshop, then later switching to bartending because the money was better and she could afford to move out of the cramped railroad flat on Ludlow Street she had shared with two roommates. Evie wondered if Son of Sam had roommates. The most talked-about man in New York, yet nobody knew anything about him. An anomaly in a city bursting with knowledge about almost everything.

New York was a city so uniquely ripe with personality that adventure lurked around every corner. Where fascination could sometimes be stoked even without leaving home, evidenced when the evening sky completed its transition to darkness and windows began to illuminate in the neighboring buildings, allowing Evie to see inside the apartments of once perfect strangers whose habits had become familiar. Seemingly average people caught in their most private moments who would become characters in the voyeuristic tapestry Evie was writing about New York life, woven together by the voice of a curious neighbor.

Through high-powered binoculars she invaded the privacy of a baldy, way too old to be playing air guitar. A couple fencing in their living room and a housewife in curlers who pleasured herself with the vegetables she would serve her husband for dinner. But the apartment of the neighbor who interested her the most was still dark. A handsome man around thirty on the ninth floor of a white brick mid-rise one avenue over who wore suits to work, drank imported beer and brought home Indian food more often than he didn't. Spent most evenings reading and, in Evie's mind, any man who picked up a book when he didn't have to was sexy. But tonight, the sexy stranger disappointed her as he had not yet come home, so Evie shifted her gaze two floors above to look in on a buttoned-down middle-aged couple sitting on their couch watching television. Boring as wheat toast, until the wife left the room and Evie saw the husband put some sort of powder in her drink and stir it well to make certain it would not be detected.

Evie's first instinct was to call the police. And tell them what? That she saw a man poison his wife from a block away. Too late anyway as the woman returned and drank the tainted beverage, nodded forward and lost consciousness. But through sharp focus, Evie could see that the woman was breathing. Saw the man poke her to make sure that she was out cold, then get up and change his clothes. Feeling like an idiot for allowing an overactive imagination to get the better of her, as all she had actually seen was a husband dosing his wife so he could sneak out of the house. Where was he going? What could be so important that he would resort to such an extreme? Her curiosity in high gear, Evie raced out the door hoping to make it to his building before he hit the street.

CHAPTER 3

Evie scrambled down the Astor Place subway steps where she dug a token from her purse then followed him onto the Number 6 uptown local. On his heels as they got off the train at Grand Central, then walked west on 42nd Street. Past office towers whose workforces had hours ago scattered back to Queens or Long Island or whatever other bridge and tunnel destination they hung their hats. Past the stillness of the public library and the serenity of Bryant Park until all of a sudden the street exploded with light and activity. The lascivious side of Times Square, where the broad sidewalks of Forty Deuce were alive with people coming and going from peep shows, sex shops and once-proud movie houses now boasting X-rated features like *Oral Annie, Inside Pussycat* and *Catholic High School Girls In Trouble*. A lewd carnival of cheap thrills, all within spitting distance of the legit Broadway theatres.

Evie hung close as her target cut off the main drag, up Eighth Avenue into a lurid netherworld of hardcore sleaze where pimps kept a tight leash on underage hookers. Where hustlers aggressively hawked joints and junk, while men of every make, model and style prowled the seamy unwashed street in search of whatever got them off, stoking the fires of Evie's fascination as she followed deeper into this carnal bazaar where the air hung heavy with the smell of cheap sex. Drugs, disease and danger. Surprised that the man she was tailing had not paid attention to anything the street had to offer until, all of a sudden, he stopped in front of an unmarked door between a scuzzy bar and a live sex theatre. Spoke to the muscular man with a towering Afro and gold chains laying heavy on the front of a skintight T-shirt who stood sentry, handed him some money then disappeared inside.

A midnight cowboy greased the gatekeeper and two stylishly dressed women on his heels did the same, leaving Evie burning to know what vice was so depraved that it could only be served up behind a secret door on a street where no attempt was made to disguise the fact that the right amount of money could satisfy any desire. A curiosity she figured would be best satisfied another night, as standing alone in a flowery sundress she was beginning to attract unwanted attention.

Evie stepped off the curb and tried to flag a taxi, but they were all occupied as the Broadway shows were letting out. She walked west on 44th Street, past darkened storefronts and commercial buildings until she reached Ninth Avenue, where there was plenty of downtown traffic but still no available taxis. She sprinted across the avenue for a bus but was a few strides too late, catching only the brown cloud of exhaust when the driver stepped on the gas. The next block consisted mostly of walk-up apartment buildings with overworked air conditioners poking out of the windows, and she was surprised that such a typical residential block could exist in the shadow of the scuz and the smut. Nearing Tenth Avenue she could see a stream of available taxis cruising past, plus the hustle and flow of normal pedestrians going to and from all the places normal pedestrians go, including a man looking lost as he turned the corner and walked toward her.

"Excuse me, miss." He was nicely dressed and had an engaging smile. "Would you be so kind as to direct me to the subway?"

"Sorry, but I don't know this neighborho ..."

Her last word choked off as the man grabbed Evie by the throat and dragged her down the steps beside the stoop of an old brownstone. One hand covering her mouth and the other now up her dress as he slammed her against the wall and ripped her panties. Fingers clawing between her legs as she fiercely struggled to free herself from his grasp. Bashed him with her knee. A near miss, provoking him to launch a powerful left hook that she barely ducked, causing his fist to smash into the brick wall of the building. Enraged as he cursed the pain and cursed her, he reached behind and pulled a nine-millimeter automatic from his waistband.

This time Evie's knee hit the target, the excruciating blow causing her attacker to drop the gun as he doubled over. She started to run, but he grabbed her ankle and pulled her back down, scraping both knees as her body thumped hard on each of the cement steps. His eyes raging with hate as he regained control of the gun and pinned her down, hovering over her.

"HELP!" Evie screamed.

He yanked up her dress.

"HELP! SOMEBODY HELP ME!"

There were apartment windows not more than a few feet above, but no lights had been switched on and no one came to her aid. Even if the people who lived above or across the street were asleep, surely her terrified screams would rouse them. Or maybe they could not hear over the rattle and hum of over-burdened air conditioners. But more than likely they just did not want to get involved, like a decade earlier when dozens of New Yorkers witnessed the brutal attack and murder of Kitty Genovese from their apartment windows and not one of them called the police. Apparently not much had changed since then, except that this time it was a young woman named Evie Eastway who was fighting for her life.

Her face red as his strong hand squeezed her throat, Evie continued to struggle until she was able to partially free herself. Scratching and clawing, ripping his shirt and further enraging him by breaking the chain that held the gold cross he wore around his neck. But for how valiantly Evie fought, in the end she was overmatched by superior strength as he jammed the gun under her chin. His other hand between her legs, fingers stabbing crudely as he tried to penetrate. Continuing to thrash, she was eventually able to snap her knees together, causing him to flinch just enough to create a struggle for the gun.

The shot was loud. Rang painfully in her ears as Evie laid on the cracked concrete and watched, in what seemed like slow motion, as her attacker fell off of her. His eyes open wide, a hole dead center in his forehead. Shock paralyzing her for several moments until she was finally able to scramble to her feet, pull down her dress and take off running toward Tenth

Avenue. Realizing just before she reached the busy thorough-fare that she still held the gun in her hand.

Evie quickly stashed the weapon in her purse, knowing that even though she had killed in self-defense, she did not want to risk calling attention to herself. The would-be rapist deserved his fate, but she did not want to have to justify her actions to interrogating police officers who may not believe her. She just wanted to go home and try to wash off the filth of a vicious assault. Deep breaths. Thinking clearly. Bolstered by an unex-plained jolt of physical pleasure as she stepped into the street and extended her arm. A taxi stopped right away.

CHAPTER 4

"Another beer, Stoney?" an off-duty mailman called to the white-haired geezer with a scraggly beard who limped out of the john. Dead-armed and reliant on a cane, the result of a savage beating he had taken from a mugger a few years earlier that had left this once-vibrant construction worker partially crippled and unable to work.

"Hell, yes!" smiled the weakened man who still believed he had the bite of a lion.

"Set us all up, Evie," said the mailman, who booked horse bets for the shopkeepers on his route and always had ready cash.

Evie worked the day shift at Jamesey's Saloon, a proud boozatorium that had propped up Soho's most fascinating characters for almost a hundred years. Where writers and sculptors bent elbows with butchers and bakers. Where factory workers and merchants debated events of the day. Frankie tossed pizza dough at Lombardi's, RayRay was a street artist and Nanette was an older woman who had the foresight to wait until her composer husband hit the big time before divorcing him. These were just a few of the habitués who haunted Jamesey's every day, and Stoney was always front and center to keep them entertained with jokes and tales of past adventures. The bar had undoubtedly been home to countless men like Stoney over the years. Men for whom alcohol fueled larger than life personalities that gave the bar a lot of its character. Men who brightened the lives of those around them. Men who, when they finally stumbled home after a long day on a barstool, were lost and alone and counting the minutes until the first beer of a new day.

A cab driver came in waving a newspaper.

"You guys hear Son of Sam killed another one?"

"He's a yellow dog coward!" shouted Stoney, who every day wore a leather vest over a white T-shirt and jeans, faded from wear but always clean and pressed. "Son of a bitch only kills girls."

"Not this time. Shot some guy up on 44th Street."

"First time in Manhattan," said Frankie.

"Let me see that." The mailman grabbed the *Daily News* from the cabbie and set it on the bar where they all saw the headline.

SAM IN MANHATTAN?

"They dug a nine-millimeter slug out of the guy," said RayRay, reading further. "Son of Sam uses a forty-four."

"Which means it's bullshit," declared Nanette as she drained her beer. She, like all the regulars, did not drink in sips. "Those assholes are just trying to sensationalize a random killing so they can sell papers."

Evie looked at the front-page photo of the body lying on cracked cement beside the stoop of the brownstone where she had left it. She understood that being put in a position to either kill or be killed made it self-defense, but nonetheless she had taken a life and was confused as to why it had given her pleasure. That was when a second look at the *Daily News* photo slapped her with the cold realization that this feeling of euphoria had come at the cost of a man's life. A man who had become more than just an anonymous corpse the moment she saw his name in print. A man who may have had a wife and kids. A man who would never enjoy another cold beer. But also, a man who would never again have the opportunity to rape another girl. She waved Stoney down to the quiet end of the bar.

Stoney relied heavily on the sturdy walking stick with a silver bulldog handle that had been a gift from the regulars on his last birthday. A broken man who looked to be in his seventies but was actually a generation younger. She poured him a shot of his favorite bourbon as he shook a cigarette loose from his pack of Virginia Slims, a brand made for women that Stoney knew no one would snatch off the bar. Lit it then slid his gold lighter securely into his vest pocket.

"What's up, girl?"

Stoney was a sweet man who had so little yet would be quick to give up his last nickel if a friend was in need, and Evie knew that she could trust him. Knew that he had been a sniper in World War Two, and that if she told him about what had happened on 44th Street he could help sort out her conflicting feelings of pleasure and guilt. But the words wouldn't come. Some things were just too private to share with anyone.

Confessing to a murder at the top of that list. But it was not murder it was self-defense, and the more Evie thought about it the more confused she became. She poured Stoney another shot and one for herself.

"I want my guitar." In a place where just about anybody fit in, ripped jeans and spiked hair stuck out like a sore thumb. "You know the band's got a gig at CB's tonight."

"Can't you see I'm busy, Ricky?"

"Boozing with this old wino?"

Stoney stood and held up his cane. "Get out before I kick your ass, you snot nosed punk."

"Not till this bitch gives me my guitar."

Stoney swung the cane and Ricky ducked, but was quickly surrounded by people quite capable of kicking his ass.

"I ought to sell it to make up for what a shitty lover you were, but it's worth giving it back to never have to see your stupid face again," Evie said as she took a pawn ticket from the back pocket of her jeans and slammed it on the bar. "Find some other chicken dumb enough to pay to get it out of hock."

Ricky snatched the ticket and made for the exit, calling back loudly as he reached the door, "This slut who gets you drunks loaded gave me crabs."

"Wrong, Ricky. You got those from your mother."

CHAPTER 5

Two on, two out and two strikes on the batter Reggie Jackson.
"Call Danny again," Jimmy told the bartender who was climbing down from adjusting the rabbit ear antenna on top of the nineteen inch RCA above the back bar of the 596 Club, a west side gin mill catering to those who had peculiar ideas about right and wrong.

"No answer, Jimmy. Want me to try his old lady's place?"

"Just find him."

Jimmy was the most feared man in Hell's Kitchen, a disadvantaged neighborhood between Broadway and the Hudson River docks that as far back as anyone could remember had stood in solidarity against outsiders. Not much had changed since before the turn of the century when the area had been controlled by ruthless criminal gangs such as the Gophers, Plug Uglies and the Whyos. And now in 1977 by Jimmy Callan, a thirty-year-old native son with fair hair and sideburns who got his muscular physique lifting weights at Sing Sing. Boss of the Westies, a vicious Irish mob that the press called the most savage organization in the history of New York City gangs.

The hands on the Rheingold beer clock moved toward ten o'clock as an oscillating fan pushed stale air around the bar that was busy with hooligans and blue-collar boozers who watched the Yankees clean-up hitter pop a foul straight back. Still two strikes.

Callan nursed a Guinness, waiting impatiently for his enforcer so they could drop in on the top man at the long-shoreman's association who had refused to cough up a bump in the weekly extortion his membership was already paying the Westies. As Callan saw it, the conversation could go one of two ways. The union boss could kick over the cash or wind up with his balls crammed down his throat; he didn't much care either way. But he did care that Danny Doyle was keeping him waiting. Hated being kept waiting almost as much as he hated the Yankees, always betting against them as he got inflated odds fading the hometown team. And losing a lot of money as the Yanks were all of a sudden hotter than the weather.

Long fly ball to right field.

Callan's eyes widened as he stood, urging the ball to drop from the sky into the glove of the outfielder whose back was against the wall, but to no avail as it landed out of reach for a game winning three-run homer. The crowd at Yankee Stadium screaming *REG-GIE REG-GIE* as the popular slugger triumphantly rounded the bases.

"DIE, YOU FUCKING RAT FUCK!" screamed Callan as he put six bullets into the RCA, exploding the screen and raining glass all over the liquor bottles on back bar.

"Dammit, Jimmy. That's the third TV this month." An impulsive outburst the bartender wished he could take back as he suffered the glare of the most feared man in Hell's Kitchen. Then tripped all over himself to apologize as he had seen men suffer the ultimate penalty for much less. "Sorry, Jimmy. I'm sorry."

"Shut up and find Danny."

"Danny's dead," said Mickey Feeney as he slid onto a barstool. He was short and wiry with light colored hair and three murder arrests to his credit before his twenty-first birthday. "Gunned down last night, around the corner on 44th Street."

"That's a block from here!" Callan was livid and signaled the bartender for a shot of the good stuff. Fired the Irish whisky down his throat then demanded another. "One block! Who would have the fucking balls to kill our guy on our turf?"

"The Gambinos." Mickey was not in favor of the association Callan had recently formed with Paul Castellano, head of the Gambino crime family, which had given the Westies clear title to the spoils of Hell's Kitchen. "You can't trust an Italian, not ever. They're nothing but niggers turned inside out. Maybe trust one of those oily pricks to make you a pizza, but don't turn your back on him for even a second. You told me that, Jimmy. You told me that a hundred times."

"The Gambinos are different."

"A Wop is a Wop, Jimmy. Unless there's something in it for them, those greaseballs wouldn't piss on you if you were on fire."

"You don't understand business, Mickey. Getting in bed with the Gambinos is going to make us rich."

"It's gonna destroy us, only you're too blind to see it. I told you from the start that this was a bad idea, and now that your guard is down they're getting ready to make a move."

"This is the most powerful Mafia family in New York. What would they want with our little patch on the west side?"

"The docks, Jimmy. Our bread and butter." Mickey saw that he was beginning to get through to his best friend. "Killing Danny was a message that we can either step aside and settle for crumbs or fight a war we can't win and lose everything."

Jimmy Callan fired down one more shot of the good stuff.

"Then I guess we better send a message of our own."

CHAPTER 6

Even after she got home from work, Evie continued to ponder the rush of excitement she had gotten from killing Danny Doyle. Was it the pride of successfully fighting off a rapist or satisfaction that she had eliminated a violent criminal before he could hurt someone else? Though she quickly realized that the last part was probably self-serving justification to keep her conscience from sniping at her. An internal battle between right and wrong that further escalated when she wondered if the fact that she was thinking about it at all was because of a subconscious desire to kill again. But Evie was not a killer. She was a bartender, and more importantly, a writer, though searching for inspiration through the windows of the same people doing the same things night after night was beginning to bore her.

Scanning the white brick mid-rise through high-powered lenses, she wondered how many more times she could suffer through the air guitar baldy butchering Townshend or Hendrix or whoever the hell he was pretending to be. Would it kill the woman violating carrots and cucumbers to change up the menu once in a while? Not to mention that most of the other people she chronicled just watched television until it was time to go to bed, causing Evie to face the reality that writing a voyeuristic tapestry of New York life woven together by the voice of a curious neighbor had been a bad idea. She had gotten off on crashing their privacy, but except for the man who had led her on a lascivious journey to Times Square, none of these people had stoked her curiosity even a little bit. Not counting, of course, the sexy man on the ninth floor who, a few moments ago, had given her a bit of a tingle when light filled his apartment.

Evie watched as he loosened his tie and went into the bedroom, out of her line of sight, then reappeared a few moments later having changed into a T-shirt and jeans and looking as if he was about to go out. Probably to dinner as he had not brought home his usual Indian take-out. Where was he going? With who? He didn't seem to have a girlfriend as she had never seen a woman in the apartment, and decided that the time had come for her to apply for the job. Follow to see where he went, who he saw, and when the moment was right accidentally-on-purpose run into him in the hope that sparks would fly. Evie quickly brushed her hair and spit out a mouthful of Listerine as she prepared to race out the door, then her expression sank as she saw him get comfortable in his favorite chair and open a book. Her opportunity for kismet doused but not her desire for adventure, Evie changed into something appropriate and caught the Number 6 uptown local.

Hair teased and wearing a skimpy tank top over a micromini, Evie looked like she belonged among the snatch traders in this netherworld of hardcore sleaze, amused by the irony that the outfit she had bought to wear to Ricky's show at

CBGB allowed her to seamlessly blend in with Eighth Avenue skanks on the make for money and dope. She eyed the sentry with the huge Afro who had the power to satisfy a writer's curiosity by granting access to whatever nefarious adventure lurked behind the mysterious door wedged between a scuzzy bar and a live sex theatre, trying to figure out the best way to approach him. It was then that a well-dressed man glided past her who apparently knew the drill, so she seized the opportunity and followed a couple strides behind. Without saying a word, the man handed the gatekeeper a twenty and was admitted inside. Evie did the same, then descended a crumbling cement stairway to a dimly-lit subterranean chamber where she choked on air thick with the gamy funk of every imaginable bodily excretion as her eyes opened wide at the lewd spectacle of both men and women pleasuring themselves as they watched other men and women having sex. Depraved sex. Sideshow sex.

Evie eyeballed unimaginable acts of perversion, wondering why a girl would allow herself to be burned with candle wax while giving oral stimulation to a German shepherd. What possible kick a man could get from having a woman lactate all over his face, and what kind of person could get off watching such humiliation. Then it became obvious that she was that kind of person, because this was just the sort of wickedness she had initially hoped to see peeping through her neighbors' windows.

The man she had followed inside was in line waiting his turn to screw a woman wearing only a black leather hood who stood chained spread eagle to the dank stone wall as if in a medieval dungeon. What kind of woman would consent to this degradation? What kind of man would want to be sixth in line? The whole set up reminding her of a party she had attended at a Chelsea loft where people had sex with sculpture. The hosts of the party were standard bearers of the Euro-trash avant-garde, validating it enough that the *Village Voice* lauded the spectacle as performance art. So, Evie figured that strangers having orgasms while watching strangers having orgasms in a stanky basement beneath Eighth Avenue was *interactive* performance art, making her think that the avant-garde should take note that they were being upstaged. Maybe she would allow the world to take note by submitting a follow-up piece about it to the *Village Voice*.

As she continued to be both amazed and appalled by the unthinkable, it became clear to Evie that the one thing all these people in the basement had in common was that they could no longer be aroused by conventional sex, needing to commit unimaginable crimes against nature and against themselves in order to get off. Making Evie think back to the adrenaline rush she had experienced by pulling the trigger just a few blocks away. Reigniting the debate with her conscience. She knew the difference between right and wrong. Understood *Thou Shalt Not Kill*. Still, she wondered what possible use any of these subterranean perverts could be to society. To themselves or to anyone.

Evie watched a skinhead using his cock as a weapon as he aggressively slammed it harder and harder into the hooded woman chained to the wall. He was not just having sex, he was committing violence, obliterating any link that may have existed between the two acts. Making Evie wonder what hole a pervert with a crudely inked white power tattoo on his ass would crawl back into after he left. And where the woman chained to the wall would go when she left. Was she somebody's wife? Somebody's mother? Maybe she was the perky third grade teacher at PS 93 but, if so, she sure wouldn't be walking to school in the morning. Whatever her backstory was, or could be imagined, Evie saw that this woman would be a great character to build a novel around. Certainly a lot more fun to write about than her boring neighbors, as one of the perks of being a fiction writer was that on paper you got to push the envelope of every taboo imaginable with zero consequence.

Words on a page, however, would not satisfy the urge that was swelling inside her as she began to understand that there never had been a link between sex and violence for the skinhead to obliterate. That not only was all sex violence, all violence was sexual. Was that why people killed, Evie wondered as she found herself helpless against the craving as the skinhead hiked up his pants and climbed the stairs toward the door. A man whose white power hatred offered nothing but misery, and would be missed only by others who offered the same. Her desire flaring as she followed him outside and down the block. The anticipation of squeezing the trigger and watching him die made her feel alive, but would her conscience allow her to take this man's life? The closer she got to him, the louder the question pounded in her head. Only a few steps behind him she zeroed in on the moment of truth.

It was only then that she realized she did not have the gun.

CHAPTER 7

"They don't serve corned beef and cabbage in this neighborhood, Jimmy," cracked Rino Reale as he stuffed his fat face with a meatball parm at a sidewalk table on the shady side of Elizabeth Street.

"Danny Doyle used to come down here to Little Italy all the time for sausage and peppers. Couldn't get enough of the stuff." Jimmy Callan sat down across the table from the Gambino soldier who had thick dark hair, sideburns and a good start on a belly that before too long would prevent him from knowing if his shoes matched. "I guess eating those gut bombs was his guilty pleasure. Kind of like fucking an Italian girl. Fun while you're doing it, but embarrassing if your friends find out."

"Don't be disrespectful."

"What's disrespectful is someone putting a bullet in Danny's head around the corner from where I drink my Guinness."

"Danny's dead?" Rino put down the sandwich and took a swig of his Pepsi.

"Night before last." Callan looked him hard in the eye. "You didn't know?"

Rino shook his head.

"Nobody in your crew said anything?"

"Not a peep."

"Nobody higher up?"

"First I've heard of it, Jimmy. On the square."

Rino ran a crew for the Gambinos. Shakedowns and protection mostly, uninspired old school rackets. A good earner, but everyone except him knew that he would never move further up the ranks. Would never get made. Held back by his reputation as a loose cannon, most notably for strong arming Dominican dealers in Washington Heights to feed a prodigious cocaine habit.

A metallic-green Oldsmobile pulled up to the curb and Mickey Feeney pushed open the passenger door.

"You don't want to do this, Jimmy."

"Relax, Rino. We're just gonna have a little talk."

"So talk."

"I'll be a lot more comfortable if we do it up on the west side," Callan told him as he liberated a thirty-eight from the Italian's ankle holster.

"Kill me and your life won't be worth a nickel." Rino scraped his hand through his hair, trying to play it cool. No dice. "Think about what comes next, Jimmy. There's no future in crossing the Gambinos."

"Get in the car."

Wedged in the middle as Mickey wheeled his green beast toward Tenth Avenue, Rino needed a bump, needed a drink, needed to be anywhere other than between those two maniacs.

"Why would I hit Danny? I had no reason to," pleaded Rino, sweat soaking through his shirt. Terrified of the pain these two sadistic Irishmen would make him suffer before finally punching his ticket. "I didn't do it, Jimmy!"

"We didn't say you did."

"Then why grab me off the street? Out of all the wise guys in the city, why roust *me*? I had no reason to hit Danny and neither did any of my crew. It don't make any sense. We're all on the same team since the big boss reached out to form an alliance."

"Why did he do that?" demanded Mickey.

"Bosses don't tell me why they do what they do."

"What do you guineas expect in return?"

"Everybody knew the Westies were being challenged. Word that trickled down was that they wanted your turf stabilized because if there's a war anywhere in the city the cops will put pressure on everybody, especially us. Peace is good for business."

"I thought they didn't tell you why they do what they do."

"They don't. That's just what I heard on the street." Rino was getting panicky. "And that's all I know. Honest to God, Mickey, I haven't heard one word about who whacked Danny. I didn't even know he was dead till you guys told me."

Callan's sister lived in an elevator building on 49th Street, and he sometimes used the apartment while she was at work. For half an hour, the three of them sat in the living room drinking beer while making small talk about girls, sports and who they had to bribe to get the summer heat to let up. But not a word about Danny Doyle. Another beer and a few lines of blow finally relaxed Rino enough that he stopped sweating, then the other shoe dropped.

"Where were you two nights ago?

"Around."

"Around where?"

"Havin' a few pops at the Mulberry."

"Can you prove that?"

"The bartender knows me. A couple guys from my crew were there."

"What time did you guys come up to 44th Street?"

"We didn't."

"So, it was just you that came up here."

"No, Jimmy. I swear I wasn't nowhere near the west side." He bit his lip, wiping sweaty hands on his pants. "Before today I haven't been anywhere near this neighborhood in months."

"Did Danny owe you money?"

"No."

"Did he fuck one of your broads?"

"No."

"Then what the hell was the beef?"

"There was no beef."

"Where did you go after you left the Mulberry Street Bar?"

"Stopped for one at the Spring Lounge then Umberto's for some clams. After that I went home and watched the tube."

"But not before you came uptown and killed Danny."

"For the last time, I didn't kill Danny!"

"Why did the Gambinos want Danny hit? Are they trying to send us a message?"

"I don't know."

"So, the Gambinos *did* have Danny hit."

"I didn't say that!" Rino was coming unglued.

"Given where you're sitting, you must know that it would be a big mistake to be more scared of the Gambinos than you are of us."

"You gotta believe me, Jimmy! I swear on my sainted mother. Take my eyes if everything I told you isn't a hundred percent legit."

Callan checked Rino's thirty-eight to make sure it was loaded.

"If you didn't kill Danny, then who did?"

"I can't tell you what I don't know."

"You got a wife, Rino?"

"No."

"Kids?"

"Please, Jimmy. I can give you money. I'll rat out whoever you want me to."

"*That's* why we rousted you, Rino. Because you're a fat rat fuck who'd sell out your own sainted mother for a line of coke. So why stay loyal to the Gambinos? Even us cabbage eaters in Hell's Kitchen know they disrespect you so much you'll never get made."

"Nobody disrespects me."

"They think you're a joke, Rino. A dumb ass. So why stay loyal to them when they aren't loyal to you? We know they fingered Danny. Just tell us which one of you oily pricks pulled the trigger and you can walk out of here right now."

"I can't tell you what I don't know," he pleaded, shifting his weight but unable to get comfortable. "You gotta believe that."

"I guess the Gambinos are right about you, because it takes a real dumb ass to get shot with his own gun."

"I'm begging you!"

Callan pressed the thirty-eight against Rino's forehead. "Last chance. Who killed Danny Doyle?"

"I don't know! I don't know!"

Rino squeezed his eyes shut, pissing his pants as he mumbled, "O merciful Jesus lover of souls I pray thee …"

"Tough Italian gangster," laughed Mickey. "These Mafia fucks don't have the balls to kill a goldfish, let alone Danny."

"Sorry, Rino," said Callan as he lowered the gun. "We had to be sure."

"Then we're okay? And I can get out of here?"

"Absolutely." Callan nodded toward the stained trousers. "Go in the bathroom and clean yourself up, then we'll drive you back downtown."

"Thanks, Jimmy." Rino said it sincerely, still shaken and grateful to be alive. "Thanks."

Callan followed him into the bathroom, then shot him in the back of the head.

"What the fuck did you do that for?" yelled Mickey.

"Who knows what that coked-up rat might have told the Gambinos if we turned him loose."

"We could have denied whatever he said. Now they're gonna come gunning for us."

"Not us, Mick. They're gonna blame this on the Dominicans." Callan set the gun on the sink and checked his hair in the mirror. "Now help me get this fat prick's clothes off and lift him into the bathtub."

Unlike most guests of the state who count the days stewing in their own hate, Callan learned the skill of meat cutting in Sing Sing. Went into the kitchen and came back with some plastic trash bags and a set of knives he made sure his sister always kept razor-sharp. Had Mickey pull up Rino by the hair, then put a serrated blade to the dead Italian's throat and cut off his head.

"You can watch from here, Rino," said Mickey as he propped the severed head at the end of the tub beside the shampoo and feminine products. "Best seat in the house."

Callan cheerfully hummed an Irish drinking song as, with the skill of a butcher, he dissected the body with a filet knife. Methodically detaching arms and legs, placing pieces of Rino Reale into several trash bags, then before packaging the rest of him, cut open his lungs and fat belly to make sure the torso would not float to the surface before the current carried it out to sea. Tossed his clothes and identification into the tub, doused it with lighter fluid then tossed in a match.

"Wanna toast some marshmallows, Rino?" yukked Mickey, almost giddy as Callan flushed giblets and gristle down the toilet.

"Quit clowning and help me finish up."

"Gotta settle his tab first."

Mickey dug his thumbs deep into the squish, pulled hard until finally popping out Rino's eyeballs. Squeezed them like grapes until they burst into milky uncongealed goop that he flicked into the flame.

Callan washed up as the fire did its job, leaving only a pile of ash that he rinsed down the drain. Used bleach to scour away residual blood, washed the knives then cleaned up the apartment as if no one had been there. Then they went downstairs and loaded the bags into the trunk of Mickey's Oldsmobile.

They laughed as they rolled Rino's head down a busy sidewalk in Washington Heights, then aimed the green beast toward Ward's Island where they would toss the bags containing the rest of him into the strong current of the East River. Congratulating themselves on a job well done, though it had not yet occurred to either of them that they still did not know who killed Danny Doyle.

CHAPTER 8

Not a lot of celebrities passed through Clifton, New Jersey, but when Vincent Price dropped off a rush job at the near-bankrupt Broad Street Laundry in 1955, the proprietor saw a sure-fire way to increase business. Change the name to attract more celebrity clientele, then plaster the wall with autographed pictures to bring in more locals.

The first part of the plan flopped flatter than a Roosevelt dime, unless you count the day Zeppo Marx stopped in to ask for directions, but that didn't prevent Marv Eastway's Star Cleaners from becoming a hit with the local housewives. Women sentenced to lives of thankless domestic drudgery made it part of their weekly routine to drop off their husbands' cleaning and check out the latest eight by ten glossies of Hollywood's biggest stars, unaware that they were bogus props the proprietor had autographed to himself. *To Marv – Best Wishes, Bob Hope … Marv – Keep up the great work, Tony Curtis … To My Pal Marv, Frank Sinatra.* Even if the women did know it was all fake they didn't care, as either way it was as close as they would ever get to celebrity, feeding a bottom line that over the years had afforded a comfortable life for Marv Eastway and his family, as well as hunting and fishing trips for himself more weekends than not.

This weekend not, as it was his wife Maxine's birthday and his only child had taken the bus from the city to be part of a family celebration. But Evie had been at her parents' house over an hour and the only time she had seen her father was when he had popped his head out of the basement door to find out what time his wife would have dinner on the table. Then without a word of greeting to his daughter, the husky man with bushy salt and pepper hair went back downstairs to tinker with the vintage Ithaca ten-gauge shotgun he had recently purchased at auction. Counting the days until duck season began in October.

"I can't believe that not only won't Dad take you out for dinner on your birthday, he has you making a pot roast. His favorite."

"I don't mind, Evie," said Maxine, a once-pretty woman with a graying pageboy cut, as mother and daughter set the table.

"What's your favorite meal, Mom? I lived in this house almost all my life and I don't know. Everything you do is for him, and from what I can see he's never appreciated it one bit." Evie knew that her mother was by nature too timid to stand up for herself, and kept pushing so that maybe she finally might. "When was the last time he took you anywhere? Brought you flowers? Told you he loves you?"

"Let it go, Evie."

"I read in a magazine that if a housewife was paid the going rate for all the different jobs she does, that she would earn close to a hundred thousand dollars a year. You at least deserve the respect of not having to bake your own birthday cake."

Special occasion or not, dinner was eaten the same way it had always been as far back as Evie could remember. In silence. Finally, it was her mother who broke the ice.

"Evie isn't working at the bookstore anymore, Marv. She has a new job."

"Is that so? What sort of work is she doing?"

"I'm sitting right here, Dad."

"Okay, Evie." He brushed a dinner roll crumb off his neatly pressed sport shirt. "Tell me about this new job of yours."

"I work the dayshift at a historic bar in Soho."

"Congratulations. Four years of college so you can sling booze to drunks."

"They're not drunks, Dad. Jamesey's is a meeting place for artists and writers."

"If they're drinking during the day, they're drunks. Maybe you wouldn't waste the opportunity you were given if you had paid your own way through Montclair State."

"I appreciate everything you did for me, Dad. I really do. And I'm using what I learned at school to become an author. I've submitted several stories to magazines and now I'm going to start working on a new novel."

"How much does it pay?"

"Writing is my passion."

"Hunting is mine, but it doesn't pay the electric bill."

"Writing is what makes me excited to get up in the morning, hoping that maybe it's the day I write a perfect paragraph. And if slinging booze to drunks allows me to pursue that passion, then being a bartender is the best job in the world."

"A son would be more practical about his future."

Marv rarely passed up an opportunity to voice his displeasure that Evie had not been born a boy, and he resented Maxine because she could not give him more children.

"I've read that bartending can provide great inspiration to a writer." Maxine smiled at her daughter. "I bet you see and hear a lot of interesting things."

"That's enough, Maxine." When Marv said it was enough, his wife knew to shut up. "I'll have some more coffee."

Marv mopped up the last bit of gravy with the last bite of his roll, then pushed his plate aside and rose from the table.

"We haven't had the cake yet," protested Evie.

Without a word, her father picked up his coffee and went back downstairs.

"He treats you like a servant, Mom. Why do you stay with him?"

"Don't say things like that."

"Do you ever think about what your life would be like if you hadn't married him? What were your dreams? What did you want out of life when you were my age?"

"I was hired by Pan Am to be a stewardess. It was a very glamorous career in those days."

"You were a stewardess and never told me!"

"Hundreds of girls applied and I was lucky enough to be among those who were chosen." Maxine liked remembering, and her face brightened with more than a hint of pride. "I was going to see the world and go to all the places I had only read about. The beach at Ipanema. The Prado in Madrid. The cafes of Paris."

"Why didn't you? What happened?"

"Your father made me quit before I even started training."

"You were married then?"

"No. But he made me choose."

"How come you never mentioned any of this?"

"It was just the silly dream of a young girl."

"It was a life-changing opportunity that was stolen away from you." Evie suffered the pain that her mother would not allow herself to feel. "It's not too late to see the world."

"Of course, it is. I'm forty-seven years old."

"Women of all ages have more opportunities available to them today than ever before."

"Women's Lib is great in theory, but for me it's not realistic." Maxine smiled at her daughter. "You were smart to move away and chase your dream of being a writer."

"What if I fail?"

"At least you'll have had an adventure. No regrets and a lifetime of memories."

"Dad gets to play the big shot with his hunting buddies by telling those phony stories about getting whiskey stains out of Dean Martin's trousers. What do you get? One eye on the afternoon soaps while you do his cooking and cleaning? The guy owns a laundry and still makes you wash and iron his shirts. Give me one good reason why you shouldn't pack a bag and create a new life for yourself."

"Because I stood before God and made a vow to honor and obey. And to stay with your father through good times and bad."

"He made those same vows, Mom."

"Let it go, Evie."

Maxine got up to clear the table, but Evie told her the dishes could wait.

"Remember our mother and daughter luncheons in the city?"

Maxine smiled at the memory of how from the time Evie was eight they would doll themselves up and spend an afternoon in New York. Luncheon among the rich and famous at the Plaza Hotel. Shopping on Fifth Avenue, where each would pick out something for the other that they would proudly carry in shopping bags from Saks or Bergdorf or Bendel, then end the day with ice cream sodas at Rumpelmayer's at the St. Moritz. Always in autumn when the leaves on the trees in Central Park blazed yellow and red, every year until Evie was old enough to have a life of her own.

Evie placed a gift-wrapped box on the table, and Maxine became teary-eyed as she opened it to find a black and white photograph in a silver frame of mother and daughter at the Palm Court at the Plaza. Mother in a tailored suit and pillbox hat. Daughter, nine or ten years old, in a frilly dress with white socks and patent leather shoes. A promise was made that they would spend a day together in the city very soon.

Evie cleared the table and did the dishes, then went down to the basement as for the first time in her life she found the courage to stand up to her father.

"You could have at least stayed at the table long enough so that Mom could enjoy her birthday cake."

"I'll have some later."

"Did you even get her a gift?"

Marv reached for a rag and a container of light oil, cleaning his newest prized possession after patterning it that morning at the gun range. The same gun range he had once taken Evie to when she had been a teenager. Taught her how to stand and how to aim a small twenty-two caliber pistol, but before a shot was fired quickly lost his temper at her lack of interest.

As far back as she could remember, Evie had done everything her father had demanded of her, but it was never enough to win his love as he continually humiliated her, degraded her and ripped away her self-respect like a bandage from a gaping wound. Again and again and again until finally, on her mother's birthday, she allowed herself to accept the cruel reality that in the Eastway house there was no possible atonement for the ultimate sin of being born female.

CHAPTER 9

Evie knew better than to turn around and look, watching the scene unfold in the mirror behind the bar as a pimp grabbed a young girl in hot pants and unconvincing blond hair, then shoved her hard out the door of the scuzzy gin mill above the circus of sexual horrors.

"Now get that ass back to work and make me some money."

The young hooker could not have been more than seventeen, yet the brutality of the stroll made her look as if she was twice that and Evie could see that this thug owned her, the same as he owned his checkerboard suit and silver platform shoes. Time was money, and the girl's meter had been running since the moment she stepped off the bus from whatever listless Midwestern whistlestop had not provided sufficient excitement to curb a teenage wanderlust, only to find out too late that ditching family and friends for dreams of Broadway would land her just a couple blocks short, on her knees in putrid, roach-infested flops. Weighed down by the stank of hopelessness and despair as she went through the motions like a cocksucking zombie, learning the hard way that not only was sex violence but that violence was sex.

Evie worked on a beer as she looked out the window of the seedy bar — probably a dead ringer for what her father envisioned when he thought of her slinging drinks at Jamesey's — knowing that it was more than a writer's curiosity that had again drawn her back to the street where everyone was either selling sex, seeking sex or exploiting sex. Only a negligible difference between the panderers on Eighth Avenue and the ad men on nearby Madison Avenue, who knew that putting a pretty girl on the arm of a man in a Head & Shoulders commercial would, within a week, result in millions of men from Hartford to Honolulu becoming dandruff-free.

Evie saw the girl in the shampoo commercial and the girl who had been bounced ass over elbows onto the sidewalk as interchangeable. The only differences being that one had an agent who controlled her career using a telephone while the other's used his fists, and one went out for drinks after work while the other was too beaten down to cry herself to sleep. In Times Square the strong devoured the weak. Preyed upon them. Brutalized them. Evie peered out at a streetscape of young hookers and old hookers. Pretty, ugly, fat, skinny. Positive that every one of them knew all too intimately that violence was sex. And as she looked out the window at the pimp in the checkerboard suit, her own violent urge began to flare.

Soul searching had convinced Evie that *Thou Shalt Not Kill* came with an asterisk that the sands of time had long ago eroded from that stone tablet. Of this she was positive. Otherwise what justification could there be for war, for self-defense or for erasing degenerate predators from the streets of Times Square so that they would never again have the chance to inflict unspeakable horrors on young girls too helpless to defend themselves?

She continued to focus on the pimp as he leaned on the fender of a flashy custom Cadillac, quickly realizing that she did not have the courage to try to lure the violent whoremonger to a fitting end. But he was not the only scum-sucker in her orbit, so she decided instead to pay $20 and evaluate the men waiting in line downstairs to defile the hooded woman chained to the dungeon wall. Choose the one who looked most deserving, wait until he finished, then follow him.

It would be that easy. But as luck would have it, it proved to be even easier than that as she noticed a familiar face across the street.

Evie slid off her barstool, hit the pavement and followed the skinhead.

And tonight, she had the gun.

CHAPTER 10

The summer sun had not yet begun to percolate as Evie walked to the bodega around the corner from her apartment building. A spring in her step as she felt good. Like she had accomplished something important as she offered a cheery smile to the middle-aged Korean man at the register as she glanced at the morning tabloids, then set them on the counter along with her usual coffee and Danish. Held out a ten but he refused it.

"On the house, Evie," said the storekeeper who was in an even better mood than she was. "Today we celebrate."

"Thanks, Mr. Kim. What's the occasion?"

"My first grandchild arrived last night. Little Anna. Six pounds, four ounces." He smiled proudly as he showed Evie a Polaroid.

"What a beautiful baby," she told him, not meaning a word of it. Then extricated herself from more congratulatory small talk and walked at a brisk pace around the corner to her apartment, eager to tear open the tabloids.

Evie sat at her writing table by the window, leafing with hurried anticipation through both the *Post* and the *Daily*

News. Frustrated that there was not a word in either about what she had done the night before. Probably happened too late to make the early editions, she figured, then switched on the clock radio beside her bed. Turned the volume loud enough so she could hear as she cleaned the kitchen, scrubbed the bathroom and tended to other domestic chores she had been putting off. There was a fresh news report every half hour, but after three cycles all she had learned was that Democrats in congress were calling for a new five cents per gallon gasoline tax increase and that a Saudi prince was bellyaching that his human rights had been violated because residents of a swank Park Avenue co-op would not allow him to buy an apartment in their building. At the top of the hour she again listened closely and held her breath.

> All news all the time. This is 1010 WINS. You give us twenty-two minutes, we'll give you the world ... The manhunt for serial killer Son of Sam has widened in Manhattan as police are saying that he may be responsible for last night's murder of a man on East 92nd Street.

"What the fuck!" Evie yelled.

> The first alleged Son of Sam victim in Manhattan had a long police record, and was associated with the notorious Hell's Kitchen criminal organization called the Westies. Last night's victim, who markings on the fatal bullet confirm was killed with the same nine-millimeter Smith & Wesson, was also

well known to police as a member of the local Aryan Brotherhood and wanted in connection with last month's bombing of a Jewish community center in The Bronx, leading to speculation from Inspector Timothy Dowd, head of the police department's three hundred-member Omega task force, that Son of Sam is turning his attention away from young girls and has possibly become a vigilante.

Evie switched off the radio as she could not stomach another word. Gulped the remainder of her now-cold coffee and the stagnant caffeine focused her anger. She knew that she should not be surprised that the media were giving the city's resident serial killer credit for what she had done, but it sounded like they were making Son of Sam out to be some kind of vigilante hero. *She* was the hero for removing both a rapist and a bomber from the streets of New York City. Not that she wanted the exposure of seeing her name in the headlines, but that yellow dog coward who did nothing but sneak up on teenagers making out in parked cars sure as hell did not deserve the credit. Where was the challenge in what he did? A jackass who couldn't even shoot straight as half those sitting ducks he only wounded. The questions pinballing through Evie's brain were no longer about right and wrong, as she wondered what kind of satisfaction Son of Sam got pulling the trigger. What was his motivation? His thought process?

Now that Evie had stopped peeping windows – with the exception of stealing late night glimpses of her sexy man on the ninth floor – she needed a new project and had given a lot of thought to the idea of basing a novel on the hooded woman in the dungeon. But the deeper she became immersed in the business of ridding the city of bad guys, the more Evie was convinced that a novel about a serial killer told from the point of view of what *really* goes on inside a killer's head would be a bestselling page-turner that would make the literary world stand up and take notice of Evie Eastway. A work of fiction that would not be fiction at all. Every urge and every emotion precise, as only a person who had actually taken a life could know. And to pull that off she would need to keep a journal of her own motivations, her thoughts and corresponding actions. She cracked open a new composition book and began to write it all down.

this makes me think of my first diary, the pink one with the lock on it that mom gave me when i was ten. i kept the key around my neck day and night so that nobody would ever know my deepest most intimate secrets, like my crush on timmy hower and how i cried for weeks when his family moved to ohio. my secrets are bigger now and will soon become deeper, darker and of greater consequence. this is more a journal than a diary, its purpose to chronicle events so that when i write my novel i will be able to reference every fact and every emotion exactly how it all happened. a lesson learned from the news, in that if you want the facts reported accurately, you need to report those facts yourself.

it all started when an innocent adventure led me to times square where i became fascinated with hookers, pimps, and the sleazy lowlifes who haunt the area. but being there alone i became nervous and walked a couple blocks west to catch a cab home, but before i could find one a man tried to rape me. we struggled and somehow i got control of his gun and shot him. when the shock wore off and i realized what i had done, my body shook with a feeling of pleasure. not really sure why. maybe it was the satisfaction of prevailing in a life and death situation. i haven't quite got it all figured out yet, but what i do know for sure is that it felt great.

it was more than a writer's curiosity or a sexual curiosity that took me back to times square a second night and then a third. drawn to a subterranean sex dungeon where i witnessed seemingly ordinary men and women pay $20 for the opportunity to masturbate while watching bizarre men and women performing sex acts so depraved that i shall never as a writer possess the talent to properly describe. it was there that i saw this skinhead who i knew was a white supremacist (who i found out later was wanted for blowing *up a jewish community center) and that momentarily placated a conscience that was still working overtime trying to dull my desire to reprise the physical pleasure i got from shooting the rapist. times square had brought me face to face with the scum of the earth. people whose very existence brought nothing but misery and suffering to those who did not deserve it, and i felt somehow that it was up to me to prevent those perverts from hurting more innocent people.*

i couldn't shoot the skinhead in the middle of a crowded eighth avenue sidewalk so i followed until i could get him alone. i waited outside while he went into two different peepshows. the definition of the word pervert does not come even close to describing how truly disgusting these dirtbags can be until you see them in action. anyway, after the peepshows, i kept a safe distance behind as i tailed this sleazebag as he caught the times square shuttle to grand central where he transferred to the number 4 uptown express. i was at the other end of the car but never let him out of my sight, watching as he emptied a pint of whiskey he pulled from his back pocket.

he got off the train at 86th and lexington, a busy corner where he went into the papaya king for a hot dog. then uptown a couple blocks where he stopped for a beer. i moved across the street from the bar as to not attract attention, but i was still able to see him through the window. he finished his beer and was about to leave when he set his sights on a woman way out of his league and ordered another one. by this time i was getting pretty antsy. eager? horny? i wanted him desperately, and how dare he make me work that hard for it. but fortunately, the woman blew him off quickly and we were once again on the move. up to 92nd where he turned down a quiet residential block. i knew a shot would ring loud, but that didn't concern me because no one had called the police when i was screaming at the top of my lungs trying to fight off a rapist, so why would anyone call this time? and even if someone had, i would have been long gone by the time the law arrived.

it was almost eleven and with no one around i could have easily stepped closer and shot him in the back, but every instinct told me that would be a letdown. darkness is never complete in the city and i needed to see his face and needed to have him see mine, but the closer i got to him the more nervous i became. my palms were sweating and my eyes open wide as i was in awe of what i was about to do. then almost upon him i began to lose my nerve, but i had passed the point of no return as he had seen me, so i called to him and asked if he could direct me to the subway. ever on the make, this creep leered as he came closer then stopped dead in his tracks when he saw the gun. he thought it was a robbery and tried to give me his wallet. begged me to take his money as a few feet away from him i assumed the stance i had been taught by my father as a teenager at a new jersey gun range. held the weapon as steady as i could with both hands and pointed it at him. the skinhead didn't beg for mercy or anything like that, he just wanted to know why. it seemed very important for him to know why, and having the power over whether he lived or died was a rush. but the kick of the gun caused me to stumble backward and MY SHOT MISSED. the skinhead lunged toward me and wrapped his hands around my neck, but before he could squeeze i closed my eyes and fired again.

*as the skinhead went down, my body
was again charged with a jolt of physical
excitement. is this why people kill? it has
to be why women kill. why don't more
women kill? even though i almost blew it
and was lucky that i was not the one dead
on the sidewalk, my confidence surged as
i made my getaway down the block and
into a taxi. feeling the same adrenaline
rush I got as a kid riding the cyclone at
palisades park, where i was scared to
death during the ride but when it was over
i immediately wanted to go again.*

CHAPTER 11

"I know you don't like to talk about it, Stoney, but …" Evie paused, then poured the old man a shot of bourbon because she *was* going to make him talk about it. "Do you ever feel guilty about what you did in the war?"

"I was a soldier following orders."

"You were a sniper, which means you got a good look at every target before you pulled the trigger. Did it give you a rush having control over life and death? A physical thrill as you watched them go down?"

"It made me sick." He downed his shot. Then grabbed a handful of his long white whiskers and slowly pulled them to a pointed end, as he often did when he was about to get serious. "Why are you all of a sudden so interested in the psychology of killing?"

"I suppose it's all this bullshit in the news about Son of Sam being a vigilante."

"What makes you so sure it's bullshit?"

"Come on, Stoney. He's nothing but a coward who shoots kids in parked cars."

"Maybe he stepped himself up in class."

"He's a putz who leaves letters at crime scenes like he's begging to be caught. Besides, the killings in Manhattan were bold and daring. The work of a real vigilante."

"You say that like you're impressed."

"Just telling it like it is." She glanced toward the drinkers at the other end of the bar to see if anybody needed anything, then backtracked the conversation. "You really never got a rush from killing in the war?"

"Truth is I died a little with every man I put down." A sadness in his eyes as he said it. "But I will tell you that some of the other snipers got their rocks off with every shot."

"But why not you? They deserved to be killed, didn't they?"

"Sixty-three men, boys mostly, whose only crime was that they had been drafted into Hitler's army the same as I was drafted into Uncle Sam's." Stoney slumped his shoulders and leaned his good elbow on the bar, smoke drifting up from between yellowed fingers. "That's why I drink, Evie. To try to forget. Which works fine until I lay in bed and close my eyes. That's when I see every one of those sixty-three faces. Every damn night."

"What about shooting someone who deserves it? Like the guy who mugged you."

"Wouldn't fix my arm and my leg, or get me my job back."

A disability pension that did little more than pay the rent on a one-room apartment. Drinking on the generosity of others. Nothing to look forward to except reliving the same day over and over until his crippled body would finally rot from the inside. Stoney had every reason to be bitter and Evie could not understand why he wasn't.

"He ruined your life for a $12 Timex and a paycheck he couldn't cash. Do you remember *his* face?"

"Like it was yesterday."

"What if he walked in here right now?"

"I'd bash that dirty bastard's head in!" He brightened as he said it. "And *that* would give me a rush."

Evie was beginning to understand that it was not killing that had goosed her adrenaline, it was justified killing. Ridding the city of criminals before they could hurt anyone else, making it suddenly clear which side to root for as guilt for what she had done continued to slug it out with a desire to do it again.

"Bottle of Beck's please," said a man in a pearl gray suit who had just walked into the bar, then gestured to Stoney. "And another shot for the gentleman."

"Thanks mister," said Stoney as he downed the shot, then got up and went to join his pals at the other end of the bar.

"From an admirer?" the man asked Evie, looking at an arrangement of flowers behind the bar.

"No such luck. Stargazers are my favorite. I pick them up on the way to work sometimes to spruce this place up a little."

The man looked familiar and at first Evie couldn't place him, but after sneaking a longer look at his reflection in the mirror behind the bar the pieces fell into place. Handsome. Dark hair, well-dressed and drank imported beer. Could his walking into Jamsey's be a coincidence or had he caught her peeping his window and followed her?

His name was Tom, and he gave no indication that anything was unusual as in between drink orders they made small talk about movies and art. Had she been to the Kenneth

Nolan retrospective at the Guggenheim? Had he seen *Eraserhead* or *Andy Warhol's Bad*? He had a quick smile and soft brown eyes, the kind a girl could get lost in, and was so easy to talk to that Evie knew his being there really was nothing more than a coincidence. An ordinary guy she had met in a most extraordinary way.

"I told the professor his class was a waste of everybody's time. That poetry is nothing but a short cut for slackers who want to be seen as creative but are too lazy to do the work it takes to become a real writer."

"I bet that helped your grade," laughed Tom, thinking Evie looked great in her flirty summer dress as a few nights later they enjoyed a first-date Indian meal.

"I understand the point of Nantucket rhymes and Valentine cards, but the rest of it serves no purpose whatsoever."

"You're a literary elitist, but your conviction is misguided. Poetry has been the premier literature of the English language since the beginning."

"Now, who's an elitist? I honestly don't understand what you can possibly see in it."

"The same way coriander and turmeric bring out the flavor of this food we're eating, a well-crafted verse brings out the beauty and the soul of its subject."

"It takes a year to write a novel but only thirty seconds to scribble a rhyme on the back of an envelope, and I still think the whole thing is a crock." Evie swatted away a fly, then took a sip of beer to dampen the fire of her lamb vindaloo. And even though her date was being obstinate, she liked what she saw across the table. Sports jacket over a T-shirt and jeans, clean-shaven with brown hair that had a mind of its own. "And by the way, the professor gave everybody in the class an A because it made him feel as if his message had gotten through to us, confirming his egotistic assumption that he should have been molding young minds at Princeton instead of squandering his talent at Montclair State."

The fly again buzzed the table, back and forth in front of Evie until eventually landing on the tip of her nose. She hated all pests, ants especially, but with flies it was more personal because they refused to take no for an answer and she made up her mind that this particular pest was going to learn that lesson the hard way. She moved her hand close, slowly as to not scare it away. Then closer still until she realized that she could not swat the fly without slapping herself in the face.

"I could say the fly is attracted because you're sweet as sugar."

"But you wouldn't," Evie told him as she swatted the fly in the direction of some other lucky diner. "Because any man who reads poetry without a gun to his head would never be so corny. Or do you write that ineffable drivel as well?"

"Ineffable drivel? Do you prepare insults from a thesaurus before all your dates?"

"Are you this insulting to all *your* dates?"

Sometimes Evie lashed out when she was nervous. A defense mechanism triggered by an insecurity about her looks. Her abilities. A lot of things, because she had never been encouraged as a child. But she was positive that all of these perceived inadequacies could be overcome by achieving success. Especially her biggest fear of all, that of being seen as ordinary.

After an awkward pause, Evie apologized. Tom too. Then they both broke out laughing, and Tom became smitten by the sexy dimples that appeared when she smiled.

"You have to look at it this way, Evie. That fly could have gone to any of the Indian restaurants on this block, but he chose this one. The best one. And he could have annoyed anyone here, but he chose you."

"Philosophy major?"

"Psychology."

"You're a doctor?"

"I'm a policeman."

Evie choked on a bite of lamb. Was this some sort of elaborate set up where a cop arranged a chance meeting at her work, then poured on the charm to lull her into a false sense of security so he could trick her into a murder confession? But if he was trying to trap her, why come out and admit that he was a cop? A fourth-generation New York City cop, he had gone on to tell her. A job that was in his blood as his father, grandfather and his father before him had all retired at the rank of captain. He had graduated from NYU in three years, joined the police department and moved up quickly through the ranks to lieutenant, no doubt in his mind that he would go all the way to the top. And even though he gave no indication of an ulterior motive, Evie would keep her guard up with first-date small talk until it was time to call it a night.

They talked about this and that, but mostly Evie just listened. Learning that most New York cops lived in New Jersey or on Long Island, but Lieutenant Thomas Vaught who, at age thirty-one, had become one of the youngest in modern department history to achieve that rank, had planted his flag firmly in the city. New York was the capital of the world and birthplace of all that was cool and exciting. He was invigorated by the fact that he could walk everywhere, and that if he varied his route by even one block it could open up an entire new world of possibilities. A record shop, a gallery, an antiquarian bookstore. A few days earlier he had walked up Thompson Street instead of West Broadway, stopped into Jamesey's for a beer and met Evie.

"You're a police lieutenant, but what is it that you actually do?"

"I command the Manhattan Major Crimes Squad. It's part of the Special Investigation Division."

"You're in charge of murder cases?"

"Not usually, unless the murder is part of a larger investigation."

"Like Son of Sam and the other two murders I read about that he's getting credit for?"

"You don't think he killed those two people in Manhattan?"

"The Manhattan killings were bold and daring, while Son of Sam is a coward who shoots girls making out in parked cars. Giving him the credit is just cheap sensationalism to sell newspapers."

"We have a task force of three hundred officers searching for one man in a city of eight million people, and it's the department's position that using a second gun in Manhattan is more than likely a ploy to divide manpower by making us look for a second killer who doesn't exist."

"A second killer does exist."

"Do you know something the police don't?"

"Of course not. But from what I read in the newspapers I think it's pretty obvious. As soon as Son of Sam is arrested, you'll see that I'm right." She took a sip of her beer. "And your job really isn't to investigate any of these murders?"

Tom was convincing when he told her that his plate was full commanding the Major Crimes Squad, making Evie finally believe that when the man with the soft brown eyes on the other side of the table had stopped into her work for a cold one, it had indeed been a legitimate boy meets girl moment.

The mood lightened and after dinner they checked out Club 57, an artist hangout beneath an old Polish church on St. Marks Place. They walked in as artist Keith Haring was doing a ventriloquist act inside a television made out of a cardboard box, first-date threads making them look more than a tad out of place among paint-stained T-shirts and girls at the vanguard of thrift store chic. Evie said hi to Patti Smith, a singer and lyricist among the first to break nationally out of the downtown scene, who she knew from when she had worked at the bookstore. Prompting Tom to remark that he did not know whether to be impressed that she knew Patti Smith or astonished that she was civil to a poet.

Evie felt a tingle when Tom took her hand as they walked up Second Avenue toward her apartment, a slight breeze making the warm summer night a little more agreeable. After assuaging her initial paranoia and seeing that he had no professional agenda, she had had a wonderful time. But dating a cop? Should it matter? It was no longer the sixties where the police were looked upon as pigs, but it was still only 1977, and nobody she knew would ever be friends with a cop, let alone date one. But this guy was handsome, knew about art and music. Could she fall for a cop? Why not? Some people liked asparagus.

CHAPTER 13

Evie got up early and aimed her binoculars at Tom's window, but reflection of the morning sun denied access. She wondered when he would call. If he would call. Opened her sweater drawer and looked at the nine-millimeter Smith & Wesson automatic, but instead picked up her journal and wrote down all the reasons why she should fully embrace a personal crusade to rid the city of criminals one at a time. Reasons her conscience refused to endorse. Refusing to back down from the position that killing, whatever the circumstance, could not be tolerated. The words *forbidden* and *evil* carved in stone. But how could evil exist inside any person who killed in the name of righteousness?

It wasn't until a couple days later that Evie figured out a way to take control of the situation, reprogramming her conscience to accept a broader interpretation of right and wrong that gave her a green light to follow the calling that would forever define her. Where she needed to be smart and calculate every move, as even one mistake would bring her virtuous crusade crashing down around her. For starters that meant staying away from Times Square for a while and plying her trade in neighborhoods where she would not be recognized, so she decided to check out the lay of the land on the upper west side. Walked up Broadway from 72nd Street and saw women lugging groceries, men shooting the breeze outside bars and teenagers crowding the ticket holders line for the 8:55 showing of *Exorcist II*.

Broadway was the main stem, too busy and too well-lit, so she cut over a block to Amsterdam and found more of a neighborhood feel as she walked past an old married couple and a young mother in gym shorts pushing a stroller. Food delivery man and a kid dribbling a basketball. Where were all the bad guys, she wondered as boots blistered her feet more with every unsuccessful block she walked. Frustration finally making her begin to understand how the cops felt, with no idea how to isolate one person in a city of eight million.

Conceding her pilgrimage uptown to be a lost cause, Evie walked over a couple blocks to Riverside Park, a narrow strip of lush greenery overlooking the Hudson River that ran all the way up into Harlem. The park was quiet at this time of night, and a cooling breeze off the water that rustled the trees gave texture to the silence as Evie made her way down a dirt pathway to a paved pedestrian and bicycle trail where she sat on a bench facing the river. The calming scent of nature was relaxing as she rested her aching feet and gathered her thoughts, beginning to formulate a list of dos and don'ts to which she would have to adhere in order to become a successful serial killer. Number one was a no-brainer; always wear sensible shoes. Number two; always have a pre-determined target or select a place with no shortage of them. Number three, and she assumed the most important, was to always have a well thought out exit strategy.

"Smoke. Smoke," called a squirrely man in his thirties with long stringy hair and a rip in the knee of his jeans, slowing down as he approached Evie without making eye contact. His tone hushed but loud enough for her to understand, reminding her of the first time she had heard someone say that. Naïve kid that she was, having lived in the city only a couple of days, she assumed the drug dealer had been asking for a cigarette. Naïve no longer with two kills to her credit, Evie sized up the dealer before deciding that hawking joints in the park hardly qualified him to be victim number three.

Evie wondered how other serial killers chose their victims. Low hanging fruit, she supposed, easily lured by the promise of sex or money. But Evie liked the element of surprise, and the look of shock on the skinhead's face when he suddenly realized that in one second he would be dead had given her a rush. She had read that when a person knows they are about to die their entire life flashes before them. Was that true? How could anyone possibly know and live to write about it? Time would have to stop so that the person facing death could review all of their accomplishments and weigh them against their regrets. Were they scared or was it a moment of peace? Maybe one day she would stretch out that final second for some unlucky bastard and ask him, then blow him to kingdom come.

As Evie enjoyed the peacefulness of the park, she saw a kid on a bicycle roll up to the dealer. The kid could not have been more than eleven or twelve years old, and after a few moments they moved away from the benches but not out of

Evie's line of sight as she shook her head in disbelief at how a kid that young was buying pot. Then saw that it wasn't pot. Small bindles meant cocaine or more than likely heroin. And selling junk to a kid, even if he was scoring for someone else, definitely qualified the dealer to be victim number three.

As the kid pedaled away, Evie scanned the park in all directions and saw that there was no one in sight. Waited a couple minutes. Still no one. Looked over at the dirt path that rose only steps away from the taxis on Riverside Drive, then when the stringy-haired dealer again walked past, Evie gestured to him.

He played it cool as he approached her. "What do you need?"

"Weed. But I don't have any money."

"Come back when you do."

Evie smiled suggestively. "Maybe we can work something out."

He looked her over, then checked in both directions to make sure that there were no other people around. "Maybe we can."

Evie pointed up the hill toward an area thick with greenery that abutted the rock retaining wall below Riverside Drive, having changed her mind about using the lure of sex as this guy was making it so easy. "It looks private over there."

"Is that where your boyfriend's waiting to rob me?"

"Forget it. I'll find somebody else."

"Chill, babe. Just being careful." He pointed in the opposite direction. "We'll go that way."

"Whatever you say."

He led her to an equally secluded area behind a huge boulder, held up a joint and told her to get down on her knees.

"Two," Evie told him.

"You better be worth it," he griped as he reached into his pocket and pulled out the second joint. That's when he saw the nine-millimeter automatic.

"Fucking bitch," he grumbled, his mind trying to choreograph a move that would knock the weapon from her hand before she could pull the trigger. Realized it would be impossible, then reluctantly offered up his stash and his money. When she didn't take it, he turned his pockets inside out to prove it was all he had. "I worked hard for this. Why don't you go rob some millionaire?"

Evie could feel her heart pumping and breath came faster as she assumed the stance and took aim. This time careful not to lose her focus. This time prepared for the kick of the gun. One shot. It was vital that he be put down with one shot.

"Okay, okay. Take it all." He reached into his sock and pulled out the big bills, frightened out of his mind as the gun was inches from his face. Stuttering, choking out the words. "I'm giving you everything I have. You don't have to do this. Please, I'm begging you!"

Engaging in conversation had brought her dangerously close to humanizing him and she squeezed the trigger just in time, the crack of the shot screaming through the stillness of the night. So earsplitting that it startled Evie, causing her to almost trip over the dead man whose body lay twisted at a grotesque angle.

"Over there!"

The booming voice was close by, and Evie scrambled through the trees to get out of there before it got closer. Only a few steps into her getaway when she saw two plainclothes policemen coming toward her, badges hanging from their necks. She did an about face and saw two more, then ducked behind a clump of bushes not twenty feet from the body of the man she had killed. Held her breath and steadied herself on all fours, trying desperately to not make even the slightest sound that might call attention to herself. She could see them examining the crime scene but was pretty sure that from that vantage point they could not see her.

"There was no time for the killer to get past us. He's hiding somewhere close by," called out the officer in charge as more police arrived. "Set up a perimeter and work your way back toward the scene. Check behind every bush and every rock, up every tree. He's armed and he's already killed once, so be alert."

What the hell happened, Evie's brain screamed. She had looked twice to make sure that the area was clear, checked the escape route and still, in a matter of seconds there were cops everywhere, leaving her no choice but to make a break for it. Running would be an admission of guilt, so she stood up and walked at a normal pace back toward the bench. Cops to her left and to her right but none in front of her. She walked as fast as she could without making it look like she was in a hurry and the dirt path back up to the street was in sight. Each step felt like a mile but she made it unnoticed. A clean escape as she could see the traffic on Riverside Drive where she would flag down a taxi and get the hell out of there.

"POLICE. DON'T MOVE."

Evie's heart stopped as a uniformed officer raced up the path toward her. In her purse, he would find the gun, barrel still warm, and it would all be over. She had no choice but to accept the reality that she was going to be locked inside a cage forever. *Her* last second stretched out. Only it was not her life that flashed before her eyes, it was her future. A future where she would never see her name on the bestseller list, never drink Mai Tais on a beach in Tahiti or wine in the cafes of Paris. Then the cop cut short her final second, just as she had cut short the final second of the man lying dead beside the boulder.

"Did you see anybody go past here?" he demanded.

"Huh?"

"A man was shot to death right over there. Did you see anybody run past? Anybody around here at all?"

"No, Officer. I'm on my way home from a friend's house."

"Let's see some ID."

Her license was in her wallet and her wallet was in her purse next to the gun. No matter how carefully she unzipped the purse and reached inside, there was no way trained eyes would miss it.

"ID. Now."

If she said that she didn't have it with her he would be suspicious. If she turned the purse away from him before reaching inside he would be suspicious. As it was, the gruff middle-aged cop could see that she was stalling.

"What are you hiding? What's in your purse?"

"Nothing."

"Are you protecting someone?"

"No."

"What did you see?"

"I didn't see anything."

"I don't believe you."

Evie could smell her body odor as she shivered from a cold sweat.

"You were near the crime scene when a man was killed. You had to have seen something. Now tell me what you saw."

"I didn't see anything."

"Something about you isn't right. What are you hiding?"

"Nothing."

"You know something and I want to know what it is."

"I already told you that I'm on my way home from a friend's house and I don't know anything."

"Maybe a ride to the precinct will help you remember."

"Okay, cop. Do you really need to know that badly? Do you really have to embarrass me like this?" Evie scrunched up her face and made a show of fidgeting uncomfortably. "I just got my period and I have to get home. I have to get home now!"

"Open your purse."

"What the hell is wrong with you? Let me go before I have an accident!"

"Open your purse."

"Do you have a daughter?"

"Four of them." He thought for a moment then half-smiled. "Okay. Get the hell out of here."

CHAPTER 14

Tom did call, the ringing phone jolting Evie from a sound sleep. Sugary patter. A date was made. It was past ten when she hung up. No time to go to Mr. Kim's for coffee, but she made time to write in her journal. Every detail of the confrontation with her victim, and how for that brief instant they had shared the most intimate connection two people possibly could until he fell to the ground and the entire area was teeming with police. She wrote down every detail and every emotion she could remember until her thoughts turned practical.

> *how come there is never a cop around*
> *when you need one, but when you don't*
> *they swarm in like a hundred clowns piling*
> *out of a volkswagen. i had it planned*
> *perfectly, from the secure kill spot to the*
> *clean escape route. but i learned that i*
> *can't just lure a target someplace out of*
> *sight, because in new york you're never*
> *completely out of sight. so how do i plan*

*for the unforeseen? i suppose the only
way is to remain focused and prepared
to talk my way out of any jam like when i
mouthed off to that cop. survival demands
that I stack the odds in my favor by being
smart and paying attention to detail. i'm
an educated woman eluding a police force
that is searching for a man, and as long as
i can keep them thinking that, this will be
a breeze.*

*NO NO NO. i can't get cocky because it
takes only one mistake to bring me down.
i need to be smarter than anybody who
did this before me. i need to read as many
books as i can about serial killers and see
how they succeeded and the fatal mistakes
that eventually brought them to justice.
i need to learn from those mistakes as
well as from my own, because another
close call like last night and this righteous
crusade of mine will be over before it ever
really gets started.*

Evie showered and got ready quickly. Her best dress, best shoes and her grandmother's pearls. After all, one did not luncheon with one's mother at the Plaza wearing anything less than her finest.

She said hello to the super on her way out of the building, making a mental note to drop off the rent went she got back.

Then was greeted by a gorgeous day as she walked to the Astor Place subway station, feeling great that she and her mother were not only reliving their happiest memories but were about to embark on new ones. Browsing the new fall styles at Saks and Bergdorf, then instead of ice cream sodas at the St. Moritz they might enjoy a proper cocktail at the Sherry Netherland. Then passing a newsstand, Evie's life changed forever as she saw the headline of the *New York Post*.

HOUDINI KILLER TERRORIZES MANHATTAN

Evie grabbed a copy and saw that Son of Sam had killed in Brooklyn at the same time another nine-millimeter murder was being committed in Riverside Park. She could barely contain her excitement as she read how a half-dozen police, on the scene almost immediately as they had been nearby in the park working an unrelated investigation, had the killer cornered until he made an impossible escape. One of the officers was quoted as saying, "It was like he vanished into thin air".

On the subway uptown, Evie tingled like a school girl as she read about the three Houdini killings and how the entire city was now in a panic as no one felt safe anywhere. When Son of Sam was shooting teenagers in the outer boroughs, most jaded Manhattanites were concerned only about the weather, uncollected trash and how many home runs Reggie Jackson hit. But now that the Houdini Killer was on their turf people were scared, with the mayor and the police commissioner running true to form with the empty promise of a quick arrest. No chance, fellas, Evie laughed. The cops had no clues and she would make sure they never would as the stakes had been raised. The media had given her a nickname, her book had a title and the game was on.

Evie carefully tore off the front page of the paper, folded it and put it in her purse. Got off the train at 59th Street and walked a few blocks west to the Plaza Hotel where Maxine was waiting outside wearing a flowery blue tea dress she had purchased for the occasion. Mother and daughter hugged, both thrilled to be reviving a tradition so close to their hearts.

Seated for luncheon at the Palm Court they ordered champagne cocktails, then without being obvious took a census of the people seated around the bright open restaurant. Mothers with young children of privilege, a smattering of tourists and a few men discussing business. But Evie and Maxine's focus was on the ladies, as recognizing famous faces was an amusement they used to share, and right away spotted a couple gossip column regulars and a long-retired movie queen from Hollywood's golden age. Jewelry suggested that most of the remaining ladies in the room were too wealthy to care about anything as gauche as celebrity.

"The woman on your right in the Chanel suit is a Kennedy," Evie whispered to her mother.

"How do you know?"

"That inbred face is a dead giveaway."

Maxine gave her daughter a scolding look, then said, "Lasagna."

"Kennedys eat lasagna?"

"On my birthday, you asked what my favorite food was. It's lasagna." Maxine allowed her memory to return her to yet another special time. "When I was a teenager, my father used to take the family to Mama Velvetella's in Passaic every

Sunday night. Red checked tablecloths, candles in Chianti bottles and an Italian crooner who looked just like Mario Lanza. They had the best lasagna in North Jersey. I was too young to know that for sure, but everybody said so."

"How come you never made it for us at home?" Evie asked, then abruptly answered her own question. "Because Dad only likes meat and potatoes."

"Don't start, Evie."

"Next time you come to the city we're going to go to this hole in the wall red sauce place I know in Little Italy. Their lasagna is to die for."

"That sounds wonderful." Maxine smiled at her daughter. "Maybe your boyfriend can join us."

"What boyfriend?"

"Ever since we got here I've noticed a certain sparkle in your eye. You're in love."

"No, Mom."

"What else could make you glow like that?"

While Evie wanted so badly to tell the woman across the table that her daughter was on the front page of every newspaper in New York, she realized the tremendous weight of the secret that she would never be able to tell anyone. But right now, she had to tell her mother something.

"It's not love, Mom. But I did meet someone."

"Tell me all about him."

"He's gorgeous and has the dreamiest brown eyes."

"Is he creative? A writer or an artist?"

"He's a policeman. Lieutenant." She saw her mother doing the math, then set her mind at ease. "One of the youngest ever in the department. He's thirty-one."

"Not to pry, but what do a writer and a policeman have in common besides sex?"

"I've only been out with him once."

"It's a modern world, Evie," she said as lobster salad was placed before each of them. "You told me that yourself. Does Lieutenant Brown Eyes have a name?"

"Tom. Thomas Vaught, soon to be the youngest commissioner in the history of the New York City Police Department."

"You say that with a lot of pride, like maybe you see a future together."

"Like I said, we've only had one date."

All through the meal they chattered like sisters. Movies. Fall fashions. Celebrity gossip. Then when it was time for tea and ladyfingers, Maxine again became a mother.

"I heard on the news about this new Houdini Killer who's murdering people in Manhattan. I hope you won't go out alone at night."

"I'll be fine, Mom."

"I already worry about all the crime in the East Village."

"You've seen my apartment. I live in a secure building."

"But what about the rest of the neighborhood?"

"It's safe, Mom."

"It's a slum."

"A lot of the buildings may be old and in disrepair, but cheap rent attracts a lot of interesting artistic people who, along with the galleries and shops and great ethnic restaurants that are opening, give the neighborhood character."

"What about Alphabet City? Mrs. Shapiro down the block has a nephew who used to live on Avenue A, and he said he had to step over needles and human filth just to get into his apartment."

"That's an exaggeration." Well intentioned dishonesty to pacify a worried mother. "Besides, that's nowhere near where I live."

"It's two blocks away."

"I have no reason to ever go anywhere near there, and neither do any of my friends. Nobody with any brains goes past A."

"What about the stockbroker who was stabbed and robbed there just last week?"

"That dumb ass was in a limo trying to buy cocaine on Avenue C."

"Are you saying he got what he deserved?"

"Of course not. But he may as well have painted a target on his back."

"Flippant remarks like that make me worry even more. And now with that psycho killer on the loose …"

"The Houdini Killer is not a psycho."

"Just promise me you'll be careful, Evie. When you have a daughter of your own you'll understand."

"You honestly don't have anything to worry about," she said reassuringly, reaching across the table and taking her mother's hand. "Besides, I have a big handsome policeman to protect me."

CHAPTER 15

"**S**omething sure smells good."

"Veal scaloppini," Evie announced proudly as she welcomed Tom into her apartment.

He handed her a bottle of white wine.

"You're sweet, Tom, but I know you're more of a beer man," she said as she checked out his blue alligator shirt and slacks, then set the wine on the kitchen counter and opened the refrigerator. Popped the tops off two bottles of Beck's.

"A woman after my own heart," he said as he took in her long brown hair that had just a bit of natural curl, her crooked smile and every last bit of what he imagined to be underneath her yellow polka dot dress. Other men might say that she was no better than average looking, but Evie could not have been more Tom's type if he had ordered her from a catalog.

He and Evie sat together on the couch, but not too close as both had first date jitters, even though they had already spent an evening together that had ended with a passionate goodnight kiss.

"Tell me about the book you're writing."

"Right now, it's just an outline. I'm still doing a lot of research." As excited as Evie was about the serial killer novel she hoped would make her a literary sensation, she knew that for now it was best to keep the subject matter a secret. Especially from Tom. "But I've been submitting a lot of short stories to magazines."

"Any particular genre?"

"I'm writing a lot about the neighborhood. The punks and the artists who have recently moved here. The immigrants and the lunatics who have always been here. Even bums on the Bowery are intriguing, with a thousand unique stories of how they hit the skids. I just wish I had the courage to do more than walk quickly past them."

"Directly or indirectly, people on the severe downside of advantage have always been catalysts for the creation of great art and music," he told her as he checked out the artwork on her walls by neighborhood nobodies that Evie hoped would someday become somebodies. "Jazz and blues are perfect examples. Even American folk music."

"Shit!" Evie bolted from the couch and dashed to the stove, pulling the pan from the flame. The sauce had burned off and the meat had started to become dry. She was crestfallen. "The dinner's ruined."

"No, it's not."

"I wanted this meal to be perfect," she groaned, looking at the writing table she had dressed up with tulips and arranged with the place settings just so.

"And it will be," he assured her, quickly commandeering the kitchen.

Evie was in awe as she watched Tom gently loosen the meat with a spatula, set it aside and scrape the brown bits from the bottom of the pan. Locate a corkscrew, add some wine and replace the veal. Then he turned the flame down as low as it would go, covered the pan and placed it back on the burner.

"I'm so embarrassed."

"These things happen, Evie."

"My mother is a great cook but I never had the knack. This is the first time I've attempted anything more challenging than meatloaf when the refrigerator needed to be cleaned out. I'm sorry I made a mess of our evening."

"Nonsense. You made a great meal and all it needs is a little steam to wake up the flavor." He took a sip of his beer and smiled encouragingly. "Go ahead and serve the salad. By the time we finish, the veal will be tender and delicious."

And it was.

"You're an amazing man, Tom Vaught." She put a Roxy Music record on the turntable, one of several LPs she had selected in advance to set a romantic mood. "Was that some old school Italian trick with the scaloppini?"

"Not all cops are Italian or Irish. I come from a very tradi-tional Polish family."

"And your mother taught you how to cook."

"The men in my family were never allowed in the kitchen. A point of maternal power, just as it had been with her mother and her mother before her."

"Then how did you know how to rescue the veal?"

"Trial and error from the first few times I left something on the stove too long."

"Do you cook a lot?"

"Usually I pick up Indian food on the way home from work, but I do enjoy cooking. Actually, I enjoy the preparation as much as the meal itself. Sometimes on a rainy weekend I like to stay in and make soup. Read a book and enjoy the aroma as it simmers all day on the stove."

"Do you cook Indian food?"

"Most of the recipes are either too complicated or require a very subtle hand. Besides, no matter how many times I tried I could never make maacher jhol as good as any of the restaurants on 6th Street, so what would be the point? I got a cookbook from my sister in Baltimore last Christmas and I like to try something new every time."

"Which I'm sure makes a lot of girls happy."

"Never anyone as pretty as you."

Evie blushed. Not just because he had said it, but because of the heartfelt way in which he had said it.

"Why do you think I stopped at Jamesey's the other day? I was on my way to Arturo's to meet some friends when I saw you through the window. I must have stood there for five minutes looking at you until I summoned the nerve to walk inside."

They sat face to face, drawing each other in. She quivered as he raked her hair behind her ear, then drew her fingers gently across his cheek. Both of them frozen in a perfect moment of anticipation until desire demanded they kiss. Then they sat back in each other's arms, gazing out the window at a nocturnal skyline of concrete and glass the way other lovers sat in convertibles looking at the stars.

"I live in that tall white brick building, and it's fascinating to see it from this perspective," Tom said. "Kind of makes me wish you had a telescope so that I could get a candid look at my neighbors."

"You're a peeping Tom?" she giggled. "Tom."

"If people leave their blinds open in this city they are pretty much inviting company. And it might be interesting to look into the lives of people I've only seen in the elevator."

Tom followed as Evie got up and slipped a Coltrane disc onto the turntable, took her in his arms and kissed her. Led her into the bedroom and unzipped her yellow polka dot dress, taking his time as he undressed her, then himself. Each of them exploring the other as they messed up Evie's perfectly made bed. Tom eventually working his tongue south until his face was between her legs.

Was this really about to happen? Evie wasn't sure that this was something that had ever happened, to anybody. Nobody had ever gone down on her or any of her friends from New Jersey. It was not something that men did. Sure, they expected girls to open wide, but she assumed that the idea of men willfully and unselfishly providing oral delight was just an urban myth you read about in *Cosmopolitan*. But Tom was a sophisticated New Yorker, and as his tongue peeled her apart like a sweet Georgia peach, Evie writhed with an ecstasy that rocketed her into outer space.

When she floated back to reality Evie only hoped she could send him as far into orbit as he had sent her, but worried that she did not have the talent, as men had always tried to jam themselves down her throat, which was not pleasant for anyone. But once Tom was inside her mouth he let it all happen naturally and she was on cruise control, loving it every bit as much as he did. Passion carrying them deep into the night until eventually they fell asleep in each other's arms.

Morning sun tried its best to sneak through the blinds, eventually succeeding in waking them up in the same position in which they had nodded off. Gentle kisses gave way to an urge for caffeine.

"I'm afraid I make coffee about as well as I cook," Evie confessed.

"Do you have the fixings?"

"Sure, but ..."

"How do you take it?" smiled Tom as he slipped out of bed.

"Two sugars, but ..."

Yeah, his butt. She could not take her eyes off of it as she watched her gorgeous lover walk out of the bedroom toward the kitchen. A few minutes later Tom set a hot mug on each nightstand, then climbed back under the covers.

"Mmm, that's good," Evie smiled, not the least bit surprised as she took a sip of her coffee. A lot better than going to the corner for the dreck Mr. Kim pours at the bodega. "Is there anything you can't do?"

"I can't screw in a light bulb."

"What do you mean?"

"The old joke. How many Polacks does it take to screw in a light bulb?"

"I don't know." She set down her coffee and wrapped her arms around her new man. "But I do know how many handsome Polish policemen it takes to screw Evie Eastway."

He proved her right. Twice. She remained firm in her belief that all sex was violence, but with Tom Vaught, it was an iron fist in a velvet glove.

"There's a street fair in Chelsea today," he said, not wanting this wonderful morning to end. "Might be fun."

"I have to work at noon."

Tom glanced at the clock radio beside the bed. "We still have time for breakfast, and I know a place that's guaranteed to be the best you've ever had."

The oppressive summer heat had moved on to torment the citizens of some other metropolis and it looked as though it was going to be a beautiful Saturday as they strolled hand in hand a few blocks down First Avenue. Past parked cars whose owners hoped to avoid smashed windows with dashboard signs that read "NO STEREO," a woman pissing in a door-way and a drunk passed out on the sidewalk spooning with an overturned trash can. But all the lovers noticed were each other as they stopped at a nondescript sliver of a storefront. Bare white walls, a Formica counter with eight stools and a stocky old woman with a bun of wiry gray hair who took orders and worked the grill. She dropped everything when she saw Tom, rushed out from behind the counter and gave him a bear hug.

"My Tommy! Too long since I see you."

"Come on, Busha, you see me every morning," he smiled. "Say hello to Evie."

"A girlfriend and you don't tell me?"

She gave Evie an examining look, making her wish she had worn something more presentable than faded jeans and a Stooges T-shirt, but that self-consciousness evaporated in an instant when the old woman smiled approvingly.

"So pretty, and such sweet dimples when you smile. You call me Busha."

"Thank you, Busha," Evie blushed. "It's very nice to meet you."

As the old lady went back around the counter she leaned across and, with a very pleased look on her face, said something to Tom in Polish.

"What did she say?" Evie asked as Busha attended to other customers.

"When we know each other better I'll tell you."

"Does busha mean grandmother in Polish?"

"You catch on quickly." He was impressed. "Until my real grandmother passed away, the two of them lived across the hall from each other for over sixty years. Two women were never so close."

"And now she's *your* busha?"

"That's how close our families were. Her husband died a long time ago and her children and grandchildren have all moved away, so she needed someone to look after. And she needed to feel useful, so she opened this place."

"And you eat here every morning."

"That I do."

"Did my Tommy tell you he was valedictor at college?"

"Valedictorian, Busha."

"Is what I said, valedictor." The old lady smiled at Evie. "He never brag, but important you should know about things like this."

"Have you ever not come in first at something?" Evie asked, only half teasing.

"I was a second child," he smiled.

Evie had never seen a restaurant so sparkling clean. The counter, the grill, even the floor was spotless into the deepest corner. That's when she noticed several live chickens making themselves at home in the back room.

"Is that legal?"

"Not even a little bit, but the health inspector is getting fat from her apple pancakes."

"Next time, pretty Evie, I make apple pancakes for you." Busha set a large plate of fresh scrambled eggs, latkes and kielbasa in front of each of them. "But today you have my Tommy's favorite. What you like to drink?"

"Whatever Tom is having."

"Two water with lots ice, coming up."

"This is delicious!" said Evie, marveling at the unique flavor as she took a bite of latke. "I've never tasted anything quite like it."

"Told you."

Evie eyed Tom as he shoveled home his breakfast. "If you eat this every day, how do you stay in such good shape?"

"Chasing bad guys keeps me fit."

"Be careful, Tommy," warned the old lady as she delivered the waters. "This new Houdini in Manhattan now."

"You don't have anything to worry about, Busha. He won't come around this neighborhood," Tom assured her, then winked. "At least if he knows what's good for him."

"My Tommy has judo belt and trophies for winning fights."

"Those were competitions, Busha. I never beat up anyone."

"Don't you worry about being safe, pretty Evie," the old woman said with a great deal of pride. "My Tommy will beat up this Houdini, tie him like pretzel and throw his dupka in jail."

CHAPTER 16

For the next couple weeks Tom and his new girl were rarely apart. He escorted her to the movies, to the theatre and, even though he knew that his appearance was way too square to fit in, took her to see the Heartbreakers at CBGB and Jayne County at Max's Kansas City. They had beers with a couple of his cop buddies and shot pool at his favorite bar with Evie's friend Manda, who had been one of her roommates at the railroad flat on Ludlow Street where she lived when she had first moved to the city. Tom showed off darts and pool trophies he had won, and let Evie win a game of eight ball while Manda beat him on the square. Tom and Evie had become inseparable. His place. Her place. The sex always more invigorating than the night before, both of them over the moon in love but too nervous to be the first one to say it.

This night it was dinner at his place where he had made a fairly successful attempt at coq au vin. A cozy night at home until his pager went off. He made a call, then put on a fresh white shirt and tie. Slipped into a light blue suit, gave his shoes a quick brushing, kissed his girl goodbye and was out the door ready to serve and protect.

It was closing in on midnight when Tom got off the elevator on the thirteenth floor of One Police Plaza and found himself in the middle of a wild party. Top brass boozing it up with detectives and uniformed officers. Reporters with a drink in one hand and a telephone in the other. All that was missing were noisemakers and party hats as dozens of people with no legitimate reason to be there kicked up their heels in the restricted area. Mayor Abe Beame stuffed cash into the shirt pocket of a man delivering reinforcement cases of scotch and bourbon from Jim Brady's, a popular cop-friendly watering hole that right now was doing less business than the thirteenth floor of One PP.

Tom understood the reason for celebration. But it was the wrong place and wrong time as, on this night of all nights, it was imperative that protocol be followed to the letter. He weaved his way through the commotion looking for the Chief of Detectives, instead finding himself face to face with the guest of honor.

Son of Sam.

He sure didn't look like much, Tom thought. A pudgy man-child with a stupid grin on his face as he sat alone at a table in the conference room. He seemed more the type to have been pinched for swiping a candy bar than terrorizing millions while evading the entire New York City police force. The serial killer, whose name was David Berkowitz, did not even react as Tom sat down across the table. His glassy eyes were empty, but still with the stupid smile.

"Why did you kill all those people?"

Nothing. Not even a blink.

"You know how we nabbed him, Tom?"

Tom stood and faced a graying man in an open-collared dress shirt who had entered the room.

"Parking citation. He left his car next to a hydrant at the scene of his last murder."

"Lucky break."

"Following that lead was good police work, Tom."

"Is it also good police work to leave a prisoner unguarded in an unlocked conference room with a party going on right outside the door?"

"He's handcuffed."

"Was he read his Miranda rights?"

"I don't like your tone, Lieutenant."

"I apologize, Commissioner." But Tom could not let it go. "Is his handwriting a match with the letters left at the crime scenes? Have ballistics reports confirmed his gun as the murder weapon?"

"He confessed, so what difference does it make? Said his neighbor's dog wanted blood from pretty young girls."

"What else did he say?"

"Just that he wanted to plead guilty, then he clammed up. Look, Tom, it was a good arrest and this whack job is going away forever. It's safe for people to walk the streets again."

"Not in Manhattan."

"Why are you here? This isn't your case."

"It's the biggest arrest in decades and puts the entire department under a microscope. I came down here to make sure that everything is done by the book, and with that mob boozing it up out there, it's a good thing I did."

"Are you such a tight ass that you begrudge these men one night to celebrate?"

"Does it also make me a tight ass if I point out that liquor is not permitted inside any New York City police facility?"

"The mayor understands that the department has been under a tremendous strain, and he waived the no-liquor policy for tonight. The boys deserve to blow off steam, and if your old man was here he'd be out there whooping it up with the rest of them." The commissioner sat and gestured for Tom to do the same, Sam remaining still as sculpture as if they weren't even there. "How is your father these days?"

"He and Mom are enjoying retirement in Florida."

"He was one of the finest officers I ever had the pleasure to serve with. Give him my best the next time you talk to him."

"I will, Sir. But what about the Houdini Killer?"

"He'll be caught just like this retard."

"And how long did that take? Houdini hasn't made a mistake or left even one clue in three trips to the plate. He's smart, and with the exception of a possible vigilante angle, so far we have nothing to go on."

"It was never reported to the press, but a fingerprint on the shell casing at the scene of the first murder belonged to the victim, meaning that he was shot with his own gun. And the shooter didn't pick up his brass from the other two crime scenes either. So, we know that Houdini is not as smart as you think he is. He's eventually going to screw up somewhere. All criminals do."

"And how many more people will die while we're waiting for that to happen? Nothing personal against Inspector Dowd and the Omega task force, but taking a year to bring this half-wit to justice is not acceptable."

"Don't try to make this a competition between you and Dowd. Why is it so important for you to come in first at absolutely everything?"

"Because it brings out the best in me, making me dig deep to succeed where others ultimately fail. And right now, that competitive drive is more important than ever because this Houdini Killer must be apprehended quickly."

"And how do you suggest we do that?"

"By being proactive and getting ahead of him rather than always being a step behind." Tom looked the commissioner square in the eye. "I'm requesting that you give me command of a squad of my own choosing. Men and women with sharp instincts who are not afraid of hard work and long hours. Officers clever enough to find a way inside the Houdini Killer's mind so that we can create our own breaks."

"There's nothing wrong with ambition, Tom, but you can't rush advancement. Your father didn't make captain until he was forty-seven. The Chief of D's already thinks you're angling for his job." The commissioner then added, knowing that he was not wrong. "Or is it my job that you're after?"

"In the morning when you and the mayor hold a press conference to pat yourselves on the back for finally catching this doofus, you'll be bombarded with questions about the Houdini Killer. Do you want to be held up to tabloid ridicule by feeding them the usual evasive double talk, or would you rather get in front of this by creating a positive buzz that assures the people of Manhattan that an elite task force has been formed that is already running down solid leads?"

CHAPTER 17

Son of Sam was toast and the tabloids would soon be all hers, a thought that propelled Evie's spirits as she sat on a bench in Washington Square Park checking out NYU students, chess players, panhandlers, musicians and people just passing through the crossroads of Greenwich Village. Indulging a writer's curiosity on the way to work as she did most days the weather would allow it.

"Smoke. Smoke," mumbled a young man in jeans and no shirt as he roller skated in front of the benches. Didn't he understand how dangerous selling joints in the park could be? Didn't he read the paper? But the Riverside killing was old news, Evie supposed, stoking her desire to scratch that itch.

It had been over two weeks since she had caused that panic at Riverside Park and, when she wasn't at work or with Tom, Evie had made use of the time by researching kindred spirits at the library, only to become frustrated at the dearth of in-depth information available about serial killers. To achieve longevity, she needed to be the best, and to be the best she needed to learn the finer points of her craft from those who had gone before her. She needed to get inside their minds and find out what made them kill. What fueled their desire to continue killing? Were victims targeted through planning or opportunity? What was the fatal mistake that led to their downfall? A lot of questions but few answers, as mostly what Evie found were just variations of news accounts and police reports. A lot of sensationalism, speculation and conjecture, causing Evie to wonder how much of recorded history was actually true. It was certainly skewed more than a bit as it was written by the winners, but how much of what was on library shelves was the real deal?

Did an outlaw named Billy the Kid really gun down eight men, or was it just a story he told to impress the barmaid at the Fort Sumner Holiday Inn? Suppose Paul Revere stumbled home drunk one night and woke up his neighbors by knocking over a few garbage cans. By the time the guy next door told the blacksmith, who told his wife, who told the butcher, who told his barber who eventually wrote it down, it could have easily become indisputable historical fact that Revere had ridden through the countryside waking up every Middlesex village and farm with news that the British were coming. History provided few checks and balances to keep stories anywhere near the vicinity of the truth, especially sensational stories like Jack the Ripper, that even at the time was based almost totally on theory and speculation. The only substantiated facts were that the women he killed were prostitutes. A sex angle. The Zodiac Killer who was making headlines in Northern California sent letters to the press saying that killing was even better than sex, further validating Evie's belief that violence was sex.

Research substantiated that Paul Knowles, Edmund Kemper and Mad Dog Taborsky were serial killers who had put impressive numbers on the scoreboard. All presumably with fascinating stories to tell, yet frustrating to Evie as she could not find one insightful word in print about any of them. Just where they were born. Where they went to school. Dates, places, victims. Nothing but cold facts that provided zero access into the inner workings of their minds. Only that many psychologists, few of whom had actually examined the men, were in agreement that they all subconsciously wanted to be caught. She did, however, find insight into the minds of educated killers who had been influenced by the writings of Baudelaire, chasing satisfaction on some greater spiritual plane only to be blindsided by the ultimate disappointment. But they weren't serial killers, they were mostly one and done and their stories of no help. Leaving Evie with the realization that all she could ever hope to know for sure about her craft would come from her own experience, that she absolutely did not want to be caught and that if she didn't get going she would be late for work.

"Looking good, girl!" called Stoney as a couple of the others wolf whistled as Evie walked into Jamesey's, reacting to a new personal style that reflected her newfound boldness of spirit. She had her hair cut asymmetrically, six inches shorter on one side than the other. Ditched the band shirts and jeans that most girls in the neighborhood were wearing and the flirty dresses that were so Jersey, for a full fashion makeover, creating a uniquely personal style. An understated mix of mod and punk that she accented with accessories from vintage shops and new punk boutiques like Trash and Vaudeville that had recently popped up on and around St. Marks Place. Tom loved the new look, but more importantly it made her feel special.

As Evie began her shift, she was surprised to hear zero discussion about the arrest of Son of Sam, as most of the barroom chatter took aim at the verdict in the case of the United States of America versus Wilton W. Millcross, head of a respected generations-old financial institution. A Wall Street firm in charge of managing, among other accounts, a pension plan for people who had spent their lives living from paycheck to paycheck. Blue collar working stiffs who had paid into the plan, many of them for forty years, and had retired comfortably on the monthly annuity until a little over a year ago when those benefits stopped. And it had not taken forensic accountants until much past lunchtime to determine that instead of being paid to the pensioners to whom it was owed, the money in the fund had instead been used by Wilton W. Millcross to purchase priceless works of art.

The middle-aged banker lived alone and kept mostly to himself, prompting Park Avenue gossip that he stayed in most nights masturbating in front of the Rembrandts and Monets that hung on his walls. He bought but never sold, and had amassed a collection that *Art Digest* had once valued at over $100 million. The harsh truth being that while he was shelling out cash for priceless works of art, the people whose money he was spending were being evicted from their homes because they could no longer pay the rent. Lives were ruined. Families were destroyed and innocent victims committed suicide. Then, finally, when the pensioners had their chance to send the thief to prison, repossess the paintings and replenish the fund, a fast-talking lawyer got Millcross acquitted on a hyper-technicality. And as public outrage exploded after the verdict was announced, he was already uptown at Christie's bidding on a recently discovered Gauguin.

"I wish I had five minutes alone with that son of a bitch."

"We all do, Stoney," agreed the mailman, who then signaled for Evie to set everyone up with another round.

"Unfortunately, that wouldn't get those people their money back," added Nanette.

"But it would sure as hell make the next guy think twice about robbing the working man," growled Stoney as the others nodded in agreement.

As the new round of shots and beers brought about a change in the conversation, Stoney drifted toward the slow end of the bar.

"How come you and Nanette never got together?" asked Evie as she noticed the older lady with fiery salon color checking him out.

"That's one hell of a woman."

"She's looking pretty good today, Stoney. Make a move."

"Not interested."

"She's totally into you. Another woman can see these things."

"Bad idea."

"Don't tell me you're shy," Evie laughed. "A man of the world like you."

"Drop it, Evie," he snapped.

"I didn't mean to upset you. It's just that I'm in love and want my friends to be as happy as I am."

"Sorry I barked at you. It's just that ..."

"You don't owe me an explanation. It's none of my business."

She poured Stoney a shot of bourbon. He downed it and she poured him another.

"You're a sweet kid, Evie." He glanced down the bar then looked away as he saw Nanette smiling at him. "Truth is that son of a bitch mugger took a lot more from me than just my watch and paycheck. The nerve damage that deadened my arm goes a lot lower."

"Oh, Stoney. I'm so sorry," she said, feeling terrible that she had embarrassed him. "I never would have said anything if I had known."

"*They* don't know," he said as he looked to the other end of the bar where the people he hung out with every day of his life were busy discussing this and that. "So, what do you say we keep this our little secret."

"Absolutely," Evie agreed, seeing the relief on his face from finally being able to share his private humiliation with someone. Then she aimed the conversation in a different direction. "What do you think about the Houdini Killer?"

It was not hard for Stoney to measure the degree of interest in her voice. "What do *you* think about him?

"He's bold and daring."

"And a vigilante."

"Says the man who wants five minutes alone with Wilton W. Millcross."

"I'd be a hero."

"Making vigilante justice sound pretty good."

"You hoping that maybe Houdini will teach that asshole a lesson?"

"Why not? He can do what the courts won't."

"By appointing himself judge, jury and executioner." Stoney took a cigarette from his pack, flicked open his gold lighter and bent his head to the flame. "Which is only justified if he's right."

"Would he be right about Wilton W. Millcross?"

"That greedy prick has an original Picasso in every bathroom, paid for with money he stole from people who worked hard all their lives and are now out in the street."

"So, it *would* be justified?"

"Just as sure as the sky is blue, my name is Gaylord Beaumont Hailstone and my cat pisses on the rug every time that damn Lynyrd Skynyrd song comes on the radio."

"Hey, Evie," called out a cab driver who had just walked in with the late edition of the *Daily News.* "Your boyfriend's in the paper."

The cabbie opened the newspaper and showed Evie a photo of the man who had made her morning coffee shaking hands with the police commissioner. Below it, an article announcing that Lieutenant Thomas Vaught had been appointed to head an elite task force to apprehend the Houdini Killer.

CHAPTER 18

"**A**rresting the Houdini Killer is going to make my career."

"*If* you catch him," challenged Evie, looking great in a white mini-skirt and loose-fitting striped top. A lone gothic earring dangling on the side her hair was shortest.

"Of course, I'll catch him." Tom did not think it possible that his girlfriend could ever look more beautiful but her new look really upped the ante. Though right now his enthusiasm was focused on his job. "The entire city is relying on me to get this vigilante off the streets."

"I thought the public looked at vigilantes as heroes."

"People are scared to death of this guy."

Tom had seen his girl that morning just long enough for coffee and a quick goodbye before he was again off to work, and had come directly from a sixteen-hour grind to meet her at the Lion's Head, a storied writers haunt in the Village that always inspired her. Except that right now she was combative, after being thrown for a loop only hours earlier upon learning that her boyfriend's mission was to send her to prison.

"What makes you think people are afraid of him?" pressed Evie.

"Why wouldn't they be afraid of a gunman killing randomly on city streets?"

"Not randomly. He's a vigilante protecting the public from real criminals."

"You can't possibly be saying that a murderer is not a real criminal."

"Wait until Houdini kills again and see what the headlines say about him."

"Headlines don't mirror public opinion."

"Headlines *dictate* public opinion. And what makes you think *you* can catch Houdini when it took 300 cops over a year to get that idiot Son of Sam?" She picked up her beer and held the bottle to her lips, looking at the man she knew would never take his foot off the gas until his mission was accomplished. Finally taking a drink, then backing off a bit. "It must have been a madhouse when they booked him last night."

"An embarrassment. The only difference between the thirteenth floor of One PP and a drunken frat party was that the officers weren't wearing togas."

"Did you actually see Sam?"

"I sat right across the table from him."

"What did he say? Did he tell you the real reason he killed all those people? Did he get a physical thrill from pulling the trigger? Did he ..."

"Whoa!" Tom held his hand up to stop the rapid-fire interrogation.

"Were his victims targeted through planning or opportunity? Did he park his car next to that hydrant because he wanted to be caught?"

"You finished?"

"For the moment."

"He didn't say a word," Tom told her, not knowing what to make of his girlfriend's pointed enthusiasm. "Just sat there with a gassy grin on his face."

"So, he's as weird as the papers say?"

"More likely insane, but court psychiatrists will make that determination." He finished his beer and signaled to the bartender for another. "And how he was able to get away with killing all those people for so long is beyond me, because he didn't seem capable of squashing a cockroach without tripping over it."

"How do you plan to catch Houdini? He's not insane, and they say he can vanish into thin air."

"Manhattan is an island, which makes it somewhat of a contained area that can be compartmentalized. And I'm selecting seasoned officers for my squad who are familiar with those areas and already have their ears to the ground through informants who see and hear things the police don't."

"Do you have any leads?"

"You sound like a reporter."

"Just a woman taking an interest in her man's career."

"Being antagonistic is an odd way of showing it. You've been climbing up my ass ever since I got here."

Tom was driven. Focused. And Evie knew that if she did not distance herself from the straight-laced lawman, his ambition would ultimately destroy her like her megalomaniac father had destroyed her mother. Survival demanding that she break up with him, and do it right away before she became any more emotionally involved. But the Lion's Head was hardly the place.

Evie excused herself and went to the ladies room, took a look in the mirror and for the first time in her life she felt beautiful. An odd moment to visualize herself that way, she thought. Was it the new look or because, even in an adverse situation, Tom always made her feel like the most desirable woman in the world? She thought that she had been in love with her college boyfriend and she thought that she had been in love with the photographer who lived above Wo Hop, but the first time she lost herself in Tom's soft brown eyes she knew that the others had been nothing more than practice. Tom Vaught had become part of her, and she racked her brain trying to come up with an idea where maybe she could have it both ways. Point. Counterpoint. Always reduced to the simple fact that she was not a good enough actress to prevent the sharp instincts of the decorated policeman she was sharing a bed with from eventually discovering that there was murder in her soul. Survival demanded she cut him loose. That the break be quick and clean. Maybe the Lion's Head *was* the place to do it.

Evie fixed her makeup. Ready to face the music. She pulled open the door and there stood Tom, blocking her path. Took her in his arms and kissed her passionately, then led her back into the bathroom and locked the door. Pressed himself against her and hiked up her skirt.

CHAPTER 19

The meshing gears of eight million movable parts created an urban soundtrack that never stopped resonating for even a second, which made it seem almost surreal to Evie that, even though the sun had set, in the ten minutes she had been leaning against the stone facade of a Wall Street bank, not a soul had appeared on the sidewalk in either direction. Not a car or taxi on the abbreviated street through which all of the world's currency passed in one form or another. Money that, it could be argued, was not even real. Just an illusion of creative accounting designed to inflate the net worth of a privileged few who had not earned a cent of it, including the man on the seventeenth floor of the building across the street who was still busy at his desk devising nefarious ways to utilize his newly minted license to steal. A fact Evie knew because for the past three nights she had shadowed Wilton W. Millcross. A creature of habit who always left his office around nine thirty, walked a couple blocks to a deli on Broadway where he bought a Snickers bar that he ate on the subway up to his townhouse on Sixty-Eighth Street between Madison and Park Avenues.

As she waited for the condemned man to show his face, Evie went over the steps of her simple plan of execution and escape, taking into account all possible contingencies should something go wrong. She would force him at gunpoint into the dimly-lit outer entrance of the office building next door to his, then put a bullet between his eyes. The shot would crack through the evening stillness of Wall Street, but by the time anyone appeared on the scene and figured out what had happened, she would have walked casually to Broadway and down the subway steps where she would make a clean getaway on the Number 4 uptown express.

But for now, Evie waited. Pondering the irony of how she had been unable to discover useful information about notorious serial killers yet, in less than an hour of scouring back issues of the *New York Post,* had uncovered pretty much everything there was to know about Wilton W. Millcross. Including the fact that he was a wealthy tightwad who was not only too cheap to hire a driver or even hail a taxi to take him home at night, he clipped coupons and did his own laundry. His only extravagance an art collection purchased with money that did not belong to him.

Perusing the *Post* had also directed Evie's attention toward other miscreants deserving of a vigilante's wrath. A fertility doctor who impregnated hundreds of patients with his own sperm. An unrepentant drunk driver who mowed down a family of five and a young woman the tabloids called the Black Widow for punching the ticket of three wealthy husbands. None of whom had as yet been held accountable by law, and by morning Evie will have decided who among them deserved the top spot on her to-do list. But for now, excitement swelled, her libido tap dancing in anticipation as Millcross was only moments away from presenting himself for sacrifice.

And right on time, he did.

"Excuse me, Mr. Millcross," Evie said politely, appearing as if out of nowhere and walking alongside him. "May I speak with you for a moment?"

"Another time."

"It's important."

The pudgy man stopped and faced her aggressively, looking to cut short the same venomous spiel he had been forced to endure far too many times in the past year. "I'm sorry your grandparents lost their money but your anger is misplaced, attested to by a jury who said that my management of the pension fund was completely within the law."

"That's not what they said at all." Evie pointed her gun at him. "You're an unconscionable thief who got lucky on a technicality."

"You are not the first person to threaten me, young woman." Not only unafraid, Millcross was cocky. And why not? He had spit in the face of both decency and the justice system and come out without a scratch. "And as you can see, I'm still quite full of life."

"This gun is a nine-millimeter Smith & Wesson. Does that mean anything to you?"

Millcross also read the *Post*, and as he quickly put two and two together his smugness dissolved into a confused panic. "You can't be the Houdini Killer. You're a girl."

"Women's Lib, Millcross," she told him, empowered by the recognition. "It's the seventies and I can be anything I want to be."

Millcross knew the Houdini Killer's reputation and that if he stood there much longer he would be a chalk outline, so he shoved her hard against the building and fled. Running like a stuffed goose as he tore around the corner, Evie a good fifty feet behind by the time she regained her balance.

He had seen her face and could identify her to the police, but only if he could get away. He cut over to Exchange Place, glancing over his shoulder every few seconds, well aware that the difference in their ages would allow her to eventually catch him if he did not escape her vision long enough to hide. But where? He could push into the lobby of a building with a security desk but knew he would be killed before the police could be called. He was slowing down and fortunately so was she, but he was rapidly running out of gas. Where the hell was a cop when you needed one? He saw a taxi coming and darted into the street frantically waving his stubby arms, but the driver had a fare and zipped past him.

His legs grew heavy as he continued to run for his life, slower and slower still, fear fueling his resolve but an out-of-shape body was unwilling to cooperate. His shirt drenched with sweat and gasping for breath, sheer willpower pushed him ahead. Half running and half walking until there was little difference. He doubled back toward an underground parking garage and, at least for a moment, seemed to have lost her. His legs now so heavy and unresponsive it was like trying to run in a swimming pool as he struggled toward the entrance. Thirty yards away. Twenty yards. Ten. It might as well have been ten miles. Over his shoulder he did not see her, and with his final ounce of strength lunged forward and stumbled, crashing his padded frame onto the oil stained concrete, then scrambled down the driveway ramp where he hid between two parked cars.

Millcross had a clear view of the entrance, but was a sitting duck. He did not deserve to be in this situation. What had he done that a hundred other bankers weren't doing who had yet to be caught? Nothing. He had done absolutely nothing wrong according to the fine print of the federal statutes, yet had been persecuted by the media, disgruntled investors and was now being hunted down in the street like a dog. Where was the justice? He gasped for air as quietly as he could, trying to get his breath back while waiting for his legs to regain enough strength to carry him a couple blocks west to Broadway. A main thoroughfare where even at this time of night there would be a lot of people. He would find a policeman and quickly a dragnet would surround the Houdini Killer. He would be a hero and all bad press forgotten. Then he saw her enter the garage and walk down the ramp, right toward him. Fear-induced bile began to well in the bottom of his throat, but he could not risk the noise of spitting so he swallowed it. Then threw up.

She reacted to the sound and stopped, not more than a few feet from him. He held his breath, but was unable to keep his body from shaking. Too weak to run. Unable to defend himself. Frightened out of his wits as he waited to be shot dead in a puddle of his own puke. Cruel headlines would write themselves. Yellow journalism would skewer his legacy. It wasn't fair. Then a man who entered the garage to claim his car saw Evie and she had no choice but to walk away. Her footsteps fading as she went up the ramp and disappeared out of sight.

Fearing that she might be lurking outside, Millcross waited a few minutes before pulling himself to his feet and cautiously edging his way up the ramp where he snuck a furtive glance into the street. He looked both ways. Then again. And once he was sure that the coast was clear, with great effort made his way as quickly as he was able toward Broadway and searched frantically for a policeman, but there were none to be found. He hailed a taxi and headed uptown, keeping continuous watch out the back window to make certain she was not following. Got out in Midtown and went down the steps of the 50th Street subway station, waited a few minutes then went back up to the street where he got into another taxi and ordered the driver to take a circuitous route that made him positive he had made a clean getaway. Proud of his daring escape, he bought a Snickers bar at a deli on Madison and ate it as he walked down his block. Would telephone the police then calm himself with a snifter of brandy while waiting for them to arrive.

"What kept you?" asked Evie as she stepped from the shadows.

"How the hell did you …"

"Unlock the door."

Confronted by the nine-millimeter, he had no choice but to do what he was told. She followed him inside.

"Turn off the alarm," ordered Evie, kicking the door shut as she faced him in the foyer.

"There is no alarm."

"Turn it off or you die right now."

He turned it off. Completely worn down mentally as well as physically, his voice trembled as he grasped at one last chance for survival. "I have money. Just tell me how much you want."

Evie put a bullet through his teeth, igniting within her a sexual explosion so powerful that she had to grab hold of a table to keep from falling. With her sleeve she wiped the fingerprints from the table then casually walked out the door, making sure to leave it wide open so that the body would be discovered in plenty of time to make the morning editions.

CHAPTER 20

**HOUDINI MAKES MILLCROSS DISAPPEAR
HOUDINI MAGIC FOR PENSION VICTIMS**

"It's vital that we catch this guy before the press turns him into a hero," bristled Tom Vaught as he flung the day's tabloid headlines into the trash in front of his newly assembled Houdini Killer task force in a briefing room at One Police Plaza.

"Freeze them out," suggested Sergeant Craig Nordby, a chain-smoking no-nonsense patrol veteran with a dark push broom mustache and reputation for street smarts and fast results who would serve as Tom's second in command.

"If we deny access to the press it will look as if we have something to hide, which will cause them to print all sorts of wild speculation. Besides, they have sources inside the department who will leak the information anyway, so it's best that we keep them in the loop so we can somewhat control it. Plus, with ballistics reports now being rushed through almost immediately, either way they get the information almost as quickly as we have it."

"Then what do you suggest?"

"That we get to work." Tom pointed to an oversized street map of Manhattan that with a black marker he had partitioned into sectors. "Twenty of you will each oversee a squad in a sector where you already have relationships with the people who live and work there. Two other officers will command at-large squads."

"What do we know about the murder gun?" asked Nordby. "Other than it belonged to Danny Doyle."

"Ballistics don't connect it to any previous crimes. And it's likely that whoever killed him was someone Doyle knew well enough to allow to get close, though the Organized Crime Control Bureau has an informant close to the Westies who says there is no one who seemed to have it in for him personally. More importantly, he also says that Jimmy Callan is going out of his mind trying to avenge the killing by taking action against outsiders even remotely connected to Doyle."

"Like rolling the severed head of a Gambino soldier down a sidewalk in Washington Heights?" asked Detective Kevin Reilly, on loan from the Midtown South Precinct near where the Doyle murder took place.

"That's right," Tom told him, then asked Patrolman Roberto Cruz from the 19th Precinct about the skinhead.

"His wallet, with the money still inside, was on the sidewalk beside the body."

"Money was also on the ground beside the body of the drug dealer in Riverside Park," added Detective Scott Green, who had been one of the first responders to that crime scene.

"Last night's murder was also in the one-nine, Berto. What's your take?"

"Wilton Millcross was killed inside his townhouse, which deviates from the pattern of street attacks. And even though we recovered a shell casing, there was no other forensic evidence or fingerprints at the scene other than the victim's. The alarm was turned off, which could indicate that, like Doyle, he also might have known the killer well, but I think that puts too big a strain on coincidence because the two victims had nothing in common. More than likely the killer forced his way into the Millcross residence, made him turn off the alarm then killed him. The killer left the front door wide open when he fled, almost as if he wanted the body to be found in time for the morning editions. In my opinion, we're looking for a vigilante who has graduated from street hoods to the big time."

"Any suggestions about where we start looking for the headline seeking killer of a banker who was hated by absolutely everyone?" Tom asked the officers.

"We start with the pensioners who were victimized," said Nordby. "That's thousands of names, I know, but we narrow it down to those who either lost their homes or committed suicide. Of those names, find out how many have relatives in the Tri-State area and start checking alibis. Talk to their friends and neighbors and find out which of them might have been angry enough to murder Millcross."

"Or," Tom countered. "We simplify the process by finding out how many victims, or close relatives of victims, attended the trial every day. Especially the day the verdict was announced, and start from there. In the meantime, we begin to assemble a profile."

"Based on what?" Nordby wanted to know. "We don't know anything about this guy."

"We actually know quite a lot. The size and depth of the footprints left in the soft dirt at Riverside Park tell us that our man is slender and stands no taller than five feet seven. None of the victims were robbed so he doesn't seem to need money. Leaving shell casings at the scene is the mark of an amateur, and if indications are correct that our man is indeed a vigilante, either he or someone close to him has probably been the recent victim of a violent crime."

"And in time all of that might add up to something." Nordby was losing his patience. "We need to collar this Houdini asshole now."

"We'll work double shifts to speed up the process, but until a pattern emerges we will proceed with traditional investigative procedures, starting with a check of the cab companies."

"That's already been done." Nordby's tone was contentious. "How are we supposed to get ahead of this guy, *Lieutenant*, when retracing our steps will put us even further behind?"

"Because maybe there was an off-duty driver that canvassers missed the first time. We check trip sheets to find out where all passengers who were picked up near each of the crime scenes around the approximate times of the murders were dropped off. I know it's a longshot, but maybe one of the drivers will remember something based on our description. There was a candy wrapper in the pocket of Millcross' suit coat, so we'll check every store and deli between his office and his home and see where he bought the Snickers bar and if the clerk remembers anyone following him. Then we send an officer to every gun store in all five boroughs to get a line on recent sales of nine-millimeter ammunition to anyone around five feet seven and slightly built." He looked at Nordby. "Anything you want to add, *Sergeant*?"

"What's the point? You seem to have your mind made up."

"Let's break for the day," Tom told the group as he handed out thick files containing copies of incident reports, interview notes, photos and other miscellaneous information pertaining to all four murders. "When we reconvene in the morning I'll give you your individual sector assignments. Until then, go home and read through these files. Then read through them again with fresh eyes when you wake up, so that maybe we find a connection between the four killings that we're missing. Remember, one clue, even the most seemingly inconsequential clue, might point us to the killer."

As the men dispersed, Nordby cornered Tom. "Why did you choose me for this task force?"

"Because there isn't another man in the department who knows the streets of Manhattan as well as you do."

"Then why do you shoot down everything I say?"

"Are you so set in your ways that you aren't capable of following a line of reasoning other than your own?"

"I'm quite capable of catching this shitheel, no matter how I might choose to do it. My record shows that."

"Or is it that you resent me because you feel that you should be in charge?"

"I turned down three promotions so that I could stay on the street where I could make a difference. And I have made a difference. My arrest record should prove that even to a college boy who's only using this task force as a stepping stone for advancement. Or maybe politics is what you're aiming for. I've worked my tail off for twenty-six years. Long hours, overtime *and* on my own time, whatever it took to get the job done."

"We may have taken different paths, but I guarantee that I put in just as many hours as you have to get the job done. And *my* record shows that."

"Cut through the bullshit, Lieutenant. What's the *real* reason I'm here?"

"I need someone who is not afraid to speak his mind and tell me when I'm wrong."

"You're wrong."

"Okay, Craig. Explain to me why."

"Get some coffee. We're going to be here for a while."

CHAPTER 21

It was pushing eight o'clock. Almost quitting time for Evie, who was getting a head start washing glasses, cutting limes and doing her other shift change side work so that she could jet out the door as soon as her relief showed up. She was wiping down the bar when the phone rang.

"Jamesey's."

Evie brightened as she heard the voice on the other end, then after a moment her expression fell and she slammed down the receiver.

"Your policeman?" asked Stoney, fingers raking his white beard as he wound down his own daily routine.

"For the first time in a week we were going to be able to spend an entire night together." She mashed her thumb on a button beside the cash register that rejected a love song that had been spinning on the jukebox. "We were going to make jambalaya from a recipe we saw in the Sunday *Times*, and I went out early this morning and did the shopping. Even stopped at Moishe's to pick up his favorite apricot rugelach for dessert."

"Sorry, Evie. That sucks."

"You know what really sucks? It was going to be a celebration, because the new issue of *Undercurrent* magazine came out today and one of my stories is in it." She set her anger aside for a moment and allowed her face to light with pride. "I'm a published writer!"

"Cheers to that!" said Stoney as he held up his beer. "What's the story about?"

"A bag lady feeding pigeons that I submitted months ago. It's just a small arts and culture mag, but it's my first published story and that makes me a professional writer because they paid me. Not much, but they paid me." Her light dimmed. "Biggest night of my life and my boyfriend bails on me."

"You can still celebrate tomorrow."

"Can we? Since he took command of that damn task force, he works day and night. Leaves in the morning before I wake up and doesn't get back until after I'm asleep, if he comes back at all. And that's not going to change as long as he continues to chase his tail trying to catch the Houdini Killer."

Stoney belched as he stabbed out his cigarette, missing the ashtray by a mile. Then pushed his half-finished beer toward the bar rail, the first time Evie had seen him surrender a glass that was not empty of its final drop, and asked if she would walk him home.

The old man relied heavily on his cane as he and Evie shuffled through a light rain toward Sullivan Street. She had walked him home before; all the regulars had when he was too drunk to maneuver on his own, but this was the first time Evie had been invited inside. As far as she knew, the first time anyone had made it past the door of the moldering pre-Civil War building.

Stoney's apartment was a basement studio with a side-walk-level window that provided a worm's eye view of all the shoes that sloshed by. One room with a pull-out couch, hinged plywood lid converting the bathtub into a counter top beside a two-burner electric stove, and a black tomcat keeping an eye on things from its perch atop a chain-flush toilet only partially concealed behind a curtain. Shelter from the storm was the only way to describe it without being unkind, but the room was spic and span as Stoney took the same pride in his home that he did with everything else. He turned on the radio, but music did not make the place any less depressing.

"Want a beer?" he asked, his stance steady and voice even as he opened the refrigerator and handed her a cold can of Piels. Less than a buck a six-pack made it his brand of choice.

"Why am I here, Stoney?" asked Evie, seeing him suddenly sober as she popped open the can and tossed the tab into an ashtray on the foot locker that served as a coffee table. "What's up?"

Stoney sat beside her on the couch, flicked his lighter and lit a cigarette.

"If you really love your policeman, you need to be the one to find a way to make it work."

"You got me over here to give me relationship advice?"

"Is there anything wrong with me wanting you to be happy?'

"My relationship with Tom is a lot more complicated than you could ever know."

"It's only complicated if you allow it to be complicated."

"You have absolutely no idea what you're talking about," she snapped, then softened and changed the subject. "That's a nice lighter."

"Solid gold," he said as he handed it to her.

"Why a buffalo?" she wondered, admiring the etched design.

"It's a bison. The old man gave it to me the day I shipped out to kill Krauts so that I wouldn't forget that he expected me to go back and work the ranch the minute Uncle Sam kicked me loose after the war. Not that I needed an incentive to go back and settle down on a thousand prime acres in the most beautiful part of God's green earth anybody ever laid their eyes on, with all the money and prestige that went along with being a Montana Hailstone."

"Why didn't you?"

"Her name was Debby, and she was pretty as the first day of spring." Remembering made him smile. "We met uptown at Howard Johnson's the day I was discharged from the army, and I held her hand as we walked through Central Park. Rode the carousel and sat on a bench just talking until it got dark. Things start slowly when it's the real thing. Did your policeman start slowly?"

"Not that slowly."

"She was going to be a teacher, so I got a construction job while she finished school. The old man never forgave me."

"Did you and Debby get married?"

"We were planning to until I fucked things up. And by the time I figured out that we could have lived happily ever after if I would have just swallowed my pride and admitted I was wrong about something that didn't even matter, it was too late. That's when the old man rubbed salt in the wound by calling me a loser and saying that I'd never amount to anything. So, I decided to stay in New York and prove him wrong." Tired eyes took inventory of the sorry one-room flop. "I guess I let my ego get in the way of that too."

"So why carry his lighter all these years?"

"It's my only link to memories of growing up, and they're good memories. Friends. Riding. Sneaking beer into the drive-in. But the nights are what I miss most, because the sky in Montana is so clear you can see halfway to heaven. I used to lay on the grass and look up at a million stars. How many stars can you see from Sullivan Street?"

"A lot of time has passed, Stoney. I'm sure your dad has mellowed with age. Why don't you make peace with him and go back and live in comfort?"

"And listen to that miserable son of a bitch tell me every damn day what a failure I am? What a disappointment I am to him? I'd rather eat cat food."

The thought of that made Evie get up and check the refrigerator. Mayonnaise, ketchup and a half-eaten can of beans kept the beer company. When she went back to the couch there was a small box on the foot locker in front of her.

"Bullets? What the fuck, Stoney?"

"With the cops on red alert, did you think you could just stroll into Jovino's on Grand Street and ask for a box of nine-millimeter slugs the same way you walked into Moishe's and asked for rugelach?"

Evie was dumbstruck.

"You shot your first victim with his own gun. That's impressive, girl, and I'm not even going to ask how you managed to pull it off. But what are you going to do when the clip is empty? Do you even know how to eject it? How to reload?"

"I didn't even know it was a nine-millimeter until I heard it on the news." She emptied her beer and popped the top on another one. "How did you figure it out?"

"All the questions about me being an army sniper, about getting revenge on the asshole who crippled me, vigilantism, whether that rat bastard Millcross deserved to die, your reaction when you saw in the paper that your boyfriend was heading the task force. Come on, Evie. You wanted me to know."

"Maybe subconsciously. But I'm glad now that you do because I need someone to confide in or my head is going to explode."

"Do you have the gun with you?"

"No."

"Bring it over tomorrow and I'll show you how to load it."

"How hard can it be to put bullets in a gun?"

"It's a nine-millimeter Smith & Wesson automatic with a spring-loaded eight-round clip. And if you did manage to somehow load it without shooting your foot off, you'd sure as hell make the rookie mistake of leaving your fingerprints on the shell casings. Now start from the beginning and tell me everything."

"It's a long story. Let's order a pizza."

Stoney made the call, then dug into the pocket of his jeans.

"My treat, Stoney."

"Like hell it is. You're my guest."

"Okay, but at least let me pay you for the ammunition."

"At three bucks for a box of fifty, bullets are cheaper than bubble gum. Now start talking and tell me why you do it.

You didn't just wake up one morning and decide to become a serial killer."

"My first victim was a rapist who attacked me on the street. I fought hard to keep him off of me, and was doing pretty well until he pulled a gun. We struggled and eventually I got control and shot him."

"Why did you kill again? The next one sure as hell wasn't self-defense."

"In Times Square, I saw how pimps destroyed the lives of girls who were too weak to defend themselves and I wanted to do something about it. I didn't have the nerve to go after a pimp, so I decided to kill one of the creepy perverts who haunt the street. At least I thought that's why I targeted him."

"Why else?"

"I can't tell you that part. It's too personal."

"I already know you're a serial killer. What could possibly be more personal than that?"

Evie fidgeted and took a slug of her beer as Stoney waited for an answer.

"Come on, girl. Spill."

"When I shot the rapist, I felt a bit of a rush and the next two times I pulled the trigger it was even stronger. Then later when I put a bullet in Millcross I had an orgasm. An honest to God sexual thrill." She sat back on the couch and crossed her legs, relaxed as her story now flowed easily. "It shook me so hard I was momentarily paralyzed. Do you think that's creepy?"

"I don't know what to think. I've never heard of such a thing."

"No different from your sniper buddies jizzing in their uniform pants every time they picked off a Nazi."

"So, it's all about sex? I thought you were a vigilante."

"Millcross was my first real vigilante target. I followed him for three days, learning his routine so that I could plan my move. Because of the work I put into it, killing him felt so much better than the others. And killing a man who had hurt so many people made me feel proud, like I had done something important. Maybe that's why I had the orgasm.

"Be careful, Evie. Pride comes before a fall."

"You're quoting Shakespeare?"

"The Bible. It means that even though you're riding high, you can't afford to get sloppy like you did in Riverside Park."

"You have no idea what happened in Riverside Park."

"Newspaper said the police stopped a young woman close to the crime scene, but let her go when it became clear that she had just been walking through the park on her way home and hadn't seen anything. It didn't take much figuring for me to know that young woman was you, and the only reason you're drinking beer with me instead of rotting in the clink is because that cop who questioned you was a moron."

"He thought I was a witness."

"A witness whose enlarged pupils were a dead giveaway that you were scared out of your mind. A witness with a gun in her purse that had recently been fired."

"I talked my way out of it."

"Because the cop was a moron."

"I got a really cool nickname out of the deal."

"Don't get cocky, rookie," Stoney warned. "The clock moves very slowly in prison."

"I'm not cocky, I'm confident. Having the power over life and death makes me feel like there's nothing I can't accomplish.

My confidence level is soaring and there's a new positivity in everything I do."

"And all that goes away with just one mistake. Like not washing the gun shot residue off your hand and clothes as soon as you get home."

"That's important?"

"Hell yes, it's important. Because if you don't your cop will sure as shit smell it. You can't allow yourself to get careless, not even for a second."

"I understand."

"I hope so, because I shouldn't have to remind you that you're playing with fire between the sheets."

"Tom loves me."

"He told you that?"

"Not in so many words."

"Until he actually says the words his only obligation is to his job and he won't think twice about locking your ass up and throwing away the key." The old man fired life into a Virginia Slim. "If you're going to continue with these vigilante killings, you have to break it off with him. And him standing you up tonight gives you a perfect excuse."

"I may be pissed off at Tom, but I'm not breaking up with him."

"You have no choice. You can't have it both ways."

"I *can* have it both ways, Stoney. He'll never suspect me because he thinks that the Houdini Killer is a man." Evie smiled. "I will *always* be able to get away with it because the cops will always be looking for a man."

"There's that cocky attitude again."

"Then why are you helping me?"

"Because you kill people who need killing, just like the pioneers who tamed the great Territory of Montana."

She sensed that there was more that he wanted to say. "And?"

"And if I don't help you, you'll sure as hell screw the whole thing up."

"Now, whose being cocky?"

"Shit!" yelled Stoney as "Free Bird" came on the radio. No time to grab his cane as he scrambled from the couch, stumbling as he raced the cat to its favorite spot on the carpet. Too late.

Evie laughed at the sight of the defeated white-haired man sprawled on the floor. So did the cat.

"I bet Nanette could keep that little pisser in line."

"Don't start, Evie."

"You gave me relationship advice, now I'm going to give you some whether you like it or not."

"Stop it, Evie."

"Are you afraid of being happy?"

"I'm afraid of being humiliated," he said as he climbed back onto the couch and drained the rest of his beer.

"When a woman really likes someone, it's for more than just sex. Nanette *really* likes you, Stoney. And as you said, when it's the real thing you start slowly. Give her a chance. She might surprise you."

"And if she breaks my heart when she learns the truth?"

"I'll shoot her."

"You gonna throw the bullets at her?" Stoney grinned and shook his head. "Some serial killer you are. Don't even know how to load the damn gun."

CHAPTER 22

Evie washed down day-old apricot rugelach with Mr. Kim's bodega coffee as she perused the early edition of the *Daily News*. Mayoral candidate Ed Koch griping about incumbent Abe Beame. Mets fans griping about star pitcher Tom Seaver being traded to the Reds. Lines of people with zero chance of getting into Studio 54 griping because they could not get into Studio 54. An excruciatingly slow news day that made Evie feel it was her responsibility to make the headlines sing.

Her policeman had called after midnight and talked her into letting him come over. He apologized profusely for ruining their dinner plans and after she finally forgave him he fell asleep, then when she woke up in the morning he was gone. No sex, no kiss goodbye, just a note saying that he had to prepare for his eight o'clock briefing and would call when he could. Lately it seemed that she had been spending more quality time with Mr. Kim, but Evie was not going to allow an AWOL lover to bring her down, so she poured the rest of the skunk brew in the sink and popped open a can of Fresca. Put a Ramones cassette into the tape player and blitzkrieg bopped her way to a positive attitude as she wrote in her journal.

*is stoney my mentor or my accomplice?
maybe both, but definitely a guiding light
to keep me focused and i need to listen
to him because he's right about me being
cocky. the power over life and death
somehow makes me feel invincible, so i
need to be smart. not just say that i'm
smart, actually be smart. because as he
said, i can't afford to be careless for even
one second. which is why i now stash the
tools of my trade securely in the air vent
above my bedroom closet.*

*learning from a man who knows from
experience what taking a life does to a
person's mind and a person's soul is going
to make me a better killer. but what about
tom? i've thought about it a lot and am
pretty sure that i can balance my love
life with my urge to kill, but with tom so
obligated to duty (or is it an obligation to
ambition?) that he is incapable of focusing
even part of his attention on me, i have to
wonder what's the point?*

*sure, there are positives, like the fact that
while he runs all over town chasing what's
right under his nose, i have a lot of free
time to chase my next headline. but stoney
is right. how can i remain with a man*

whose sole purpose in life is to send me to jail? what kind of future does that leave us? do we have any chance at a future at all? my only hope is to stay one step ahead of him until the police department finally gives up and disbands the task force, then we can live happily ever after while i go on killing happily ever after. but how long will that take? months? years? i love tom and i want to spend the rest of my life with him, but am i just some hopeless romantic dreaming of the impossible?

the other night i followed that creepy fertility doctor for the second time. so far, his routine hasn't varied by even a step, so getting close to dr. bernard ulmer should be a piece of cake. a weasel-faced runt who has an ego so colossal that he actually believes he is doing the world a favor by impregnating patients with his own sperm. i can't even imagine the horror that new parents feel when they first glimpse the child they moved heaven and earth to create and see the hideous creature they are stuck with, just like the 216 other couples forced to raise a sideshow curiosity they did not conceive together. he's been indicted and will eventually stand trial, yet some people are so desperate for a

*baby that they continue to pay him crazy
money in hopes of defying the odds that
they won't be burdened with the human
equivalent of a cross-eyed three-legged dog.
leaving it up to me to send this narcissistic
piece of crap to that special corner of hell
where the worst of the worst are forced to
watch episodes of my mother the car on a
continuous loop forever. and ever. and ever.*

*i have the day off, so i'm meeting my mom
for lunch, then maybe afterward i'll stop
by the record store and see manda. i feel
guilty for ignoring her, for ignoring all my
friends, and for what? a boyfriend who,
when he shows up at all, is too tired to
fuck me?*

The rain had moved on and taken the humidity with it but heavy cloud cover continued to blot out the sun, gifting the city a cool reprieve from the dog days of summer and Evie was eager to dress for it. Snug-fitting black sweater over a black mini-skirt and tights. Red Chuck Taylor high tops and an oversized man's watch that dangled from her wrist like a bracelet.

Her first stop was the supermarket, where she filled a cart with meats and vegetables and fruit. Bread and canned goods and snacks. Took a cab to Sullivan Street where she stocked the subterranean kitchen of the man she feared had been eating cat food. Then they got down to business.

Evie was an eager student as Stoney showed her how to do more than just stand and aim. He taught her how to work the safety. How to eject the clip and reload it, using a glove so that she would not leave fingerprints on the shell casings. Practiced until she got the hang of it, then put the nine-millimeter Smith & Wesson automatic back into her black leather shoulder bag and zipped it shut. Walked Stoney over to Jamesey's so that he could continue his day in proper fashion, then ventured east to Mulberry Street where her mother was already waiting at a window table in the little red sauce joint that served the best lasagna in Little Italy.

"Cute outfit, and I *love* your hair," smiled Maxine, overwhelmed by her daughter's dramatic change in style. "I've never seen a cut like that even in a magazine."

"Thanks, Mom." Evie told the waiter to bring them each a glass of Dago Red, then looked at her mother's pageboy hairstyle that had been the same for decades. Modestly applied lipstick and rouge that did little to compliment what could be a pretty face. "Let's get you a makeover."

"I'm too old for that."

"No, you're not. It'll make you look ten years younger and give you a fresh outlook about everything. After we eat, let's go uptown to Bloomingdale's."

"You're sweet, Evie, but maybe next time. If I don't beat the rush hour traffic it could take me hours to get home."

Mother and daughter each took a census of the small dimly-lit restaurant with muted strains of Caruso floating through the air. No wealthy socialites or faded movie queens, not even a stray Kennedy. Just a handful of locals who knew the score and a few tourists who had gotten lucky by wandering into the right place. Red checked table cloths, murals of the Sicilian countryside and aromas wafting from an open kitchen that made both women ravenous with anticipation.

"Here's to creating new memories," toasted Maxine, as she and Evie clinked glasses. "And by the way, I saw a picture of your Tom in the newspaper. He's even more handsome than you said he was."

"I guess."

"You guess? What's wrong?"

"Nothing."

"Come on, Evie. Every time you call me you can't stop talking about him."

"I never see him anymore because he's working day and night trying to catch the Houdini Killer. He comes over late and is gone by the time I wake up. Leaves me notes. It's like dating a pen pal."

"He's got an important job to do."

"Eighteen hours a day? Every single day?"

"He's a policeman. It's his duty."

"It's his obsession."

"Good for him. Because I'm still afraid for you walking the streets at night with that killer on the loose."

"The streets are safe, Mom. At least from Houdini, because he's a vigilante who only goes after criminals. He's a hero."

"If that's how you talk to Tom, no wonder you two are having problems." Then she softened. "But I'm sure it won't be long until he catches this killer, then the two of you can pick up right where you left off."

"Not likely."

"Sounds like you're not so sure it's work that's taking up his time. Could he be seeing someone else?"

"Believe me, Mom. Right now, all Tom cares about is his job."

"Men lie, Evie."

"Is that what Dad does? Lies to you about where he is when he's really chasing other women?"

"Your father has never lied to me."

"I suppose that's true, because when a man has complete control over a woman he doesn't have to lie."

"Stop it, Evie."

"You don't have to put up with it, Mom. You have options, why don't you explore them?"

"I didn't come all the way into the city to be ridiculed. I get enough of that at home."

"That's exactly what I'm talking about."

"This is supposed to be a nice lunch, Evie. Don't spoil it."

"I'm sorry, Mom. I didn't mean to get on your case like that, but I love you so much I can't help myself." Evie picked up a bud vase that held a single white rose. "This flower is beautiful, don't you agree?"

"Yes, I do."

"Vibrant and full of life?"

"What's your point?"

"This rose was you when you were hired to be a stewardess with Pan Am." Evie poured the water from the vase into the ashtray. "And this is what Dad did. He didn't allow you to grow. Didn't allow you to flourish. How do you think this rose is going to look tomorrow? The day after? In twenty-five years?"

"Is that really how you see me? As a dead flower?"

"I see you as an amazing woman whose best years are in front of you if you would just take control of your life. It's not too late, Mom. Get out of Clifton and see the world, or at least stick up for yourself enough to make Dad wash his own dishes once in a while."

"I'm supposed to take relationship advice from someone whose boyfriend treats her like a pen pal? Is that what brought on this condescending attitude? Or has that new hair style made you feel like you're better than everybody else?"

"You're supposed to enjoy life, Mom. You've earned that right."

"It's *my* life. Why don't you concentrate on getting your own affairs in order before criticizing mine?"

Evie stood by everything she said but regretted the harsh manner in which she had said it, and Maxine felt bad about lashing out at her daughter who she knew was right. But neither would swallow their pride and they sat in silence for several moments. Maxine broke off the end of a breadstick and dipped it in olive oil. Took a bite, then blinked first.

"How is your novel coming along?"

"I'm finding more inspiration every day."

"That's great. What's it about?"

"I'd rather not say until it's finished."

"Writer's superstition?"

"Something like that."

"Well, I'll be the first in line at B. Dalton to buy it when it comes out. Your father and I will be so proud."

"He won't even notice."

"What a thing to say."

"But I'm going to make him notice. Just wait, Mom. I'm going to prove to him that I can be more successful than any son. More successful than anybody's son, and that I'm not just some biological typo."

"I know he doesn't always show it, Evie, but your father is very proud of you. He loves his daughter."

"He's a fucking bully."

"What has he ever done to make you say such a horrible thing?"

"You know exactly what he did." She spit the words angrily, then shook off the ugly memory with a slug of wine. Wondering if it was possible for her mother to be so far under the thumb of a domineering husband that she could repress the most traumatic event of her only child's life as if it had never happened. "How can you not remember that afterward I cried for days and refused to ever again play with dolls? What seven-year-old girl is scared to play with dolls?"

"Please, Evie. You promised you wouldn't spoil our lunch. Can you tell me anything about your book?"

"It's going to shoot to the top of the bestseller list and they'll make a movie of it. I'll be on the *Today* show, the *Tonight* show and every show in between. Dad's hunting and fishing buddies will no longer care about his bullshit stories about getting stains out of Dean Martin's pants, they'll want to hear all about his famous *daughter*. Marv Eastway will never again be able to ignore his daughter."

"Sounds like you plan on becoming another Hemingway."

"Why not? Hemingway was a legend."

"That legend grew more from his larger than life personality than from his books. Do you have a secret life I don't know about?"

"You never know, Mom. One day I might surprise you."

The lasagna did not disappoint, and as they ate the conversation took a chatty turn toward fashion, movies and celebrity gossip. Uncle Joe's mid-life crisis Corvette and Cousin Sue's trip to the Grand Canyon.

"You know, Mom, there is so much to do in the city and it always seems like just when we get started you have to go home. Next time we should go to the Museum of Modern Art or maybe the theatre. You used to tell me all the time how much you loved the theatre."

"I was younger than you are when I saw *Guys and Dolls* and *South Pacific*. Those were such great shows. And in *The King and I*, Yul Brynner gave every girl in the theatre goose bumps." Then a hint of sadness in her voice. "I haven't been to a Broadway show since."

"Then let's go to one. We'll dress up and have an early supper at Sardi's." Surprised that she still had her mother's attention, Evie went for the closer. "We could see *Annie* or the revival of *The King and I* that's playing at the Uris. Pick whatever show you want and I'll get tickets. You can leave a casserole for Dad so all he has to do is put it in the oven. He does know how to work the oven, right?"

"He knows how to work the refrigerator when I'm not there to get him a can of beer."

Mother and daughter shared a laugh.

"Then you'll do it?"

"I don't know, Evie. Talking about it is one thing, but I'm not sure I could."

"You can spend the night at my apartment. Maybe give me some cooking tips, because I've been working really hard trying to get better in the kitchen so I can cook for Tom." Evie reached across the table and took her mother's hand. "Promise me you'll at least think about it."

After the meal, Maxine took an Instamatic camera from her purse and had the waiter take their picture that she would put in a silver frame and give to her daughter for her birthday. They enjoyed espresso and cannoli down the block at La Bella Ferrara, then Evie walked her mother to her car so that she could beat the traffic back to New Jersey in time to have dinner on the table at the appointed hour.

The weather was still cool and invigorating as Evie walked from Little Italy in the direction of Bleecker Bob's, a record store in the heart of Greenwich Village where she found her friend Manda, packaged tightly in a very low-cut blouse and leopard-skin slacks, alphabetizing a rack of forty-fives. Today her hair was red and straight as she almost always wore wigs, changing color and style more days a week than she didn't. It had been a slow day and her boss agreed to cut her loose early, so she and Evie found the nearest barstools and spent the rest of the afternoon bitching about their boyfriends.

A shameless flirt, Manda eyed the bartender. Cheap sex with strangers was her thing no matter how much she might or might not care for her current beau, and she would think nothing of taking this guy in the back for a quickie. But not just now as her focus was on schooling Evie with relationship advice and, though little of it applied to she and Tom, one tidbit Evie took to heart was to totally ignore him until he came to his senses. If he did, she would know that they had a future together. If not, there were plenty of fish in the sea.

"You need to treat yourself to some fun, Evie."

"I thought that's what we were doing."

"You can drink anytime. I'm talking about some real fun," said Manda as she nodded toward the bartender. "Check out that bulge in his jeans. Take him into the bathroom."

"I couldn't."

"Why not? Your cop has made it pretty clear that his job is way more important than you, so have a little fun." Class was again in session. "Just because you've never had a quickie with a stranger doesn't mean you shouldn't. Lose your inhibitions and get back in the swing of things."

"How would I even go about asking him?"

"You flash a suggestive smile, then slowly walk toward the bathroom. Unless he's gay, he'll follow."

It seemed almost chaste compared to the things she had seen on Eighth Avenue, but even after a couple shots of tequila, Evie still could not bring herself to have sex with a stranger in a barroom toilet. Because even though Tom didn't seem to care at the moment, she was in love enough for both of them to believe that he would eventually get his shit together. Then watched in amazement as one smile from Manda led to a bathroom tryst that led to free drinks the rest of the afternoon.

More beer, more shots and a lot of girl talk left Evie shitfaced. She knew that the smart thing would be to pick up some sesame noodles and go home and watch TV, but instead she found herself on a bench across the street from

Dr. Bernard Ulmer's Fifth Avenue apartment that overlooked Central Park.

CHAPTER 23

Every night at nine o'clock Dr. Ulmer took his evening constitutional around the Reservoir, entering the park at 85th Street, completing the circle back to Fifth Avenue then calling it a night. A boring man with a predictable life that would make it easy for Evie to confront him, pull the trigger, then keep walking to the other side of the park and vanish into the hubbub of west side. Though tonight when he appeared in front of his building in a golf shirt and windbreaker, Ulmer threw her a curve as he had the doorman whistle for a taxi. Then as he got in and sped away, Evie jumped into the street and frantically waved her arms to flag a taxi of her own.

"Follow that cab!"

"In the movies, the fare always offers the driver an extra twenty not to lose him."

Evie slid a twenty-dollar bill through the cash slot of the protective Plexiglas partition that separated the front and back seats.

"Now step on it!"

The driver was more than up to the task, staying on Ulmer's tail all the way down to 14th, then zig-zagging west to Christopher Street where the target got out. Evie followed, looking out of place as the only woman on a shadowy side street of gay bars and sex shops that reminded her of a homosexual Eighth Avenue, though the closer she looked, the more any similarity faded. She did not know what blemishes might appear in the unforgiving light of day, but at night the street had somewhat of a cozy charm and, although there was a lot of activity in the shadows, there was zero desperation in the air.

Ulmer walked slowly, looking more than a bit out of place himself as a middle-aged square swimming upstream through a surge of much younger, better looking men aggressively flaunting their sexuality. He paused to check out the action through the window of every bar as if he desperately wanted to go inside but did not have the nerve. Eventually making his way the few short blocks to where the street ended at the river, all of a sudden seeming to find his nerve as he headed toward a rotted wooden structure, one of several long-abandoned shipping piers that jutted out above the water. Evie stayed way back as the area, unlike the fraternal vibe of Christopher Street, looked both seedy and dangerous as dozens of shirtless men lurked in tight shorts and in jock straps. Ulmer went inside, on the heels of a muscular man wearing nothing but work boots and a thick mustache.

As she watched from across the street, Evie figured that this tail job had been a complete waste of time because if Ulmer got back into a cab to go home or walked back up Christopher Street before going home, she would have no chance of getting him alone. But that would not be the case, as after a few minutes Ulmer walked away from the dilapidated pier and headed down West Street along the river as Evie tailed him stride for stride from the other side of the street. One long block, then another, then three more. The area was mostly warehouses and light industry that had been shuttered for the night and she wondered where he could possibly be going. Then Ulmer crossed the street, Evie ducking into a doorway as he passed right in front of her. No one around. The time to hit him was now.

Evie picked up the pace to get within striking distance, but by the time she did she heard voices. People staggering out of the Ear Inn, a time capsule booze and eats joint that had propped up the west side waterfront since the regulars wore three-corner hats. Ulmer went inside and ordered a drink. Evie wanted to steady herself with a shot of tequila, but thought better of going inside as she did not want witnesses to remember the woman who followed the victim out of the last place he was seen alive. So yet again, she cooled her heels across the street.

Ulmer finally showed his face and Evie followed closely this time, but he seemed spooked by a group of drunken men loitering outside an Irish bar on the other side of the street. His fear of gay bashing taking him through a confusing maze of short blocks, and by the time he led Evie around a corner onto Vandam Street, she had had quite enough cat and mouse, forcing him at gunpoint behind some trash cans inside the loading dock of a printing company.

He tried to give her his wallet but she slapped it out of his hand.

"Then what do you want?"

"Shut up, you narcissistic piece of shit."

"I'll give you anything you want." Ulmer was both confused and terrified, spittle flying as he begged. "Just don't hurt me. Please don't hurt me."

"Why not? You hurt hundreds of women who trusted you by impregnating them with your own repulsive jizz."

"You don't understand."

"Is it because you're gay and can't have kids of your own?"

"I'm not gay."

"I could see that at the pier."

"I am *not* gay!" His voice trembled as he fidgeted, shifting his weight from one foot to the other.

Evie could not believe that a man with a gun pointed at him would spend his final moments denying his sexuality. "Nobody cares that you're gay, Ulmer."

"I have a Park Avenue practice and could lose everything if people found out. That's why I can't go into gay bars where I'd have a chance to meet someone nice, because I can't risk being recognized. So I go to the pier, because whatever I do has to be completely anonymous."

"If you wanted a kid of your own, you could have figured out another way."

"What other way?" Sobs trapped in his throat. "You have no idea what it's like to be gay."

"There's always another way, Ulmer. Preferably one that does not destroy other peoples' lives. How could you have ever looked in a mirror and thought that mass-producing kids in your creepy image was a good idea?"

"You don't understand."

"You keep saying that, but one thing I very much understand is that I'm about to do the women of New York a great favor."

Watching Ulmer drop to the pavement shocked her body with a jolt of excitement that was cut short before it had a chance to take hold as she heard footsteps running toward her.

"The shot came from over here."

"Check the other side of the street."

An afternoon of boozing had led to the carelessness of moving in on the target before checking out the area, and Evie knew it was only a matter of moments until she would be discovered huddled next to a fresh kill with the murder weapon in her hand.

"Look in every doorway, behind every trashcan."

The voices were too disorganized to be police, leaving Evie to fear the one thing scarier than the police. She crouched beside Ulmer's body, the blood leaking from his head smearing on her high tops as she sensed that they were only a few feet away. Frightened to her core as she could not withstand a beating and she certainly did not want to die, especially as the *victim* of vigilante justice.

Spooked by shadows that appeared on the wall behind her, Evie felt as if she was under water and did not know which way was up. More footsteps approached and she could hear the men speaking softly, which meant they knew she was there. Her heart slammed against her chest as she struggled to control her breathing. In and out slowly but steadily, fighting the urge to gulp for more air. Her free hand smothering the ticking of her oversized watch as she was scared that even the slightest sound would be magnified in the stillness and give her away, in the unlikely event that her position had not already been compromised. Her only chance to escape would be to fire a shot in the air and scare them into retreat, then run like hell the other way. She gripped the nine-millimeter automatic, ready to spring into action the instant they moved even a step closer. Any second now. Shoot then run. Her legs cramped from squatting. The perspiration of fear stinging her eyes but she didn't dare move her hand to rub them. Shoot then run. Shoot then run.

"Get your asses back to work," yelled a voice from down the street.

"Let's go, guys," one of them said as footsteps began to retreat. "We can call the cops from a pay phone."

"Forget it. Looks like nobody was hit and the shooter's long gone."

Evie peeked her head out from the loading dock and watched five men in Con Ed hard hats go back around the corner where they were working to repair a ruptured gas line. She waited until the last one was out of sight before allowing herself a series of deep breaths followed by a weighted sigh of relief, then cautiously eased back into the street and walked away.

"Evie," came a voice from behind.

She walked faster.

"Evie Eastway."

Nowhere to run. Nowhere to hide. No choice but to stop and brace herself for the end of the line. Fright tied her stomach into a knot and frustration made her want to cry. But Edmund Kemper didn't cry. Mad Dog Taborsky didn't cry. And, by God, neither would Evie Eastway as she turned to face the music. Instead, finding herself face to face with her ex-boyfriend Ricky.

She stood stunned for a moment, then pulled herself together and put her arm around Ricky as if she was glad to see him. Led him to a darkened doorway where they could not be seen.

"How long were you standing there, Ricky?"

"Just walked up. Why?"

"What did you see?"

"Nothing." He gave her a curious look. "What are you doing around here?"

"What did you see, Ricky?"

"I told you. Nothing."

"It doesn't matter. You saw me and eventually you'll figure it out and tell the police."

"I don't tell cops anything. Ever. So, whatever this is, if anybody asks, I never saw you. I was never even here."

"You expect me to believe that?"

"I swear, Evie. I won't say a word to anybody."

Evie pointed the gun at him.

"Are you crazy? What the hell are you doing?" He panicked. Stumbled backward and bumped into the door. "I told you, I won't say a word to anybody! I swear! Please, Evie, you gotta believe me!"

"Maybe I do and maybe I don't," she told him calmly. "But one thing I know for sure is that you can never trust a junkie."

The shot screamed loudly through the deserted street, but this time Evie would not be cheated. Screw the nosy Con Ed crew, she thought, bracing herself as sexual lightning shot through her body. Looked at Ricky, dead at her feet, then smiled and said out loud, "At least you finally gave me an orgasm."

Sirens closed in from two directions. She took off running in a third.

CHAPTER 24

A knock on her door jolted Evie awake. Then a loud banging as she shook out the cobwebs and put on her robe, fearing that the massive screw up of stalking Ulmer when she was drunk had led the police to her apartment. Terrified as she knew it would not take them long to find the gun, the box of ammunition and her journal in the air vent above her bedroom closet.

"Evie, it's Tom. I know you're in there."

Relief followed quickly by anger. "Go away!"

"Come on. Open up."

Not wanting him to create any more of a scene in front of her neighbors, she opened the door and he pushed his way past her, demanding to know about Richard Hansen.

"I give up. Who the hell is Richard Hansen?"

"Your ex-boyfriend."

"You mean Ricky?" Evie was no actress but knew that she had better become one in a hurry, as Tom was an experienced detective who would pounce on even the most subtle misstep. "He wasn't a boyfriend, just somebody I knew. Besides, how the hell do you know about him?"

"The drummer in his band said you used to go up to his loft all the time."

"So what, Tom? It was before I knew you. And anyway, what about him?"

"He was murdered last night by the Houdini Killer."

"Oh, my God!" She was pleased with her surprised reaction. "How? What happened?"

"There were three bindles of heroin in his pocket. Was he a drug dealer?"

"You can't ignore me for days, then all of a sudden show up unannounced and grill me like I'm some sort of criminal."

"Was he a drug dealer?"

"He was a junkie. That's why I broke up with him."

"What was he doing over on Vandam Street?"

"How the hell would I know?"

"Have you spoken to him recently?"

"Fuck you, cop." Standing stiffly with her arms crossed, she no longer had to act.

"I have a job to do, Evie. Don't make it more difficult."

"Then don't bully your way in here and interrogate me like I'm a fucking suspect."

"I have to follow every lead."

"I'm not a lead, I'm your girlfriend. At least I thought I was."

"Look, Evie. We have to check out every coincidence, no matter how seemingly insignificant, and this is important as it's the first actual connection we've been able to make." He sat on the couch and she followed, leaving a lot of space between them. "Houdini killed Bernard Ulmer last night. You've probably read about him in the paper, the fertility doctor under indictment for impregnating patients with his own sperm.

Anyway, Hansen was killed moments later right across the street, and when we found drugs in his pocket we assumed that he was another criminal vigilante victim. But now that I know he was a user, it makes sense that he was just passing by after having scored and probably witnessed the Ulmer murder, and that's why he was killed as well."

"You could have learned that by asking nicely."

"I'm sorry, Evie, I really am. I shouldn't have barged in here and given you the third degree."

"Were there any other witnesses?"

"Some Con Ed workers heard the shots, but unfortunately they didn't see anything."

"You find any other clues?"

"A smudged fingerprint on the wallet we found beside Ulmer's body was no help, but there were a couple partial bloody footprints made by a Chuck Taylor sneaker that led in the direction of the second victim. And the fact that the Houdini Killer was wearing a brand of sneaker popular with both playground basketball players and East Village punks means that he's probably young, which we can add to the profile we're putting together."

"Profile? What else do you know about him?"

"He's slender and no taller than five feet seven. It's not a lot, but every little bit gets us closer to eventually having enough for a police artist's sketch."

"When will you realize that you're never going to catch this guy? Whether you have a sketch or not, he's one man in a city of eight million."

"We caught Son of Sam and I'm going to catch the Houdini Killer. After I leave here I'm taking the train up to Sing Sing to interview convicted murderers for any tidbits of information that might help me get inside his mind."

"You're pushing a rock up a hill."

"This isn't the first time you've been antagonistic toward me when it comes to the Houdini Killer. I'm supportive of your writing, why can't you be supportive of my job?"

"If you were even the least bit supportive you'd know about this," she snapped, grabbing her copy of *Undercurrent* magazine off the coffee table and throwing it at him.

He leafed through it and saw her story. "This is great! Why didn't you tell me?"

"When would I have done that, Tom? You're never here because your job is more important to you than I am."

"That's not true. You're very important to me."

"Then find a balance."

"I come over after I'm finished with work. Or at least I try to."

"You fall asleep, then sneak out before I get up, so why bother coming over at all? I know that you can't stand to lose at anything, but you're real close to losing the best thing that ever happened to you if you don't start treating me as more than just an afterthought." She looked at him for a long moment, wanting so much to love him and wanting even more for him to love her back. Then stroked her fingertips lightly across his cheek and kissed him. "We're not broken, Tom. We just need to spend time together. How about I see if one of the other bartenders can cover my shift so I can go with you up to the prison?"

"You want to talk to murderers?"

"None of them can help you get into the mind of the Houdini Killer."

"No offense, but what could you possibly know about it?"

"I've been spending a lot of time at the library, trying to understand what my boyfriend is up against. And I can tell you that those guys rotting in Sing Sing are nothing more than basic garden variety lowlifes who pulled the trigger out of jealousy or greed, and not one of them can give you even a hint as to what motivates Houdini. Don't you know anything about serial killers?"

"I've reviewed countless studies and psychological profiles."

"Paul Knowles killed three strangers in San Francisco the night his girlfriend dumped him. Why did he kill them instead of killing her? And afterward, what motivated him to keep killing?"

"I don't know."

"Court records say that Edmund Kemper killed ten people because he was a paranoid schizophrenic, which is a cop-out, meaning they either didn't know the real reason, or more than likely didn't care because they already had him locked up. What really motivated him to keep killing after his first victim?"

"I don't know."

"Okay, Tom. Here's an easy one. Tell me about Jack the Ripper."

"He killed prostitutes."

"And they never caught him, even though he was in a contained area right under their noses." She softly shifted gears. "I don't give a damn about Sing Sing, but I was hoping that maybe afterward we could take the train further up the river to Cold Spring and have a nice lunch. Browse the shops."

"I can't. I'll have to get back and brief Sergeant Nordby."

"Tonight then. I still have all the fixings to make jambalaya."

"I'm sorry, Evie, but we're coordinating a stakeout in Chelsea. It's only a hunch, but Nordby has information from a source that makes him think that's where Houdini will strike tonight."

"A hunch? Your way of finding balance in our relationship is to blow me off again because some cop has a fucking hunch?"

"What's with you lately? At first, I figured that this new confidence of yours was because you were happy about us. But now, every time we talk about my job you become combative."

"Maybe if you were around more often I *would* be happy about us."

"When I arrest this guy, I'll make it all up to you."

"Quit pushing around the same useless words and make it up to me now."

"It won't be long until I have him behind bars, I promise."

"Get it through your thick head that you will *never* arrest the Houdini Killer. Which leaves us nowhere."

"Maybe tonight you can catch that new James Bond movie you've been wanting to see. Or better yet, stay in and work on your book."

"I don't need you to find things for me to do while you're out chasing your tail."

"I'll come over as early as I can."

"Don't bother, Lieutenant. You've made your priorities painfully obvious."

"Please, Evie. You have to understand the enormous pressure I'm under."

"To make an arrest or to make captain? You're just pretending to protect the people of this city, because to you Houdini is nothing but a stepping stone to personal advancement." She folded her arms across her chest and cast him a cold stare. "Is that what I am, Tom? A stepping stone to someone better?"

"That's not fair, Evie."

"I've seen firsthand what happens when a woman with big dreams takes a back seat to her man's ambitions. Over the years she becomes nothing but a dead flower with nothing to look forward to except more of the same. It's sad and it's cruel and I'm not going to allow you to do it to me." She got off the couch and flung open the door. "Now get the hell out of here. I don't ever want to see you again."

CHAPTER 25

The target was having dinner with a friend at El Charro, a Spanish restaurant on a quiet Greenwich Village block. The Black Widow. A tabloid moniker earned after three rich husbands had mysteriously dropped dead. Quite an accomplishment for someone only twenty-seven years old and, according to Evie, who had become hyper-critical of other women since her makeover, looked like a triple-bagger. But just how eye-catching did a woman have to be to attract men forty years her senior? She figured that proper table manners and proficiency in the sexual arts were probably qualification enough.

Dressed for function and not style in jeans, dark shirt and a pair of old PF Flyers (she had tossed her bloodied Chuck Taylors into the trash behind an Ethiopian restaurant a half dozen subway stops into Brooklyn), Evie had parked herself on a stoop across from the restaurant. Focused. Sober, and aware of her surroundings. Figuring it best not to call attention to herself by lurking too long in one place while the target finished her meal, she took a stroll around the neighborhood. Wondered how it would feel to pull the trigger on a woman.

Curious whether the thrill would be as sexually charged as it was killing a man. Then as she headed back toward the restaurant she saw something painted on the side of a building that stopped her dead in her tracks.

HERO HOUDINI

The mural was two stories high. Red block letters amid a field of gravestones. Six of the gravestones marked with the dates of her six kills and the rest were blank, ready to be filled in. Evie squeezed her eyes shut, then opened them to make sure she wasn't dreaming. Stepped out of the way of foot traffic on the busy corner, swelling with pride as she stared at what was to her more of a masterpiece than the ceiling of the Sistine Chapel.

CHAPTER 26

"**W**hat makes your informant so sure that this child molester is Houdini's next target?" Tom was aggravated that two dozen officers were wasting valuable hours that could have been put to more productive use elsewhere. That it was past midnight and he was choking on Nordby's secondhand smoke in the back of a steamy painter's van that served as a mobile command post on West 26th Street, waiting for a killer who was not going to show up. "How could he possibly know such a thing?"

"His information has led to a lot of arrests."

"And how many times has he blown smoke up your ass for the money?" Tom fired back as he sweated inside his light blue suit, wondering if maybe the streetwise sergeant was so keen on the stakeout because some of the payola had stuck to his fingers.

"He wouldn't do that."

"Because snitches are so honorable? Houdini has never killed after eleven and we've wasted an entire night for nothing."

"There's still time."

"And he's never killed two nights in a row." Tom was angry, mostly with himself for allowing Nordby to lead him on this fool's errand. "So, why tonight?"

"What do you care, as long as we catch the guy?"

"This tough cop persona you've created for yourself might play with the younger officers in the squad, but I can see right through you, Nordby. You can't even begin to understand the selflessness it takes to be a team player, so self-involved that you don't even care that this failed grab for credit is causing the squad to waste countless man-hours on the unsubstantiated say-so of some two-bit rat who lined his pocket by feeding you a steaming plate of bullshit." Then Tom baited his second in command. "Or did you line your pocket too? Is that why you keep declining promotions, because you make more money on the street?"

Nordby swung, but Tom was ready for it and blocked the punch just as a voice crackled through the van's trunked radio receiver.

"26th and Tenth. I've got eyes on a suspicious-looking white male in his mid-twenties matching the description, walking south. Five-foot seven, one-forty. Bushy brown hair, jeans and white Chuck Taylor high tops. Looks hinky wearing a baseball jacket on such a warm night."

"Fall back, Logan," ordered Nordby, checking a street map marked with the locations of all plainclothes officers deployed in the stakeout area. "Danny, he's coming right toward you. You have the eye?"

"Got him, Sarge."

"All positions, stand by," commanded Nordby, coiled tightly and ready to strike as he looked smugly at Tom. "This is it."

"Target stopped at the corner. Looks like he's adjusting something inside his jacket."

"Walk past him, Danny. Don't spook him," ordered Nordby. "Logan, you still have eyes on him?"

"Roger that," the officer confirmed through his walkie-talkie. "He's still on the corner looking like … He's mobile. Heading east on 26th."

"Perimeter positions, secure both ends of the block, then take him when he approaches the building." Nordby glared at Tom. "Looks like this tough cop came through, *Lieutenant*."

"So far I've let you operate this stakeout, but don't for one second forget who's in charge," Tom said as through high-powered binoculars he watched the suspect walk toward them, then snatched the radio transmitter from Nordby's hand. "Hold all positions and allow target to enter the building and go up to the third floor. Repeat, hold all positions. Don't make a move until he knocks on the apartment door or attempts to enter."

"There's no reason to let him get so close," argued Nordby. "Take him now."

"We need to catch him in the act. If we brace him just because he matches the profile, any indictment could be tossed."

"Not if he's holding the Houdini murder gun."

"He could say he found it. He could say anything."

"But we'd have him. Locked up and off the street."

"For how long? Without an actual connection to the murders, a good lawyer would have him back on the street in a matter of hours."

"Then let's look the other way while he drops the hammer on this kiddie raper." Nordby took the last hit of his Camel then tossed the still-lit butt into a paper coffee container. "One skel in the morgue and the other locked up forever. A win-win."

"Don't even joke about a thing like that."

"Just following orders. The commissioner said to do whatever we have to and he'll make the pieces fit later."

"Since when do you talk to the commissioner?" Tom put down the binoculars as the target came clearly into view and approached the building, telling the officers to continue to hold their positions, then faced Nordby, "We're doing this by the book so that the D.A. has as much admissible evidence to work with as possible. So, you can either follow *my* orders or go back to regular duty."

"You're letting the power of this command go to your head."

"Or I can *demote* you back to regular duty."

As Tom saw the target enter the building he kicked open the rear door of the van, then he and Nordby sprinted across the street. Tom motioning for peripheral officers to follow and led them quietly up the stairs to the third-floor landing, only a few feet away as the target walked down the hallway and knocked on an apartment door.

"POLICE! FREEZE!" yelled Nordby, his thirty-eight service revolver trained on the target.

Officers quickly converged, slamming the suspect against the wall and cuffing his hands behind his back. Frisked him and found a puppy that had been asleep inside his jacket.

"What the hell is wrong with you?" Tom screamed at Nordby.

"Your orders were to wait until he knocked. He knocked."

"On the *wrong door.*" Tom was livid. "This kid is *not* the Houdini Killer!"

As officers stormed inside and scared the crap out of a nerdy-looking college student playing a game of Pong on his console television, other apartment doors cracked open to see what the racket was all about, including the occupant behind the *right* door. A serial pedophile the courts had been unable to bring to justice, who had escaped the wrath of the Houdini Killer but come perilously close to being licked to death by a four-pound Pomeranian puppy.

"Nothing to see here, folks," Tom told the curious neighbors, as he took a close look at the suspect whose jacket was on the floor and whose pants pockets were turned inside out. "Sorry for the disturbance. Please go back inside your apartments."

"He had this," Tom was told by an officer who held in his hand a joint and a pack of rolling papers.

"That's it?"

"That's it.'

"No gun?"

"No, sir."

"Check with B.C.I. for priors and warrants," Tom instructed the officer. "And if he comes up clean, let him go."

"Let him go?" squawked Nordby in disbelief. "Our *by the book* commanding officer is kicking loose a drug dealer caught in the act?"

"He's just a kid with some weed."

"*Delivering* weed, and that makes him a dealer."

"And what do you suppose happens to the credibility of this task force when word gets out that we tied up two dozen officers for half the night just to rough up a kid with one joint who had gone to his friend's apartment to play a video game?"

Thoroughly disgusted, Tom turned his back on the scene and walked down the stairs.

"Okay, I admit my informant sold us a bill of goods," conceded Nordby as he followed Tom out of the building and into the heavy night air, lit a cigarette and leaned against the surveillance van. "But we can't just sit around with our thumbs up our asses waiting for this scumbag to make a mistake. We have to follow every lead, no matter what the source."

"Don't you understand that it's better to control a situation rather than react to it."

"By wasting time interviewing psychologists and jerking off lifers at Sing Sing? We need to be aggressive. We need eyes and ears on the street because somebody knows something."

"Nobody knows anything, Nordby. How could they? Unless an informant *is* the killer, how could he possibly know when and where Houdini will strike?"

"You don't know a fucking thing about real police work."

"Tell you what, Nordby. You go back on the street and get jerked off by some more snitches. In the meantime, I've taken control of the situation by manufacturing a villain so perfectly tailored to the profile that the Houdini Killer won't have any choice but to go after him."

"A decoy?"

"A phony slumlord who is about to skate on several counts of murdering young children. I've recruited a traffic officer from the East Bronx to play the part. He's been set up with an office and an apartment. I've created a backstory and a routine that will leave him vulnerable to ambush, while plainclothes officers from the task force cover him every second of his day." Tom loosened his tie and top button. "The *Post,* the *Daily News* and *Newsday* have all agreed to play the story up big for however long it takes. Even the *Times* is on board. Radio and TV as well. The fake news stories will play into everything we know about this vigilante killer and he will not be able to resist the bait. The first story is set to run tomorrow."

Nordby was equal parts stunned by the wide scope of the operation and angry about being kept in the dark. "You put this elaborate plan into motion without even consulting me?"

"Good night, *Sergeant.*"

Tom walked toward Ninth Avenue to catch a taxi home. He was exhausted, but doubted he would be able to sleep as he awaited the morning editions.

CHAPTER 27

Unable to force down any more of Mr. Kim's foul brew but unwilling to walk an extra block to the Greek diner, Evie opted for a bottle of orange juice to go with her morning Danish. And with no caffeine to jolt her vision into focus, did not immediately notice that below her headlines in both the *Post* and the *Daily News* was the photo of a slumlord accused of endangering children. But after skimming the story, Evie was certain that by tomorrow the rent collector would be as forgotten as yesterday's baseball scores, while a mural on Sixth Avenue would continue to scream enduring testament to her legend.

> *i got back to el charro just as the black*
> *widow and her friend were leaving.*
> *followed them over to macdougal street*
> *where they ducked into a noisy bar and*
> *stayed for what seemed like forever until*
> *finally calling it a night with her friend*
> *heading toward the park while the widow*
> *walked across the street to minetta lane,*

a somewhat isolated shortcut to sixth avenue where she could get a cab home. i followed, and within moments asked her for a light, shot her then got into a cab that took me back to my home.

the jolt of sexual lightning i absorbed from killing the widow was every bit as powerful as when i kill a man, proving that murder doesn't discriminate and has a unique thrill all its own. a bigger thrill than seeing the mural? for now i'll call it apples and oranges. i have not lost sight of the fact that my purpose in killing criminals is to make new york a safer place, but it doesn't mean that i shouldn't take pride in the thrill of recognition, as anonymous as it may be, that goes along with it. i get such a rush whenever i see a houdini headline or hear the name on the radio or overhear people talking at work or in restaurants or when i'm out shopping. i would probably jump out of my skin with excitement if it said evie eastway on the side of that building or in the headlines, and what a kick in the ass that would be to tom. show him just how stupid the great policeman was to ignore me. i hate him so much right now that i think it would almost be worth it to out myself in order to see the look on his face.

what if i did take credit for being the houdini killer by writing my book as a memoir? sure, i would have to disappear to maintain my freedom, but my legend would explode and i could enjoy the attention from afar. people say they see hitler flipping burgers in argentina, and even though it's only been a couple weeks since elvis crapped out on his toilet, already the crazies are claiming to have seen him in all sorts of ridiculous places. but i would really be alive, and evie eastway sightings would be more common than seeing ufos. and because i would be a fugitive, every sighting would be investigated, meaning that the name evie eastway would still be newsworthy if i lived to be 100.

how hard could it be to close one chapter of my life and begin another? all i would have to do is move away and start over in a town where nobody knows me and i've been thinking lately how nice it might be to live on a beach. i've never been arrested or fingerprinted which would make it easy to establish a new identity. i found a wallet the other day and the driver's license description fits me. i haven't gotten around to returning it yet and now don't think i will. her name is carol caldwell and she has red hair. i've often wondered if i would be better looking as a redhead. i know for sure that the black widow is better looking with that hole I put in her head.

if i reinvented myself somewhere else i would miss my mom, but maybe it would force her to ditch clifton and finally see the world. my dad would probably change the name of his business to serial killer cleaners and get rich selling all of my childhood toys, with a big mark up on my barbie if he was man enough to tell the story of why. they would put my picture on the wall at jamesey's and stoney, god bless him, would spend every day of the rest of his life telling the story about how he taught me how to load the gun. and again, there's tom, who would be disgraced and probably fired from the police force and end up washing dishes at busha's. it would serve him right for choosing ambition over me.

but it's all just a romantic illusion. that's all it can ever be as i must remain true to my duty of giving people protection, hope and belief that there is real justice in the city. so i will gladly settle for being an anonymous folk hero. besides, i can't

disappoint the artist who is waiting to fill
in the dates on so many more gravestones.

Evie closed her journal and began to think about who was most deserving of being her next victim. The firebug who torched an animal shelter? The priest who lost his ecclesiastical ring up some alter boy's ass? She looked again at the photo of the sleazeball slumlord with a fat face and aviator glasses who had trespassed onto the front page. Her front page. Figuring that alone was enough to qualify him to be next.

CHAPTER 28

"You look silly in that hat," Evie laughed good naturedly at the brand-new Yankees baseball cap that crowned Stoney's long white mane.

"I think he looks adorable," cooed Nanette, as the three of them shared a table at a bustling Szechuan joint in the heart of Chinatown. "And you should have seen him at the game, drinking beer and scarfing down Yankee Franks. He had the time of his life."

"Plus, we beat the crap out of the Twins," beamed Stoney, speaking loudly to make sure he was heard over the din of clattering dishes and competing conversations. "And we're going again Sunday, right baby?"

"That's right, lover."

"Hey, maybe ..." He slammed the breaks on his thought.

"Maybe what?" asked Nanette.

"Nothing," he replied, relieved that he had caught himself before suggesting that they make it a double date.

But Evie knew what he had been about to say. Loved him for thinking it and even more for stopping short in an attempt to spare her feelings. Life had been dealing to Stoney from the bottom of the deck for a very long time, and Evie would not begrudge him happiness just because Cupid had kicked her in the ass. It had been two days, two and a half if she was counting, and if Tom had ever cared for her at all he would have called by now to apologize. Flowers or a card. Even a note tied to a rock. But not one word, which confirmed the painful conclusion that she had never been as important to him as she thought. Just an available late-night piece of ass. A stepping stone to someone better. A model or an actress would seem an appropriate trophy, or maybe the proper accessory to his ultimate ambition would be a woman of wealth and position. All you had to do was look at Page Six of the *Post* to see that New York was lousy with beautiful daughters of prominent families. Families whose money and highly placed connections could boost a charismatic son-in-law beyond the police commissioner's office all the way to Washington.

As far as Evie was concerned, Stoney and Nanette had more class than any of those society jerkoffs, and it made her feel good that they cared enough to treat her to a dinner of soup dumplings and Mongolian beef as a thank you for pushing them together. But Evie needed more beer if she was going to continue watching love blossom across the table while the wounds from her own breakup had not yet begun to scab.

"This food is delicious, Nanette. Out of all the places in Chinatown, how did you discover this one?"

"You kiss a lot of frogs before finding your prince." She planted a wet one on Stoney's cheek, then helped him properly grip his chopsticks. "No different with restaurants."

The waiter brought another round of beers and Evie finally began to relax. Enjoyed getting to know Nanette away from the bar, finding it interesting that she had once been a singer who had done well for herself doing jingles and session work. Had supported a struggling composer for twenty years, working the glove counter at Gimbels after recording gigs had dried up, while her better half stayed home trying to arrange musical notes into combinations that would jump up and dance. And when he finally succeeded in pulling it off, she felt it only fair that her suddenly flush husband now support her, so she divorced him. Got the deed to a bright, airy loft on Wooster Street, not far from Jamesey's, and a monthly alimony check that would more than cover all the booze and ball games she could ever enjoy.

"This beer's going right through me," said Nanette as she rose from the table, then winked. "I'll give you guys a chance to talk about me."

The fiery redhead was in her fifties and the lines on her face showed every minute of it, but she had the hourglass figure of a centerfold half her age, and Evie watched Stoney admire it as she slalomed through the tables of the busy restaurant on her way to the ladies room.

"So, I guess I don't have to shoot her?"

"She's an amazing woman, Evie," Stoney said, feeling as if he was the luckiest man on earth as he stuffed his mouth with a scallion pancake, the one thing at the table he could eat without chopsticks. "And I don't just mean that bitchin' body of hers."

"What about … you know?"

"You told me that when a woman really likes a man it's for more than sex, and that I should give Nanette a chance. And you were right, Evie. That lady and I have found all sorts of new and exciting ways to please each other."

"Wear that baseball cap to bed and see what happens."

"Don't think I haven't," he grinned. Then became serious. "I feel like I've known her all my life. I told her everything, Evie. Growing up on the ranch. About how the old man turned on me. Even about the war and those sixty-three boys I killed. And you know what? She helped me put things into perspective so that I don't have to be passed out drunk to get to sleep at night."

"You've been drinking all day."

"Just beer. No more of the hard stuff from now on. Nanette too. We decided that we're going to start enjoying life."

"Did you tell her about Debby?"

"Every last detail."

"But not our secret?"

"Never." Stoney was a man of honor, the one thing that no one could ever take away from him. "And by the way, nice job on that Black Widow last night."

"Why thank you, sir," she replied, accepting his compliment ever so formally.

"And did you read about that asshole slumlord in today's paper?"

"Just skimmed it," Evie told him. "Do you think he should be next?"

"Paper says his building has rats, *inside* the apartments. A seven-month-old baby was almost eaten alive and four other kids are getting rabies shots. Do *you* think he should be next?"

CHAPTER 29

BABY JESSE DEAD

dentical headlines were splashed across the early editions of
both the *Post* and *Daily News* that Evie had spread out on
her writing table, looking at photos of Baby Jesse clutching
his teddy bear and doing all the other adorable things that
babies do. Any maternal instincts she may have had were buried deep, but the sweet smile on the innocent face of Jesse
Norberto Rodriguez stirred them up. A child who could have
grown into a man with unlimited potential, but before saying
his first word or taking his first step, a slumlord's rats made a
feast of him as he cried helplessly in his crib.

> *i have no appetite for my breakfast as*
> *reading the gruesome account of baby*
> *jesse's death makes me want to puke. so*
> *does the fact that the fat-faced fuck who*
> *murdered him gets his picture on the*
> *front page. MY front page. i have to kill*

*this asshole slumlord and i have to do it
quickly. vigilante justice for the family
and for the city. but a bullet to the brain
would be too merciful for this monster.
maybe immobilize him with a shot to
each knee cap, then turn loose a bunch
of starving rats to feast on him. could I
pull that off? where would i get rats? how
does one wrangle rats? i bet stoney would
know. if not, i have all day to try to figure
something else out because tonight after
work i'm going after this douchebag. but
there will surely be photographers and tv
news crews camped outside his apartment.
and there are sure to be cops. how to get
past them just one more thing i'll have all
day to figure out.*

Evie took a bite of raspberry Danish that she had gotten at the Greek diner, having taken the long way home as to not get busted cheating on Mr. Kim, then washed it down with a sip of coffee that was definitely worth the subterfuge. Since she would be stalking her victim right after work, she put on the uniform. Black shirt, black jeans and PF Flyers. The nine-millimeter zipped securely in her purse as she walked to Washington Square Park where she sat on her usual bench, only instead of seeking a writer's inspiration, this time she locked into a killer's vision.

CHAPTER 30

No cops. No TV news crews. Not even a cub reporter as Evie scoped out the Slumlord's residence from a diner on the corner of a quiet neighborhood nestled on the east side of the upper east side. The tabloids provided the address, and a quick look at the mailboxes would provide the number of the apartment that sheltered the notorious baby killer. After that it would just be a matter pressing the buzzers of a few neighbors that would undoubtedly grant her entry into the building. Then what? Just knock on his door? Would he let her in? Why would he let her in? Was he even home?

As Evie continued to surveil the five-story brick building so did Lieutenant Tom Vaught, staked out in a flat across from the phony Slumlord's digs, a vantage point that offered no view of the diner. He scanned the block as street lights had just come on, confident of success in apprehending the Houdini Killer as he had deployed task force officers through-out the building as well as at strategic points in and around the immediate area. And knowing that all the Houdini kill-ings had occurred between sunset and midnight, Tom was preparing to put his decoy in play.

"Hold your position," Tom ordered, speaking on the telephone to a policeman inside the decoy apartment. "There's someone on a bike rolling up in front of the building."

Evie saw him too. A kid making a food delivery who bypassed the buzzers and walked right inside. Focusing harder through the twilight, she saw that the frame was askew and that the security door did not completely close, meaning that she could walk into the building just as easily as the delivery boy. But then what? Evie still had no way of getting a man in the public's crosshairs to open his apartment door, and figured that if he did not show himself she would return the next night. And the next. However long it took until he did. Unnecessary forethought as, all of a sudden, opportunity was immediate as she saw the Slumlord walk out of the building alone. Round face, aviator glasses and a red track suit. On the move.

Evie grabbed her purse and readied herself to take off after him, then froze as the target walked right toward her. Into the diner. Past her table. So close that she almost gagged on his cologne. Watched as he settled in at the counter, chatting up the waitress as he put a knife and fork to work on a king size helping of meatloaf and mashed potatoes. An unrepentant asshole who had allowed an innocent baby to die in the most cruel and unconscionable way imaginable, whose presence only a few feet away could not have been more of a gift had he been wrapped with a bow. Or so Evie thought, unaware that there was a plainclothes task force officer at the end of the counter and two more in a booth by the entrance, on high alert to not let the decoy out of their sight and to pounce on anyone who made even the slightest move toward him.

Evie waited impatiently to follow the Slumlord home after he was finished eating. But what if this fat slob, who had just prolonged the wait by ordering pie, walked off in a different direction? Up York Avenue or, even more precariously, into the park by the East River. She knew from experience that a lot could go wrong in a public park after dark, especially this particular park as it was home to the mayor's official residence.

Evie noticed the undercover policemen exchange glances but, not knowing that they were policemen, thought little of it. Her thoughts focused on the fact that no matter where the Slumlord might walk off to that he would eventually return home, and she would be inside his building waiting for him to show his fat face. Easy. Force him inside his apartment at gunpoint as she did with Millcross. Easy. No time to choreograph the karmic theatricality of rats, but once she had him alone would nonetheless make him suffer unimaginable pain before finally putting him down, then casually walk away to wait for the morning headlines.

Don't get cocky, rookie.

She could hear her mentor's words as clearly as if the old man was seated across the table from her, but she was not cocky and with seven kills already on the scoreboard Evie was no longer a rookie. Experience making her wonder if this set up was too easy. No news crews. No police and no angry protesters. The most hated man in New York City casually strolling into a diner and flirting with the waitress as if he had not just killed a baby and sent four more kids to the hospital for rabies shots. Why had he not been arrested? What was she not seeing? She pondered the situation for a moment, finally deciding that there was nothing she was not seeing. That the opportunity really was as easy as it looked and she would be a fool not to take advantage of it.

Evie put money on the table, checked the nine-millimeter automatic in her purse and walked toward the door, noticing that the man at the end of the counter looked her way before again exchanging furtive glances with the two men in the booth. Went out into the night air and gave the five-story brick building a final appraisal. Nobody around. All clear. Bloodlust surging as she started across the street to wait for the baby killer to present himself for execution. Glanced back at the diner and saw that the two men in the booth were now staring straight at her. Figured that there was indeed something she was not seeing, and was smart enough to know that the security door to the Slumlord's building would still be broken tomorrow.

"**Y**our plan is short-sighted in that you failed to take into account any one of a number of contingencies."

"The plan is working, Commissioner. And I can assure you that every possible angle is covered."

"Except for the public outrage over your fictitious baby being eaten alive by rats."

"And there will be even greater outrage tomorrow when the press reports that the district attorney's office has refused to indict, citing a lack of evidence." Tom stood his ground as he was being raked over the coals in the commissioner's office on the fourteenth floor of One PP, an inner sanctum known to the rank and file as the Emerald City because they knew that none of them would ever see it. Forced to justify what had become known as Operation Slumlord only days after it had been put into motion. "That outrage should be all it takes to incite the Houdini Killer into making his fatal mistake."

"You had better be right, Lieutenant, because there will be rioting in the streets if you lose control of this narrative." The commissioner got up and poured himself a glass of water from a pitcher on the credenza, then turned his back to Tom.

Looking out the window for several moments to let him stew. "It took a lot of convincing for me to get Morgenthau on board with this charade of yours, and if it doesn't result in a quick arrest he's going to blow the whistle, because there's an election coming up in a few months and he can't afford to alienate voters by becoming known as the district attorney who couldn't even indict a baby killer."

"We'll have our man in custody long before it comes to that. Today the tabloids buried all Houdini coverage on the inside pages and, because headlines are what drive all high-profile criminals, that will definitely motivate him to take action against the man who has stolen what he feels is his rightful place on page one."

"You're cocky, Lieutenant. The truth is that you have no idea what's going on inside that killer's head."

"All we have to do is keep ramping up the media's slumlord coverage as scheduled and I guarantee that ego will demand he make a move against our decoy, and when he does, my team will be on the spot to arrest him."

"You guarantee a lot of things, Lieutenant, but so far I've seen no results. Unless you count roughing up a kid and his puppy. What the hell were you thinking?"

"We had a tip, Sir."

"And you decided to act upon it? Your decision?"

"I gave the final okay."

"Based on what?"

"I was told that this informant had been instrumental in helping the department make several arrests in the past, and that there was no reason to doubt him."

"Unless your informant *is* the killer, how could he possibly have known when and where Houdini would strike? Squandering two-hundred man-hours that could have been put to more productive use elsewhere on the say so of some street snitch was a bad decision, Lieutenant."

"Yes, Sir."

"Did I make a mistake by putting you in charge of this task force?"

"No, Sir."

"Then if you want to remain in charge, I suggest any future decision-making be based less on snitches and theoretical psychology, and more on the tried and true methods of hard-nosed police work. You need to utilize Sergeant Nordby more."

"I discuss strategy with Sergeant Nordby every day."

"He says he was not in the loop on Operation Slumlord."

"I didn't want to risk any slip ups, so, other than yourself, Morgenthau and our media liaison officer, everything concerning the set up was on a need-to-know basis."

"And your second in command did not need to know?"

"Not at that time, Sir."

"Nordby is a valuable asset, Lieutenant. He turned down multiple opportunities for promotion to remain on the street where he can make a difference."

"So he keeps telling me. But in getting to know him better, I think it's possible that his motivation to stay where he is might have had more to do with personal gain."

"That's a serious accusation. Do you have evidence to back it up?"

"No, Sir."

"Until you do, keep your opinion to yourself and utilize Nordby's experience to make a quick arrest. Because if you don't, not only will we have to come clean with the public, which will subject the department to fierce ridicule, but we'll be right back where we started with a serial killer on the loose and no leads."

"Operation Slumlord will work, Commissioner."

"Stop saying that and *make* it work."

"Only a few days ago you were one hundred percent on board with this plan, and I can't believe that a little heat from the D.A., who I might remind you was also totally in favor of this, has caused you to get cold feet." Tom leaned forward in his chair and challenged his boss. "You're the best commissioner in a generation because you've never been afraid to do what you believed to be right. Always stood by the men under your command no matter how much heat you faced. What changed? How is it that you're all of a sudden scared of a little public pressure?"

"Watch it, Lieutenant."

"Or is it political pressure? Are you afraid that if Ed Koch wins the mayoral race that you'll be out of a job if we don't arrest the Houdini Killer fast enough? Back me up so that we can get this murderer off the street and the public can stop living in fear."

"The public isn't scared of Houdini, and right now I'm not even sure they want us to catch him. There's Hero Houdini graffiti popping up all over the city and I saw several Hero Houdini bumper stickers on my way to work this morning. What they're scared of is that you made them think that rats ate a baby and we won't lock up the man responsible."

"We will make a quick arrest, then issue a statement explaining how and why Operation Slumlord was put into action and that it succeeded as planned. With no dead baby and the Houdini Killer on ice, it will be a red-letter day for both the city and the department."

"Save the speeches and make the fucking arrest, because what the city and the department really need is closure. And don't worry about this headline whore walking on a technicality, because you know as well as I do that he'll get his rocks off by feeding the press every grisly detail."

"Unless he wants another year of headlines by using a trial as his forum."

"He wouldn't be the first killer to hang himself in his cell."

"Or to be shot trying to escape?"

"Just get the son of a bitch and we'll make the pieces fit later."

"Everything is going to be done by the book."

"You will do *whatever* it takes to get this job done, Lieutenant. Because if you don't, I won't have to look very far for your replacement."

It suddenly became very clear to Tom why Nordby and the Commissioner were suddenly thick as thieves. His boss *did* like Operation Slumlord, but political survival necessitated a fall guy should the plan backfire. Tom would be hung out to dry, while Nordby would be the man counted upon to step in and get his hands dirty doing whatever it took to get the job done.

"I was on the beat with your old man and have known you since you were born, so nobody understands better than I do that the pressure to arrest the Houdini Killer is compounded by the intense pressure you put on yourself to succeed. But you're pushing too hard and letting that pressure consume you twenty-four hours a day. I know how smart you are, Tom. How hard you work and that you will eventually catch him. But this self-inflicted stress is effecting your judgment. Take a few days and go somewhere to relax."

"I can't do that. Not when we're so close to making an arrest."

"The press already has the daily information we want them to release. A task force detail will have eyes on the decoy every second, and Sergeant Nordby can take charge of anything that comes up while you're away."

"All due respect, Commissioner. I need to be here."

"Don't worry, Tom. If we catch him while you're on vacation you'll still get the credit."

"This is not about getting credit for the arrest. It's about you getting me out of the way so that your personal hatchet man will have a clear field to ensure that the Houdini Killer is dead before he can be arraigned."

The commissioner angrily rose to his feet, palms on the desk as he leaned threateningly forward. "One more outburst like that and you will no longer be a policeman."

"You can't fire me, because the press would want to know why and you'd be scared that I would tell them." Tom stood and faced his boss unafraid. "You assigned me to do a job and I'm going to finish that job."

"I'm not asking, Lieutenant." The commissioner opened the office door. "Give Nordby his orders then get out of town. Far out of town. No newspapers, no television and stay away from the telephone. For the next few days you've never heard of the Houdini Killer."

CHAPTER 32

"You telling me you wouldn't fuck Farrah Fawcett?"

"I'm just saying that Lindsay Wagner's better looking," countered RayRay as he and the mailman argued over which was the sexiest of the current TV cuties.

"You know she's not *really* a bionic woman, don't you?"

Back and forth it went until Stoney chimed in that his Nanette made both actresses look like roadkill, then boasted about how they were going to Yankee Stadium again Sunday, as if none of the lifelong New Yorkers at the bar had ever been there. The lovebirds had not been more than inches apart all afternoon, giving Evie no opportunity to update Stoney on last night's aborted Slumlord mission and get his insight on her plan to go back and put a bullet in the rat bastard's head just as soon as her shift ended.

Time dragged, as work days tended to do when you had something to look forward to afterward. Maybe Manda would stop by, as she often did, for a beer on her way to the record store. Evie thought about playing the jukebox but, as with any bartender, even favorite songs grew tiresome when you heard them several times a day. She knew better than to slow down the clock by watching it, so instead kept herself busy cleaning the back bar and doing side work, but her mind was focused on murder.

"Hey, Evie," called out the mailman. "Let's have another round."

As Evie was setting everyone up, all of a sudden they stopped talking. Stopped drinking. Every one of them looking toward the other end of the bar where Tom Vaught stood with a bouquet of stargazer lilies. Evie ignored him as she rang up the sale. Made him twist in the wind as she busied herself polishing glasses and cutting fruit. Silence in the bar as all eyes were fixed on Evie to see what she would do. Finally, she walked over to her ex-boyfriend, took the flowers and tossed them into the trash.

"Are you that clueless to think flowers are going make up for how deeply you hurt me?"

"I'm sorry, Evie." He meant it. "You were right about everything. I put my job ahead of you and I apologize. Please give me ... Please give *us* another chance."

High drama for a Jamesey's afternoon and the regulars hung on every word. The mailman tossed some money on the bar.

"Fifty bucks says she tells him to take a hike."

"Easiest fifty I'll ever make," said Nanette, as she matched the stake.

The longer he stood there, the angrier Evie became. "Get lost, Tom."

The mailman laughed as he reached for the money.

Nanette slapped his hand away. "Not so fast."

"Let's get out of the city for a few days," Tom said to Evie. "My friend Harry lent me his cabin on Blue Mountain Lake up in the Adirondacks. No television. No telephone. And, most importantly, no job to get in the way."

"Are you fucking deaf? I told you to get lost."

"I'm sorry it took me so long to get my priorities straight. You mean everything to me, Evie, and I want us to spend some time alone together with no interruptions so I can prove it to you."

"You can't make time for a lousy dinner, you disappear for days and now you want to take me to the mountains? I don't buy it, Tom. What's the catch?"

"If I don't make things right with you, I'm going to regret it every day for the rest of my life."

Evie saw Stoney and Nanette frantically signaling her to quit playing hard to get, but she stood firm.

"Please, Evie." Tom was begging. "Please say you'll go with me."

CHAPTER 33

"**Y**ou promised that you wouldn't let your job get in the way," scowled Evie as Tom's rented Pontiac Bonneville rolled past Albany toward Saratoga Springs. "But that's all you've been thinking about for the past hour."

"You're a mind reader?"

"I'm a girl who won't spend days trapped in the middle of nowhere with a workaholic whose mind is still in the city. Especially when I blew off something really important last night to get ready for this trip."

"Do you want me to turn around and go back?"

"Are you really willing to give up on us that easily?" Evie asked, then realized that only a day earlier she had been willing to give up on the relationship just as easily. Figured that couples were always going to have differences and saw that she needed to look at the big picture of forever and always, and that if they were to have any chance at all, she would have to meet him halfway. Pointed to a roadside drive-in up ahead. "Pull in over there. That place is going to fix us."

"Hamburgers are going to fix us?"

"The key to happiness."

The place was bustling with local teenagers and vacation-ing families, enjoying America's favorite food at communal picnic tables in the fresh country air with upbeat sounds of Chuck Berry and the Beach Boys wafting through outdoor speakers. Evie and Tom washed down burgers and fries with chocolate milkshakes. Stuffed themselves until they could not eat another bite, then ordered apple pie.

"Growing up in the city I never had a chance to go to places like this. Eating outside made these burgers taste so much bet-ter, and I'm so full I might have to loosen my belt," he joked. Feeling good as he realized that it had been days since he had seen humor in anything. "And you were right, Evie. This is a great place for an attitude adjustment. Not just because of the food, it's the people too. That kid who moved his bike so we could park. The family who offered to change tables so we could sit together. Why is everybody here so nice?"

"Because they have no reason not to be."

"And that's the key to happiness?"

"All you have to do is learn to enjoy simple pleasures, then the things that matter most in life will fall neatly into place. Now come on. Let's go work off these calories," Evie said as she got up and disposed of their trash, then took Tom's hand, dodging cars as she led him across the road.

"Miniature golf?"

"What's the matter, tough guy? Afraid of getting beaten by a girl?"

Over the bridge. Through the windmill. Between the dinosaur's legs. Score tied after nine holes as their competi-tive juices flowed. Around the loop de loop. Into the clown's mouth. Across the drawbridge into the castle. And when it was all over, Tom Vaught had indeed been beaten by a girl.

He was so good at absolutely everything that Evie was positive Tom had lost on purpose, which showed just how hard he was trying to win her back. And as they fired up the Bonneville and continued north, she sat close and could tell by his relaxed body language that stress had indeed disappeared. She was not naïve enough to believe that burgers and eighteen holes of putt-putt were a cure-all, but felt confident that as a couple they were off to a good start.

"Harry said that to stock up properly on provisions, we'll need to stop at a grocery store before turning off the main highway. It will still be a bit of a drive from there, but he said that our best bet is Lake George."

"Are we going to do a lot of cooking?"

"Every meal."

"Good. Because I brought a shopping list."

They stopped at a supermarket and filled a cart with everything they could possibly need to feed themselves for days. Meat, fruit, vegetables, bacon, eggs, pastries. And lots of snacks. Plus, a second cart filled with beer and assorted beverages.

"Can you think of anything else?" Tom asked.

"We need chives."

As they located them, Evie added that they also would require a whisk.

"Harry assured me it's a well-equipped kitchen. Anything else on your list?"

"Champagne. Taittainger pink champagne."

Tom grinned at the exactness of the request, and was told by the grocery clerk that they would have to go to the liquor store down the street. So, they did. Picked up the bubbles and got back on the road.

The hamlet of Blue Mountain Lake was barely a speck on the map, but the lake itself was awe-inspiring, bordered tightly all around by a majestic forest. Harry's cabin, like most in the area, was secluded and would have been impossible to find without spot-on directions, which fortunately they had. The structure was decades old, built mostly of logs and had a wide porch overlooking the lake which was not more than twenty yards away. There was a row boat tethered to a short dock and a tire swing that extended out over the water. Inside was a stone fireplace and, as advertised, a well-equipped kitchen with almost-modern appliances. Also, as advertised, there was no television and no telephone. Not even a radio. Only the heady residual aroma of burnt embers and ash, which made them feel as if they had been transported a million miles away from civilization, providing Tom with the confidence that thoughts of the Houdini Killer would not be able to crash the party.

They walked down to the water and skipped stones then explored the grounds, wondering if the back and forth chirping of a couple birds high in the pines were expressions of love or conflict. Both Evie and Tom hoping that their own back and forth during the coming days would be more in line with the former. They cracked open a couple cans of beer and sat close on the porch swing, not saying much as they took in the magnificence of a mountain dusk as the setting sun dropped the temperature. Not cold enough to justify a fire, but they were city slickers who were going to squeeze every bit of enjoyment out of such idyllic surroundings, so Tom brought in some logs and kindling from the wood pile on the side of the cabin and built one.

They kept dinner simple with steaks and corn on the grill. The evening was wonderfully romantic as they took things slowly, relaxing on an overstuffed couch in front of the fire until eventually falling asleep in each other's arms.

Day two came to life as the smell of bacon woke Tom from the best sleep he had enjoyed in weeks. Aroused by the sight of his girlfriend wearing an apron over a pink bikini as she put together a mountain breakfast that she served on the porch.

"Sorry I didn't make coffee," said Evie as they gorged themselves on eggs, muffins and fresh-squeezed orange juice. "But you know I suck at it and I didn't want to ruin your meal."

"It would be impossible to ruin this meal."

Her smile sparkled, as she had worked very hard the past few weeks to improve her skill in the kitchen. But his compliment had been aimed at more than just her cooking.

"And the secret to good coffee is simple," he added. "Other than getting quality beans and grinding them yourself, all you need to do is put an egg shell, best if it's a dry egg shell, in the filter to take away any bitter taste."

"As simple as that?"

"As simple as that. I'll buy us a proper grinder when we get home."

Evie liked the way he said *us.* Then she let out a shriek and sprang from her chair.

"What is it? What's wrong?"

A terrified Evie pointed under the table. "ANTS!"

The frightened look on her face told Tom that he had better not laugh.

"You're afraid of ants?"

"Please, Tom. Get rid of them."

He went inside, got a broom and swept the little monsters off the porch. Then took his girl in his arms.

"I'm sorry, Tom. I know it's ridiculous, but ever since some girl put ants in my sleeping bag one summer at Panther Lake, I've been petrified of them."

After assuring her that he would shoot any ants who dared to come back, they sat down and finished their breakfast, talking about what they might do with their day and deciding that no plans would be the best plans. Then she asked him if he liked the Yankees.

"My dad took me to the stadium when I was ten and got Mickey Mantle to autograph a ball for me." Remembering that day put a smile on his face. "You've probably noticed it on the dresser in my bedroom. Whenever I'm having a particularly bad day I pick up the ball and squeeze it tightly, and immediately I feel better."

"When's the last time you went to a game?"

"Not since last season. Have you ever been?"

"Nope."

"Would you like to go sometime? It's a lot of fun."

"So I hear. Maybe we could double date with Stoney and Nanette from my work. I think you'd really like them."

"Sounds perfect," he said as he leaned back and rubbed his full belly, if toned abs could be considered a belly. "A few more of these big meals and I won't be able to fit into my clothes."

"I could say the same."

"Not the way you look in that bikini. You're the sexiest, most beautiful woman I have ever seen." He had said those words to her before and meant them, but never more than at this moment.

Together they cleared the table and did the dishes. A usually annoying chore that right now seemed quite pleasant as Evie hummed a happy tune while Tom's fingers tapped out an accompanying beat on the counter. When he had finally wiped and put away the last plate, Tom disappeared for a moment then came out of the bedroom in his swimsuit. Evie took off the apron, then hand in hand they walked down to the lake and stood at the end of the dock.

"It's freezing," she said as she stuck a toe in the water.

"It's invigorating."

"Aren't we supposed to wait thirty minutes after we've eaten?"

"Quit stalling. It's just water."

"Then you go first."

"Tell you what," Tom said. "Take my hand and we'll jump in together."

As she reached out her hand he pushed her in.

"YOU DIRTY ..." The last of it heard only by the fish.

Tom laughed as he watched her splash around, then jumped into the water. Rubbed warmth into her arms until all was forgiven, then held her close and kissed her. Pent up passion ready to detonate as he removed her bikini bottom and lifted her onto the end of the dock. Standing in the water he pulled her legs apart.

"Tom, stop. Someone will see us."

"Who? There isn't a soul around in any direction."

"What if somebody across the lake is watching with binoculars?"

"Then we'll put on a show he'll never forget."

She thought of Tom's neighbor who had sex with the vegetables she served her husband for dinner, figuring that the woman must have been aware that she was being watched and had been putting on a show for the neighborhood. A sexual exhibitionist just like the woman in the dungeon below Eighth Avenue, who understood that performing the unspeakable in front of an audience would get her off in ways that conventional intercourse never could. Evie invited her man inside.

Tom tickled her with his tongue, hitting all the right notes until she filled the mountain air with shrieks of delight, not caring who heard or saw them. Then he climbed onto the dock and they locked bodies together, reacquainting their flesh in ways they had not before tried until Evie again exploded in wild climax. Maybe not a murder climax, but she screamed so loud that if the people across the lake had not been watching, they were sure as hell watching now as the lovers laid naked on their backs facing a warming sun.

"That was the best sex we ever had," Evie said sweetly, stretching like a satisfied kitten.

Tom rolled over and kissed her gently on the lips. Smiled, then kissed her again. "That was the best sex *anyone* ever had."

They swam some more then took the boat out. Grilled bratwursts as they enjoyed the serenity of the view from the porch, each of them totally at ease with the world. After a while, Tom built another fire, then together they drank beer and munched pretzels while doing the prep work for a dinner of barbecued ribs and potato salad.

"Is Busha the only one who calls you Tommy?"

"She's the only person who has ever called me Tommy."

"What did she say to you in Polish that first morning you took me to the diner? You said you'd tell me when we knew each other better."

"She said that she looked forward to dancing at our wedding."

They lost themselves in each other's eyes. It was love. The real thing. The forever and always kind. He said the words.

"I love you too, Tommy."

Day three began the way all days should, Evie thought. With champagne. She and Tom clinking juice glasses because the kitchen wasn't quite as well-equipped as Harry had made it out to be. Then she told Mr. Forever and Always to keep out of the way because she was making a very special breakfast.

"I've told you how much I love James Bond, right?"

"I know you've seen all the movies."

"I've also read all of the books, including the short stories. There's one where Ian Fleming has Bond in New York where he reveals his special recipe for scrambled eggs. I've never made it because I never had the right person to make it for."

"May I ask what exotic ingredients are in this top-secret recipe?"

"Nothing exotic at all. Salt, pepper and an entire stick of butter. You whisk the eggs over a very low flame until they're slightly more than moist. Add more butter, finely chopped chives then, most importantly, serve with Taittainger pink champagne." She playfully shooed him away. "Now go out on the porch and wait. I've already set the table."

The eggs were indeed worthy of a Double-O spy, and they both agreed that champagne for breakfast was something they needed to make a habit of. The rest of the day was pretty much a carbon copy of the one before, and they relished every moment of it because the following morning it would be time to aim the Bonneville south toward reality. Evie understood that Tom had to get back to work, and the fact that he had spent the better part of three days without even a whisper of his job, showed her that he was indeed making the effort to find a proper balance between ambition and the woman he loved. Then over a dinner of venison chili and cornbread, he knocked her over with a feather by saying that he did not want to leave their enchanted love nest and that the New York City Police Department would have to get along the best it could without him for an extra day.

CHAPTER 34

Over the bathroom sink Evie scorched an egg shell with her hair dryer, an added twist of her own as she attempted to make a great pot of coffee for her man who had gone out for a paper their first morning back in the city. Hearing his key in the lock she raced back to the kitchen, afraid that Tom might laugh at her innovation, but instead saw that he was preoccupied with the front page of the *Daily News.*

SLUMLORD HANGS SELF IN CELL

Evie smiled to herself, pleased that the scumbag had taken the coward's way out so that she did not have to bother figuring out how to wrangle rats or worry about whether or not the security door had been repaired. But she did not understand why Tom seemed so upset.

"This is a good thing, right? He'll never be able to kill another child."

"He didn't kill anyone."

"Maybe not actually, but he was still responsible for what happened."

"All the newspaper stories were fake, Evie. It was a sting I created called Operation Slumlord that was intended to get inside the mind of the Houdini Killer and lure him into the open by providing a tailor-made vigilante target. Poke his ego by motivating him to kill the man who took him off of the front pages."

"Are you telling me that there never was a slumlord? How is that possible? I saw him with my own eyes."

"What? What do you mean you saw him?"

"In the newspaper," she said matter of factly, pleased with her quick save. "His picture was in the paper and there were stories about him every day."

"He was a decoy. I had a squad of task force officers keeping him under tight surveillance day and night so that the second Houdini made his move he would be arrested."

A shiver shot through Evie as she realized that those men staring at her as she left the diner had been cops, and that she had come ever so close to walking right into that arrest. The supreme irony being that if Tom had not shown up at Jamesey's begging her to go away with him, his trap would have eventually worked.

"So, there was no Baby Jesse?"

"Nope."

"How could you have known that the papers would bump Houdini to the inside pages?"

"Because they were all in on it," he told her as she poured them each a cup of coffee. "I not only planted every story, I dictated placement. But the one thing nobody counted on was a public outcry over the district attorney's refusal to indict a baby killer. With the election coming up, both he and the commissioner were afraid that they might lose their jobs in November if they didn't pull the plug quickly. I threatened to make waves if they didn't give the plan more time, so they waited to make their move until I was up in the mountains with no outside contact."

"But having the slumlord commit suicide doesn't make any sense."

"It actually made a lot of sense. Because not only were the commissioner and the D.A. able to save face by pretending to arrest the Slumlord and charge him, they avoided responsibility for inciting the public outcry by not having to come clean and admit the entire thing was a hoax."

"But they didn't catch Houdini, so what was the point? The whole thing was a complete waste of time."

"Hey, this is really good," Tom said as he sat beside her and took a sip of his coffee.

"I added a little twist of my own," she smiled, with more than a hint of pride.

"And you're right about the whole thing being a waste of time, which has me back to searching for one man in a city of eight million."

"It was a brilliant plan, Tom. It really was," Evie told him, still shaken from hearing how close she had come to being caught in the trap.

"Thanks for saying that. It means a lot to me." He leaned close and kissed his girl. "You know, this is the first time we've ever agreed about anything concerning the Houdini Killer."

"Maybe that's because this is the first time you've opened up to me. Shared what's going on with your job the way other couples do."

"I'm glad I did, because being able to talk about it has taken a lot of the pressure off me as I prepare for the shit storm that's ahead of me today."

"How do you want your eggs?"

"James Bond style."

"We don't have any champagne. Besides, I imagine you've got a lot of asses to kick and we can't have New York's preeminent police lieutenant going to work with a buzz on."

The eggs were served sunny side up and the second cup of coffee was as delicious as the first, then with the promise of a special dinner, Evie sent her man off to battle. Went into the bedroom, stood on a chair then with a screwdriver removed the cover from the air vent and took out her journal.

> *i was so smart thinking that the cops*
> *would never catch me as long as they kept*
> *looking for a man. so smart in thinking*
> *that i was always one step ahead of tommy*
> *when he was really ten steps ahead of me.*
> *well it's time to actually BE SMART and*
> *admit that not only am i in over way over*
> *my head, it's clear now that everything i*
> *did was driven by ego. chasing headlines.*
> *the physical pleasure. the self-importance*
> *of thinking that i was helping the people*
> *of new york city, when the reality is that*
> *for every bad guy i killed there were still*
> *a thousand more on the street. and just*
> *because some guy painted a mural doesn't*
> *make me a vigilante hero serving the*

community because every last bit of what I did was to serve myself. and thinking that I could do the impossible by balancing love and murder was the most ego- driven thing of all.

MEA CULPA. I QUIT.

because if i don't quit, i know now that i will sure as hell eventually be caught by the man who makes my heart melt every time he looks at me with those dreamy brown eyes. the orgasms with tommy are not as earth shattering as the orgasms i got from pulling the trigger, but the combination of sex and love i get from tommy sends me further into orbit than a dozen millcrosses or black widows ever could.

i'm not sure how long it will take, but when the police finally figure out that the houdini killings have stopped, they will disband the task force and my tommy will be assigned to a new project, hopefully one with regular hours where success is not measured by the arrest of evie eastway. and because the houdini killer will have never been caught the legend will continue to grow. to energize me and fuel my

*creativity as long as i live. as intended, i'm
going to use this journal as a guide to write
a novel based upon a fictional serial killer.
and i'm going to spend every minute i'm
not sitting at my smith corona making my
man as happy as he makes me.*

*i'm not scheduled to work today, but i'm
going to stop by the bar and see stoney. so
much to tell him about operation slumlord
and about falling in love at the cabin on
blue mountain lake. i wonder how he'll
take it when i tell him i've fired my gun for
the last time? he won't have me to mentor
any longer, but being in love himself he will
understand why. after jamesey's i'm going
to buy a proper coffee grinder and some
gourmet beans, then spend the rest of the
afternoon preparing chicken paprikash
from a recipe that tommy pointed out
a couple weeks ago in a magazine, then
greet my love with a kiss and a cold beer
when he comes home from what will
undoubtedly have been a hard day at work.*

Evie replaced the journal and screwed the cover back on
the air vent. Took a long relaxing bubble bath, then slipped
into a vintage pink paisley mini-dress she accessorized with
a matching Bakelite necklace and bangles. Checked herself

out in the mirror and had no doubt that it was going to be a wonderful day.

CHAPTER 35

Evie licked the chocolate sprinkles off a Mister Softee cone as she sat on her usual bench in the park, taking in a view that included Frisbee players and musicians singing for their supper. Pretty much the same scene as every other day, except this time Evie looked upon it not as a writer seeking inspiration or a killer finding focus, but as a typical New Yorker delighting in one last day of playing hooky before returning to work. Thinking that for how wonderful it had been to get away on a romantic adventure, it was equally great to get back to the city and be reminded of all the reasons why she had moved there in the first place.

Window shopping added a half hour to the ten-minute walk to Jamesey's, and as she entered the bar the mailman popped quickly off his stool and took her aside for a private word.

"NO! NO! NO!"

Stoney was dead. Beaten to death by a mugger.

RayRay moved down to make room as Evie joined the regulars.

"How could that happen to him *twice*? When? Where? What exactly happened?"

"It was three days ago," said Nanette as she returned from the ladies room and hugged Evie, her own grief so crippling that she had no more tears to shed. "He went out to cash his pension check, feed the cat and pay his rent. The mugger must have followed him from the bank, then attacked him by that crazy sculpture bar on Watts Street. Emptied his pockets. Wallet, lighter, even took his cigarettes. The detective said evidence at the scene made it look like Stoney had tried to fight back, but the mugger took away his cane and repeatedly bashed his head in with the heavy bulldog handle, almost beyond recognition."

Envisioning that made Evie want to puke.

"Were the mugger's fingerprints on the cane?"

"They didn't even check."

"The lighter is distinctive. Did they check the pawn shops?"

"The cops aren't going to check a damn thing," groused Nanette as she slugged down a shot of bourbon. Back on the hard stuff as for the past three days she had been drinking for Stoney. Handed Evie a detective's business card. "He was nice enough, but obviously just going through the motions. Didn't come right out and say it, but it wasn't hard to read between the lines and see that he had other cases that were more important to him than the brutal murder of a sweet man who was on his way to feed his cat."

"Stoney and I had talked about trying that new fried chicken place up on Bleecker. Maybe if I would have stayed in town and taken him to lunch he would still be alive."

"I've thought the same thing over and over," Nanette told her. "We were going to go to the bank together, but I stayed in the shower so long washing my hair that he got tired of waiting and went alone. You can't beat yourself up over *what ifs*."

How true, Evie thought, as she all of a sudden realized that if she had stayed in town she would not have been eating fried chicken with Stoney, she would have been in jail.

Both women sat quietly for a while, frustration driving their anger until finally Evie asked if his family knew.

"I called his father. Said that I was a friend of his son Gaylord and that I had some very bad news. Told him what happened. I fudged a bit, okay a lot, by telling the old man how much Stoney missed him and was planning a trip back to Montana to make things right between them. I laid the blarney on thick, trying to give the old man a loving memory of his son." Nanette steadied herself with another shot, trying unsuccessfully to control her anger. "And you know what that miserable asshole told me? Said he didn't have a son, and hung up."

CHAPTER 36

"This is the cop who refuses to investigate Stoney's murder," said Evie, cursing the injustice as she handed Tom the detective's business card.

"Ben Bassham. He's lazy and has a reputation for cutting corners."

"Is there anything you can do?"

"I'll talk to him in the morning," he assured his girlfriend as she sat beside him on her couch.

"Stoney was such a sweetheart. I wish you could have known him."

"Old man with long white whiskers who drank bourbon?"

"I forgot that you bought him a shot that first day you walked into Jamesey's." The thought of that moment pleased Evie, but not enough to quell a rage that had been boiling all day. "Tell this Bassham to get off his ass and check the pawn shops to see if somebody hocked Stoney's lighter. It's solid gold with a bison etched on the front, and the killer's fingerprints would be on it. And all over Stoney's cane, which he already has."

"I'm not his commanding officer, so I can't order him to do it. But the police department is run on favors, and I'm pretty sure that Detective Bassham would consider it a win to be owed a favor by me."

With her man stepping up to take charge, Evie felt confident that Stoney's killer would be made to face the music. But the wheels of justice moved slowly and no matter how hard she tried to hold it together, it was not going to be fast enough to keep her from flipping out and losing her shit.

"Please don't be mad at me, Tommy. But I just remembered that I promised to go over to Nanette's. I know I didn't make the dinner I promised and that I'm ruining our night, but she's all alone. Do you mind if I go and see her?"

"Take care of your friend," he told her, knowing that Nanette would be just as much comfort to Evie as Evie would be to her.

But Evie did not go to that airy loft on Wooster Street to comfort Nanette, she took the subway to a place where she knew that she could satisfy her rage. A rage that gained steam with every step as she marched with purpose up Eighth Avenue where she would slaughter every pervert waiting his turn to ravage the hooded woman chained to the wall of the sex dungeon. Then realized that while seemingly a victim, the woman chained to the wall was actually very much in control, getting her rocks off pulling a train the same as she was about to get hers off pulling a trigger. Women's Lib, and Evie was not going to rain on a sister's parade. But someone in that dungeon was going to die.

Firepower in her purse, Evie pounded the pavement past snatch traders and general riff raff toward the towering Afro who stood sentry. Slipped him a twenty and, as she was admitted, immediately realized that one narrow doorway would not provide a viable exit. So, she decided to exorcise the pounding fury that continued to possess her by following the first creep who left and shooting him dead. But for the longest time no one left, forcing Evie to be proactive as she smiled at two men in expensive suits gawking like teenagers at exhibitions of sex with food, gerbils, midgets and grandmothers.

It wasn't long before the three of them were walking up the steps, the men trying to convince her to go to their apartment but Evie told them that she had a better place. A more daring and exciting place. And without question, as horny men always did, they followed. Across Eighth Avenue and west on 44th Street. Past Ninth Avenue, down a fairly nice residential block of mostly brick buildings with overworked air conditioners poking out of the windows, then down the steps beside the stoop of an old brownstone.

"Here?" they both asked.

"Drop your pants."

Evie did not have to tell them twice. And as pants and underwear fell around their ankles, both looked up to find themselves facing the business end of a nine-millimeter Smith & Wesson automatic. They did not beg for their lives or offer money, just stood frozen with shock as two shots cracked through the night air. Did they deserve to die? She didn't care, as the rage that sent her off the rails had turned Evie into a garden variety lowlife who murdered two men just because she was having a bad day. A rage that still demanded satisfaction.

CHAPTER 37

The *Daily News* called them the Trouser Twins and the *Post* christened them the Perv Brothers. Two more dead bodies credited to the Houdini Killer, sensationalized because the victims were shot with their pants down. But they were not vigilante killings and Evie had not even gone out to get the morning papers, her focus instead on the Yellow Pages as she made a list of every pawn shop below 59th Street.

Evie knew that Detective Bassham was lazy, so even if Tom was able to get him to check the pawn shops, when he eventually got around to it there was no way he would check them all, so she got one of the other bartenders to again cover her shift and set out to do the leg work herself. The list was long and the locations scattered, so she grouped them by neighborhood. Logic indicating that she start nearest the crime scene and work her way uptown. Questioning gruff men in places that looked and smelled like an attic needing to be cleaned out after an old person had died, and after a few stops it became routine. *Do you have a gold lighter with a bison etched on the front? In the past few days, has anyone pawned a lighter like that or tried to sell you a lighter like that? A bison looks like a buffalo.*

Some of the pawnbrokers were nice, probably because she was a girl in a miniskirt. Some did not like being asked cop-like questions by someone who was not a cop. Some flat out told her to get lost. But she soldiered on, all the way up past 14th Street with no luck. Then after having to explain several more times that a bison looked like a buffalo, and being told several more times that no one had seen Stoney's lighter, frustration set in and she called Manda to meet her for lunch at the Old Town Bar.

The place had been going strong for over eighty years, and Evie liked sitting near the end of the bar where she could watch food come down from the kitchen in a dumbwaiter. Over burgers and a couple beers, Evie filled her friend in about Stoney being killed and the search for his lighter. It was Manda's day off and she agreed to help check the pawn shops, so they divided the list and got back to it.

It wasn't long before Manda hit pay dirt.

CHAPTER 38

There had been no answer when Evie pressed the buzzer for Larry Webb's apartment on the top floor of a blighted walk-up building on 11th Street around the corner from Avenue B, so she waited. And waited, until the street lights came on and dusk eventually dissolved into a chilly early September night. Wearing a black sweatshirt over dark jeans, her patience grew thin as she continued to wait for the man who had murdered her friend to come home. Was this scumsucker out drinking up Stoney's pension money? Was he lurking in the shadows somewhere waiting to mug another helpless old man? Evie didn't care how long it took, she would wait. Her surging rage eager to administer a death that would be slow and merciless. Righteous torture as punishment for an unspeakable crime. Unlike anything she had ever done and not yet sure what sort of nightmare she would unleash, but confident that when she looked him in the eye all the pieces would fall into place.

Another thirty minutes passed. Forty-five. Evie had not eaten since the dumbwaiter burger, so she walked to the corner for a quick slice and a Yoo-hoo, and when she got back saw that the lights in the fifth-floor walk-up had been turned on. Her target was home. Missing his entrance and not knowing if he was alone put her at a disadvantage, but that was not going to prevent Evie from exacting revenge. She pressed the buzzers for lower floor apartments and quickly gained entrance to the building. Walked quietly up five flights of stairs and stood outside Larry Webb's apartment door. She heard the television but no voices. Readied herself then knocked.

"Who is it?"

She knocked again, then could see a shadow behind the peephole where he was looking at her. He opened the door. A once-muscular man who had gone to flab and tipped the scales at somewhat more than 250 and somewhat less than a Chevy. With thick dark hair everywhere except on the top of his head, wearing only soiled Jockey shorts and a wife beater. A creepy smile as he invited her into his one room flop. Bed, television, dirty clothes and empty beer cans on the floor.

"Don't you ever clean this dump?" Evie coughed. "The smell in here could gag a maggot."

"You don't like it, you can leave." Smile gone. The thought that he might get lucky right behind it. "What do you want, anyway?"

She produced the nine-millimeter. Pushed the door shut with her foot.

"You're robbing the wrong apartment, girlie." He was deferential to the gun, but not at all afraid of the woman holding it, then told her in a conversational tone. "There's nothing here worth stealing and I don't have no money."

"You spent it all?"

"All what?"

"The money you took from my friend, Stoney."

"I don't know no Stoney, I don't know you and I got nothing here worth taking. So, don't let the door hit you in the ass on the way out."

"He had long white hair and a beard. Wore a Yankees cap. Remember him now?"

"I never saw nobody looks like that."

"Stoney was a sweet man with a good heart who loved his girlfriend and going to ballgames. He walked with a cane that had a silver bulldog handle. You bashed his head in with it the other day on Watts Street."

"Get the fuck out."

"You smoke Virginia Slims?"

"I'm no fag and anybody says I am is gonna take a beating." Then he dialed back the machismo, following her eyes toward Stoney's cigarettes on a table by the bed. "One of my broads left those."

"No matter how much money you paid her, I can't even imagine what sort of vile skank would ever allow a pig like you to touch her."

"Watch your mouth."

"Or what, Larry?"

"You got the wrong guy, wrong apartment, wrong everything. I didn't know your friend, so whoever sent you here give you a bum steer."

"It was a pawnbroker on 47th Street. He says you sold him the gold lighter that Stoney always carried with him."

"Must have been somebody else."

"Your name and address were in his transaction records because you were stupid enough to show him your real ID."

"Somebody must have stolen my wallet. I haven't been that far uptown in years."

"This will go a lot easier on you if you admit what you did."

"I didn't do anything."

Evie turned the volume on the television way up.

"Take off your underwear."

"First you accuse me of offing your friend, and now you want to fuck me?"

"Do it."

"I don't trust you."

"Small dick, Larry? Is that why you're so shy?"

Gun pointed at him, he had no choice but to do what he was told. Trying to conceal the embarrassment that she was right as he stood before her naked except for a sweaty wife beater stretched to the limit by his fat belly.

"Now shove that shit-stained underwear in your mouth."

"No fucking way."

Evie put a bullet in his kneecap and he crashed to the floor, screaming in pain.

"I said to put it in your mouth. Now do it!"

Shot and humiliated, he did what he was told.

"All the way. Cram it in as far as you can."

No choice but to again do as he was told. Panting with great difficulty through his nose. Bleeding as he pulled himself up onto a wooden chair, then with his good leg started to scoot it aggressively toward Evie.

"You may have stolen his money, but the one thing you couldn't take from Stoney was his pride. And I'm haunted by the thought of him on the ground completely helpless. The torture of knowing that he was about to die as you hit him again and again, bashing in his skull."

Still defiant, his face burning red as he tried to scream at her through the gag. Hate in his eyes as with great difficulty he inched the chair closer.

"Do *you* feel helpless right now, Larry?"

Enraged and fighting through the pain of a crippled knee, he was almost close enough to get his hands on her.

She shot his other knee.

As she watched his eyes bug out, Evie knew the indecipherable screams filtering through the soiled gag were now pleas for mercy. Shot up and naked everywhere that mattered, he was as helpless and pathetic as any man could be.

"How does it feel knowing that *you* are about to die?"

Bravado had dissolved to a whimper as he knew that he was finished. But Evie was not finished. She assumed the position and held the nine-millimeter with both hands, then aimed it between his legs and squeezed the trigger.

He writhed in pain too excruciating to imagine as blood pooled on the chair beneath where his balls used to be.

"That wasn't for what *you* did to him. That was payback for what that first creep did to him. But I suppose that wasn't really fair, was it Larry? So, I tell you what. I'll give you one chance to get out of this alive, which is a lot more than you gave Stoney. Do you want to live?"

An anemic nod pleaded for mercy.

"Then this is what you need to do." She stepped behind him, bent her knees and with great effort pushed the chair across the small room to the window, then opened it wide. "Just fly away and all of this will be forgotten. You can fly, can't you, Larry?"

Helpless to prevent the horror that awaited him, tears streaked his face as he closed his eyes.

Evie slapped him hard. "Wake up, asshole. I don't want you to miss one second of this ride."

Hatred had given Evie superior strength, and she needed every ounce of it to tilt the chair forward so that his head and arms lurched across the window sill and hung over the side. She could not think of a more terrifying way to die than being pushed out of a window head first and staring down at the rapidly approaching concrete finish line. It would be the final Houdini killing. The most spectacular and most satisfying. And although Larry Webb's death would not provide closure, justice will have been served for Stoney and Nanette.

Now that she had leverage, Evie was able to hoist his legs and slide the fat man's bloody carcass out the window. She watched with delight as his face smashed into the sidewalk, his neck crumpling like an accordion. Then she dropped to her knees, the flames of orgasm burning her loins with an intensity that she was positive no other woman on earth had ever felt.

CHAPTER 39

How was a slightly built man able to drag someone twice his size across a room, lift him up and push him out the window? Did he have help? There was no forced entry, so was it safe to assume that the victim knew his killer? He was castrated and gagged with his own underwear, which points to personal motivation. A jilted lover? Could the Houdini Killer be homosexual?

These were only a few of the unanswered questions that Tom had been trying to make sense of all morning. Cross-referencing a mountain of files from the previous killings with preliminary reports on the torture and mutilation of Larry Webb. A crime so different from all the others that, aside from a ballistics match, there was not one similarity to connect it to the other Houdini killings.

Tom sat at his desk staring at the files, knowing that buried somewhere in those hundreds of documents was a clue. A connection that would point him in the direction of a killer. This time he would review the files in reverse chronological order, starting with the Perv Brothers, as there was a sex angle to that double murder just as there was with the killing of

Larry Webb. He would pore over every page again and again until something popped. It always did. Eventually. And usually it proved to be something obvious that he had glanced at a dozen times without really seeing it. And he would keep looking until he found it, but before he could again get started, Detective Ben Bassham walked into his office. Tall and wiry, bushy brown hair and eyes that said he would rather be on a barstool somewhere. But at the moment very pleased with himself.

"I circulated a flyer to every pawn shop in the city with a description of the gold bison lighter and got an immediate hit. Pawnbroker up on 47th Street bought it the other day from, and you're never going to believe this, your Houdini victim from last night."

After beating his brains out trying to find a lead, any sort of connection, the laziest cop on the force walks into Tom's office and makes him a present of one. But it was a lead that raised questions to which he was afraid of learning the answers. The coincidence of Evie's connection to Richard Hansen could be logically explained away, but her connection to a second Houdini victim could not be as easily blown off.

"Thank you, Detective. I owe you one."

"Maybe more than one. I haven't gotten to the best part yet." He sat down across the desk. "I interviewed the pawnbroker and he said a girl came into his shop yesterday and asked specifically about the lighter, and after some haggling he sold it to her for eighty bucks. Then she offered another twenty for the name and address of the guy he bought it from, but he held out for a blow job behind the counter."

Tom cringed as the coincidences implicating his girl-friend began to add up. But he knew that there was no way the woman he knew, the woman he loved, could possibly be involved even peripherally in a grisly torture killing. And that if she would have gotten the name and address of the man who sold the lighter she would have given it to him and let the department do its job. *Wouldn't she*? Then, afraid of what he might be told, Tom asked the $64,000 question.

"Did he describe the girl?"

"A real looker, and I don't blame him from taking the hummer instead of the twenty."

Tom knew that Evie was desperate for the name, but also knew that she would not go down on her knees to get it. *Did he know that*?

"I knew this was a priority for you, Lieutenant, so I had the pawn broker give a description of the girl to a sketch artist."

Tom looked at the face of the girl who had gotten down on her knees and let out a sigh of relief as, with curly blond hair and blue eyes, this girl in the sketch could not have possibly looked more different than Evie. And, coincidences aside, he felt guilty for even suspecting the woman who was going to be his forever and always.

He took a closer look at the sketch and had a feeling that he had seen this girl somewhere before. He had a good memory for faces, but couldn't place her. The hair wasn't right. Probably just reminded him of someone. Tom knew that it was highly unlikely that this girl, or any girl, had killed Webb, or Millcross or any of them. But he was positive that the girl in the sketch knew who did. *She knew the Houdini Killer*, and if they could find her, they could sweat her into giving him up.

The only problem was that she looked like a thousand other girls you would pass on the street every day.

CHAPTER 40

"**I** want you to fill in the blanks on Larry Webb," Tom told the man he did not trust but had been ordered to utilize. "He had a sheet of priors a mile long, burglaries and muggings mostly, but it's possible that his last mugging turned deadly. I want to know everything there is to know about this scumbag, so canvas his neighbors, local merchants and bartenders. Everybody who lives or works within a three-block radius of his apartment."

Nordby lit a cigarette, exhaling a tight stream of smoke across the desk at the man he did not trust but had been told to take orders from.

"Then I want one of the at-large squads to retrace our steps on that double hit on 44th Street. Find that one thing we may have overlooked."

"Why do you always insist on doing the same things over and over?"

"The same reason we always ask witnesses the same questions over and over. Because they usually remember something they had previously forgotten. Do *you* have anything new on the Perv Brothers?"

"They both sold shoes at the Gucci store on Fifth Avenue and they lived together in the same apartment, so you can do the math on that."

"They had separate bedrooms, Nordby. And even if they were gay, the important thing is to find out what crime Houdini was avenging. He does not kill randomly, which means that he knows about a crime they committed that we don't."

"I ran both names through B.C.I. and they came back clean."

"These guys had their dicks out in public, which makes me very much doubt that it was the first time. Keep checking."

"I told you. Neither one of them has any criminal history, perverted or otherwise, in New York state."

"Then check nationally."

"Do you have any idea how long that will take?"

"Find out when they moved to New York and where they came from, and if they knew each other before moving here. That should narrow down your search."

"Digging up dirt on victims is a waste of time."

"Do what you're told, Sergeant. There was a reason Houdini lured them to the same spot on 44th Street where he killed Danny Doyle. That's a connection. Which makes me suspect that, one way or another, it might have something to do with Jimmy Callan, because word on the street is that he's offering a $25,000 dead or alive bounty on the Houdini Killer."

"You're getting way off track."

"I want you to use any sources you have in Hell's Kitchen to keep an ear to the ground so that we can take a closer look at everybody even slightly connected to Danny Doyle and find things that don't add up. And for me, Jimmy Callan's involvement does not add up."

"Because he's doing the job we're supposed to be doing?"

"For once, why don't you try aiming that brain of yours in a positive direction instead of always being so quick to criticize. What is Callan's motive for offering this money? Is it possible that he knows the Houdini Killer and wants to shut him up before we catch him and he spills something incriminating? We need to know what Jimmy Callan knows."

"We need to know what Evie Eastway knows."

"What connection could she possibly have to any of this?" snapped Tom. "And I suggest you think very carefully before you answer."

"She was Richard Hansen's girlfriend, plus Larry Webb killed Gaylord Hailstone, who was a regular at the bar where she works." Nordby planted his feet on the desk and blew a smoke ring. "And not only does your girlfriend have a double connection to the Houdini killings, she's the one who got Webb's address from the pawnbroker."

Tom slapped Nordby's feet off his desk, then shoved the sketch of the girl from the pawn shop in his face.

"This is *not* Evie Eastway. It doesn't look anything like Evie Eastway. This girl could be anybody, which means that your bullshit accusation is totally unfounded. Now get the hell out of here and do what I told you to do."

"You're a dirty cop, Vaught. You're trying to cover the whole thing up, and I won't let you get away with it."

"From the very beginning you've had a bug up your ass about me. Why?"

"You may have made lieutenant at thirty-one, but you didn't earn it. A college boy who somehow conned the brass into believing that you could do better police work with your face in a book than by paying your dues on the street where crime is real."

"That's it?" Tom almost laughed. "Nothing tangible? Just a petty grudge because I went to college while you were shaking down streetwalkers and yeggs? That I used reason and logic instead of intimidation and violence to advance in rank faster than you did? A lot of officers have left you in the dust."

"But *you* didn't earn it."

"I selected you for this task force because I thought you were a good policeman, but I see now that you're nothing but a simple-minded thug."

Nordby smashed Tom with a left hook that sent him crashing backward against a filing cabinet. Viciously beating him until Tom shook off the blows and began to pummel the bigger man. Lamps broken and furniture knocked over as they traded punches until Nordby pinned him on top of the desk, squeezing his neck in a strangle hold until Tom managed to free himself then get Nordby into submission by twisting his arm behind his back.

"You are dismissed from this task force and re-assigned back to regular duty."

"We'll see what the commissioner has to say about that."

"And if you ever again mention the name Evie Eastway, I will beat you within an inch of your life."

"Fuck you, Vaught."

With a quick upward thrust, Tom snapped Nordby's arm.

CHAPTER 41

Finally getting around to taking a stab at jambalaya, Evie stood at her kitchen counter chopping onion and bell pepper and reflected upon what had been a satisfying afternoon. She had gone to the Waverly Theater and saw the latest James Bond movie, *The Spy Who Loved Me*, then on the way home ducked into St. Mark's Bookshop and picked up a collection of Bukowski poems for Tom and a new book of Raymond Carver stories for herself. Found a funky eyeball necklace at Manic Panic, then stopped by a thrift store where twenty bucks scored a sweet 50s biker jacket that made her eager for the trees in the park to kick off their annual autumn spectacular. When crispness in the air would reinvigorate her feeling that there was nothing she could not accomplish. She wondered what percentage of the world's great masterworks had been created in autumn.

Following the recipe exactly, Evie put shrimp, andouille sausage and a dozen other ingredients and spices into a heavy pot on the stove over a low flame so that it would be ready when Tom got home from work. She relaxed on the couch with a cold can of Fresca, put her feet up and began to compose what would be the final entry in her journal.

> *the image of larry webb's face smashing*
> *into the sidewalk like a rotten watermelon*
> *will forever fill my heart with joy. whenever*
> *i am having a bad day, all i will have to*
> *do is remember the pride of enacting that*
> *justice and i'll smile. just as whenever i see*
> *an old man wearing a yankees cap i will*
> *think of stoney and smile.*
>
> *so i suppose i have received closure after*
> *all. not only for losing stoney but for the*
> *spectacular, yet short lived, career of the*
> *houdini killer. finally it's time to begin*
> *writing my novel, while devoting the*
> *remaining hours of every day to pleasing a*
> *man who is both charming and handsome.*
> *virile, urbane and can always be counted*
> *upon to do the impossible. my agent 007 –*
> *tommy vaught.*

CHAPTER 42

"One more thing, Berto." Tom switched the phone to his other hand after spending the past half hour making personnel moves and reissuing orders pertaining to Larry Webb and the Perv Brothers. "The report on the Riverside Park murder mentions a potential female witness who ran off before she could be properly questioned. The only description noted is that she was female and in her twenties, so I want you to track down the officer who spoke with her and show him the sketch of the blonde from the pawn shop. Get on it ASAP and we might finally catch a break."

The remainder of Tom's afternoon was spent attempting to justify his hunch about Jimmy Callan. In police work a hunch was usually nothing more than an educated guess, a gut reaction not based on fact but on years of experience. And Tom's experience told him that something was definitely not kosher about the boss of the Westies offering a $25,000 dead or alive reward for the Houdini Killer. Why would Callan put a price on his head, especially with the police already turning the city inside-out looking for him, unless he had something to lose should the cops catch up with him before he did. Danny

Doyle had been both muscle and bag man, so could he have been robbed of money that Jimmy Callan was desperate to recover?

Tom had assembled copies of every piece of paperwork the New York City Police Department had on James Callan. Convictions and acquittals. Known associates and his connection to the murder of a rival, only a few months earlier, that had given him complete control of Hell's Kitchen. Some assumed that the Gambinos had ordered the murder to forge an alliance with the Westies, but most in law enforcement believed that Callan had ordered the hit. If that were true, then it was beginning to make sense to Tom that the man he paid to commit the murder could have been the Houdini Killer. And the $25,000 bounty was part of a scheme to eliminate him before he was arrested and had the chance to rat out Callan in exchange for a lighter sentence.

A Callan/Houdini connection made sense. The only thing so far that had. But he couldn't prove it. As it was, Tom needed a lot of things to fall into place before he could prove anything about anybody, but was positive that one minor detail would be the catalyst to make all the dominos fall and point him directly to the Houdini Killer. Could the elusive Riverside witness be that catalyst? Step by step Tom had investigated by the book, only to feel as though he had been trying to assemble a jigsaw puzzle with one piece missing from the box.

Frustration was setting in and he needed to clear his head, but how was that possible when he lived and breathed this case. Lived and breathed every case. The only time he had even come close to completely putting work out of his mind in his ten years on the police force were those magical days at Blue Mountain Lake, and it made him wonder what it would be like to withdraw from society and live out his days enjoying sex and scrambled eggs among the pines with the gorgeous woman he loved more than he could put into words. But he knew it was a dream that his ambition would never allow.

Nordby hadn't told Tom anything about Evie that he had not already known. Her link to Richard Hansen could be written off as coincidence because he probably had dozens of friends and acquaintances. Everybody had dozens of friends and acquaintances. But oblique as the Hansen connection might be, could the Stoney/Webb connection also be dismissed as coincidence? No matter how much Tom did not want them to, facts added up that Evie might somehow be involved. He knew both logically and in his heart that it was all nothing more than circumstantial and wanted to disregard it exactly the same way that he had told Nordby to disregard it. As a bullshit accusation that was totally unfounded. Yet if the situation was reversed and Tom had found out that Nordby's girlfriend had a double connection to the Houdini killings, he would not stop digging until he found absolute proof of her guilt or innocence. What kind of policeman would he be if he did not investigate his own girlfriend with equal diligence?

It had been a very trying day and, even though it was not yet six o'clock, Tom organized the documents on his desk and called it quits. On his way to the elevator he stopped in the men's room, then standing at the urinal in mid-stream heard the lock on the door snap shut.

"Sergeant Nordby is at the Bellevue ER with a broken arm," the commissioner told him. "It's a severe break that will require surgery so they can reattach the bone with a plate and special screws. Barring complications, the doctor says the arm will be in a cast for a minimum of six weeks."

"That's what happens when you start a fight you can't finish."

"Seems he got in at least one good shot," said the commissioner as he pointed to Tom's eye that had begun to color and swell. "Is there anything else I need to be made aware of?"

"Sergeant Nordby has been dismissed from the task force, which I assume you already know or you wouldn't be here. My new second in command is Berto Cruz from the one-nine."

"He's inexperienced."

"Cruz has good instincts. Knows how to follow orders and respects the chain of command."

"That may be, but I can't condone the fact that you put a valued officer out of commission."

"Valuable to you, maybe, but not to the task force."

"You won't be of value to anyone, Lieutenant, unless you put the cuffs on this damn Houdini Killer. And I don't care how the fuck you do it, just do it."

CHAPTER 43

"She cheat on you with other man?"

"No."

"She give you that black eye?"

"Of course not."

"Then nothing else matter," said Busha as she fed the chickens in the back room of the diner that had just closed for the day. "My Jozef had little secrets he think I don't know about, like sneaking off for beer when supposed to be working late. But none of that matter if you are in love. Are you in love, my Tommy?"

"More than I can put into words," he said, as he bagged the day's trash against the wishes of the self-sufficient old woman whose pride insisted that she do everything herself. "But this goes way beyond love."

"Nothing ever get in the way if love is strong." Busha snatched the trash bag away from him and carried it to the door. "Pretty Evie a wonderful girl and you lucky to have her."

"I know that."

"She cook for you?"

"Yes."

"She give you the sex?"

"Busha!"

"You think about her all day when you at work?"

"I do."

"Then do not be glupi. You do whatever it take to keep her."

"It's not that simple, Busha,"

"You make simple. I see in your eyes she is best thing ever happen to you. Don't be idiota and let her get away."

"What if she's involved in something illegal?"

"Look other way."

"I'm a policeman."

"You come here for my advice, you take my advice. When in love, nothing else matter."

"Please try to understand that this is a lot more serious than sneaking off for a couple beers. If Evie is involved with this and I look the other way, I could lose my job, and if she's innocent and finds out that I'm investigating her she'll leave me."

"Decide what mean more to you, your woman or job."

"They're equally important. Evie and the department both mean everything to me."

"Then you must find way to have both."

"That's not possible."

"Forget what they teach at college and listen to your busha. Just because in sixty years I never leave neighborhood, does not mean I do not know how the world work. You want something, you take it."

CHAPTER 44

"**T**he fact that my straight arrow boyfriend beat the crap out of someone is sexy as hell," gushed Evie as she pressed a package of frozen corn against Tom's swollen eye. Then took the lid off the pot and stirred the jambalaya, unleashing a burst of savory aroma that dominated the kitchen. "The only thing that could make it more exciting would be if I would have been there to see you do it."

"The fact that my girlfriend is turned on by violence is more than a bit disconcerting." He said it with equal measures of surprise and concern, then took his seat at the table by the window as Evie plated and served the meal. Dug in, then quickly cooled the Cajun heat with a long swallow of beer, smiling at the cook as he declared the food delicious.

"You're not just saying that?"

Tom's left hand held the frozen bag of corn while his right shoveled home another heaping forkful of jambalaya. Then another.

"Honest to God, Evie. The sausage and chicken are so tender they almost melt in my mouth, and you nailed the perfect balance of spices. It's like eating in New Orleans. You'll see when we go there."

"We're going to New Orleans?"

"Even a cop gets vacation time. We're going everywhere."

As Evie imagined all the exotic ports of call they would one day visit, Tom told her that the Houdini Killer's latest victim, Larry Webb, was the mugger who murdered Stoney.

She acted properly surprised, then asked how he knew.

"A woman had been making the rounds asking about the gold bison lighter you told me about, and she found it in a pawn shop on 47th Street. Used her feminine charms to get the name and address of the man who sold it." He took the police artist sketch from a pocket of his suit coat that hung on the back of his chair. "Is this Nanette?"

"Maybe thirty years ago," Evie laughed. A lot of relief in that laugh. "Does she know that the mugger is dead?"

"Not yet."

"I can't wait to see the look on her face when I tell her tomorrow at work." While continuing to play it cool, Evie's stomach knotted as a closer look saw that the police sketch of Manda was as spot on as a photograph. "So, you're saying that this woman is the Houdini Killer?"

"That's doubtful. But she most certainly gave Houdini Webb's address." He held the sketch in front of her face. "Are you sure you don't know her? Have you ever seen her?"

"Sorry."

"Think hard, Evie. Is she a customer at the bar?"

"Not that I've ever seen."

"A relative, maybe?"

"Stoney's only family is in Montana."

"Well, she has some connection to him. And when we find her, and we *will* find her, we can expect that she will lead us directly to the Houdini Killer."

"Do you have anything to go on other than this sketch?"

"I thought she might also be a potential witness who fled the scene of the Riverside Park murder before she could be questioned, but the officer who confronted her said that she was not the girl in the sketch. Said that the girl in the park had long brown hair. Could be anybody."

"This girl in the sketch could be anybody."

"I've got half the task force pounding the pavement looking for her. It won't be long until we pick her up."

"How you expect to find one blonde in a city full of them?"

"Trust me, Evie. We will."

But Evie knew they would not, as first thing in the morning she would tell Manda to ditch the blond wig at the bottom of a dumpster somewhere in the outer boroughs. She checked Tom's eye and saw that the swelling had gone down, but not all the way. "I'm glad you beat the shit out of the asshole who did this to you."

"It was Sergeant Nordby."

"A cop fight?"

"We had a disagreement about the focus of the case and he took a swing at me."

"Other than your mystery blonde, what *is* the focus of the case?"

"What do you know about a criminal gang called the Westies?"

"Irish mafia, right?"

"The word mafia gives them way too much credibility. They're more of a glorified street gang."

Tom gave her a basic overview of the Irish ghetto that was Hell's Kitchen and its hundred years of mob rule, up to and including the Westies. He told her in frightening detail about the crimes of Jimmy Callan, including the fact that he was suspected of cutting off the head of a Gambino soldier and rolling it down a busy sidewalk in Washington Heights.

"And now he's after you?"

"Not me. But he's emerged in the investigation as a person of interest."

"He can't go bowling with some guy's head and just walk around bragging about it." She cringed at the thought of her handsome lover being decapitated. "Can he? Why isn't he in jail?

"From the time he was nine years old, Callan has been arrested for everything from mopery with intent to creep all the way up to murder one. He's not particularly smart and doesn't hide behind top criminal lawyers like the Italian mobsters do, yet somehow prosecutors have never been able to convict him of any of the top charges." Tom's voice was riddled with frustration. "If there was ever a criminal who deserved to face the business end of the Houdini Killer's nine-millimeter, it's Jimmy Callan."

"I can't believe you just said that."

"Words spoken in the heat of the moment," Tom quickly backtracked, then took a deep breath. A sip of beer. "You know that I would never in a thousand years seriously suggest such a thing. It's just frustrating that a murderer who doesn't go to very much trouble to conceal his crimes continues to cheat justice. And now he's flaunting it as well by offering a $25,000 dead or alive bounty on the Houdini Killer."

"What?" blurted Evie, imagining herself headless. "Why?"

"My guess is that it has something to do with Callan ordering the hit on a rival a few months back that gave him clear title to Hell's Kitchen. If the man he paid to do the actual killing was the Houdini Killer, he may be tying up loose ends."

"Houdini isn't a hit man."

"He might be. Until last night we didn't know that he went in for torture and sexual mutilation."

"I don't buy it."

"It's not uncommon after high profile mob hits for the contractor to be eliminated so that there is no connection between the person who ordered the hit and the man who pulled the trigger. Which in this case makes sense, because twenty-five grand would be a small price to pay to silence the Houdini Killer before he has a chance to trade all the things he knows about Callan for a lighter sentence."

"Houdini is facing ten life sentences. What kind of break could he possibly hope for?"

"Maybe a chance at parole."

"After a thousand years?"

"Who knows? The justice system is far from predictable."

"But isn't Jimmy Callan doing you a favor by going after the Houdini Killer?"

"He's creating a distraction. Even more work for the task force whose time and resources are already stretched to the limit. Besides, placing a dead or alive price on someone's head, anyone's head, is no different than murder for hire."

"Why don't you arrest him?"

"No admissible evidence. Not yet anyway. Meanwhile, every night Callan sits in the 596 Club waiting for someone to come in and claim the reward."

"You're getting yourself all worked up, Tommy. You need to relax," Evie purred as she unbuttoned his shirt and ran her fingers through his chest hair. "Why don't you forget about work for a while and join me in a hot bubble bath?"

"If you don't mind, I'm going to finish my beer and unwind a bit," he said as he got up and looked through her records, then slipped one onto the turntable. "I'll join you in a few minutes."

As pink bubbles rose in the tub, Evie knew that Tom's hunch about Jimmy Callan was all wet and that the dead or alive bounty would never come close to touching a single hair on her head. But the Houdini Killer's retirement had been designed to put an end to the task force, and now that the lunatic Irishman had become a focus of the investigation she saw no end in sight.

As Evie massaged the bottoms of her feet with a soapy loofa, Tom compartmentalized a thorough examination of drawers, suitcases and shoeboxes. Looked under the mattress, the bottom of the laundry hamper and the back of the closet. Discovering nothing that would in any way implicate his girlfriend's involvement with the Houdini killings. Then in reverse order he searched again with the same result, feeling guilty for ever having suspected her in the first place.

CHAPTER 45

Runners on second and third, two outs and two strikes on the batter Reggie Jackson as Jimmy Callan's eyes were glued to yet another new rabbit-eared RCA. Tonight he had attempted to change his luck by putting his money on the hometown Yankees, who were making a strong run at the pennant, only to find himself down by two runs in the bottom of the ninth inning. He tensed as Jackson took a big swing, launching a long foul ball into the stands.

"A single ties it and a homer wins it," encouraged Mickey Feeney. "You got this, Jimmy. You got this."

Aside from a few dodgy characters and a street-weary tart, it was mostly just the regular crowd of blue collar boozers propping up the 596 Club. Die hard Yankees fans smart enough to keep their mouths shut when Callan was betting on the other team were tonight screaming at the television, urging their hometown hero to win the game with one mighty swing of the bat. But instead, that mighty swing sucked the air out of the room as Jackson struck out and the game was over.

The bartender dashed for cover, but tonight Callan did not shoot the television. Just sat quietly. Then after a few moments told Mickey to find out where Reggie Jackson lived.

"You can't kill him, Jimmy."

"Who's gonna stop me?"

"Use your noodle. The whole city would be lookin' to lay boots on you."

"Then I'll cut off his arms," the pissed off Irishman countered, then took a pull from a pint of Guinness. "He can't play baseball with no arms."

"Stop talking crazy."

"You can't expect me to just let this go, Mickey. I have to teach this wanker a lesson that he can't fuck with a man's bankroll."

"Are you Jimmy?" interrupted Evie as she walked over to his table.

"What the hell do you want?"

"I'd like to talk to you." She gave Mickey a look that said get lost. "Privately."

The boss of the Westies checked her out. Dark jeans and a dark shirt. Brim of a baseball cap pulled low. "Don't flatter yourself that I'd ever wet my pecker inside the likes of you."

"Don't flatter *yourself* by thinking I could find it without a magnifying glass."

Callan bolted to his feet, transferring the hatred he felt toward Reggie Jackson to the girl who suddenly realized that she needed to choose her words a lot more carefully when she did not have a gun in her hand.

"I'm here for the reward."

"Piss off."

"I know who the Houdini Killer is and I want the money."

"Can you believe the balls on this gash?" Callan grumbled to Mickey, then glared at Evie. "You think you can just walk in off the street and expect me to believe you know who the Houdini Killer is? Who the hell are *you*? Tell me how *you* know?"

"Do you want Houdini or do you want to play twenty questions?"

"What I want, little mouse, is to know why I should believe anything that comes out of your fucking mouth."

"Just because I'm a woman doesn't mean I don't know who put a hole in your pal Danny Doyle and all the others, and you're an idiot if you don't listen to me."

"She's full of shit, Jimmy." Mickey stood and confronted her, an extra degree added to his annoyance when he realized that Evie was taller than he was. "Let me toss her ass in the street."

"Get your creepy paws off me," Evie barked at Mickey as he roughly grabbed her upper arm. "I can prove to you who killed Doyle. I know things about the killing that weren't in the newspaper."

"Like what?"

"His hand was bloody, and probably broken, from punching the brick wall on the side of the stoop where it happened," Evie said as she yanked her arm away from Mickey's grasp and made herself comfortable at the table beside Callan.

"Even if I could verify that, what would it even mean?"

"Then how about this? Houdini ripped the gold cross off Doyle's neck in the struggle and the police kept it as evidence. I'm sure his family never got it when they returned his wallet and the rest of his things."

Callan looked at Mickey who shrugged his shoulders.

"Let's assume for a minute that I believe you. Who's the Houdini Killer?"

"The money first."

"The name first."

"I know you wouldn't be stupid enough to keep that kind of money in a bar full of lowlifes. Where is it?"

"Be careful not to push me too far."

"Where's the money, Jimmy?"

"Never mind where it is."

"You don't have it, do you?" denounced Evie boldly, as cocky as if the nine-millimeter in her purse was in her hand. "You make yourself out to be some kind of neighborhood big shot by offering a reward for information, then when I bring you that information, it turns out that you don't have the money to pay me."

"This is the last time I'm gonna warn you to watch that mouth."

"Or what, Jimmy? Are you stupid enough to kill me *before* learning what I know? If you really have it, take me to the money and I will not only tell you who the Houdini Killer is, I'll put you face to face with him."

"It's a load of crap, Jimmy," bristled Mickey. "Let me crack this bitch in the kisser."

Callan was not convinced either way, but Evie's ballsy confidence had stoked his curiosity. "You'll put me face to face with the Houdini Killer?"

"As soon as you take me to the money."

"I'm sure I don't have to tell you what will happen if you're not on the level."

"Just take me to the damn money."

Callan looked at Mickey. "Get over to my sister's place and tell her to go to the movies."

"Damn it, Jimmy. Can't you see this broad's playing you?"

"Now, Mickey."

He didn't like it, but did what he was told.

"What's so important about Danny Doyle that you would offer a reward to find his killer?" Evie asked as they watched Mickey's metallic-green Oldsmobile peel away from the curb up Tenth Avenue. "Or is it maybe that it's not about Doyle at all? What's your real interest in the Houdini Killer?"

"You want the money, or do *you* want to play twenty questions?"

"You want the name? Tell me why you want him so badly."

"That's not part of our deal."

"I haven't seen any money yet. Why are you stalling?"

"Keep your shirt on."

"Want to kill the time talking about the Yankees?"

"You got balls, I'll give you that," the Irishman growled. Anger tempered with confusion as no one ever dared to talk to him that way. "But if you don't deliver the Houdini Killer, I'll cut them off. And that won't be all I cut off."

"I'll deliver. Now tell me why you want him so badly."

"He came onto Westies' turf and gunned down one of our own, and for that I'm gonna cut him into so many pieces that the undertaker won't be able to find them all to glue his ass back together." His tone was icy. His words laced with hate. "Nobody gets away with that. Nobody. And to send that message, twenty-five grand is a bargain. Now let's go. We're gonna take a walk."

Evie unzipped her purse as they walked in silence up Tenth Avenue, her courage surging as she noticed a parked car with a Hero Houdini sticker on the bumper. Trying to figure all the angles should it become necessary to defend herself against this insane butcher, while hoping to make those contingencies unnecessary by seizing control of the situation the second she got him alone.

Still not a word between them as they walked around the corner on 49th Street and entered a building a little nicer than most in the neighborhood. Rode the elevator to his sister's fourth floor apartment, making her think back to the thrill of killing Wilton Millcross in the privacy of his foyer. Uninterrupted. Able to take her time before putting him down. Able to revel in the aftermath. And now Jimmy Callan was offering her similar seclusion, where he would take his place in the history books as the Houdini Killer's final victim. After which, Evie Eastway would hail a taxi back to the East Village to enjoy forever and always with the man of her dreams.

A half-eaten plate of tuna casserole and a glass of wine were on the table as if someone had left in a hurry. Callan told Evie to wait while he disappeared into the bedroom, returning a moment later with a banded stack of hundred dollar bills that he dropped onto the glass coffee table where Rino Reale had cut lines of blow moments before losing his head.

"There's your money. Now tell me who the Houdini Killer is, and where he is."

Evie reached into her purse and pulled out her gun.

"You fucking bitch! You're ripping me off?" He was furious, but more so with himself for allowing her to lure him into a trap. "You used that whole line of bullshit to set me up for a robbery?"

"I'm not robbing you, Jimmy."

"Coulda fooled me."

"I never had any intention of taking your money." She picked up the stack of bills with her free hand and gave it a closer look, then dropped the bundle into her purse. "But things change when they become real. Talking about this kind of money is one thing, but when you actually touch it and when you smell it, it becomes something altogether different. And a girl can accomplish a lot when she has $25,000 tucked away for a rainy day."

"You won't live to spend a penny of it."

"You held up your end of the deal, which quite frankly surprised the hell out of me, and now I've held up mine."

"What the fuck are you talking about? The deal was that you put me face to face with the Houdini Killer."

"This is a nine-millimeter Smith & Wesson automatic."

"That supposed to mean something?"

"Danny Doyle's nine-millimeter Smith & Wesson automatic."

"You telling me *you're* the Houdini Killer? Don't make me laugh."

"Suit yourself. But this is going to play out the same way whether you believe me or not."

"You really expect me to believe that *you* killed Danny?"

"I was walking toward Tenth Avenue to catch a cab when he came up to me and pretended to be lost, and before I knew it he had one hand over my mouth and the other up my dress. I fought back, and that's when he punched the brick wall and got so angry that he pulled this gun."

"And I'm supposed to believe you took it away from him?"

"He's dead, isn't he?"

"So, why kill me? You already have the money."

"This was never about the money."

"Bullshit. What's more important than money?"

"One last headline that will guarantee the fairy tale ending that every little girl dreams about."

"What kind of crazy shit is that? I don't get it."

"A guy like you never could. Goodbye, Jimmy."

Evie steadied the nine-millimeter with both hands, as it would be the last time she would ever fire a gun and she wanted the shot to be perfect.

"Drop it, bitch," yelled Mickey Feeney as he charged out of the bedroom with a thirty-eight pointed at her head.

Evie stood her ground. A Mexican standoff, with her gun on Callan and Mickey's aimed at her.

"If you don't drop it by the time I count three, I'll put a fucking bullet in your head," threatened Mickey, hoping for the latter as he really wanted to kill her. "One …"

Before he got to two, the apartment door was kicked open and two men with guns of their own were on them in a blink. One aimed at Callan and one at Mickey. Mickey's still aimed at Evie while hers remained trained on the Irishman.

"Who the hell are you?" one of the gunmen demanded of Evie.

"Who the hell are *you*?"

"Back away, lady. I don't know what your beef is with this creep, but we were hired to take him out so he's ours now. Walk away while you still can."

She didn't budge, adrenaline giving her the nerve to stand her ground. But with Mickey's gun still aimed at her head, there was not much else she could do.

"Did you really think we were going to let you get away with whacking Rino?" the other hitmen asked Callan.

"I didn't kill Rino."

"All you had to do was talk to the bosses and they would have set you straight that none of the Gambinos had anything to do with whacking your man Doyle and it would have been business as usual. But like the hot-headed Mick you are, you had to fuck up a good thing and now you and your crew are gonna lose it all. Because after we kill you, the Gambinos are gonna take control of the docks plus everything else in this shithole neighborhood."

"Fuck you, you guinnea prick," snarled Mickey as he turned his thirty-eight in the direction of the hitman.

"What was that? I didn't quite catch it."

"I said that if you spaghetti bending half-jig Gambino moth-erfuckers don't get out of this apartment right now, you are fucking dead."

"That's what I thought you said," he replied calmly, then blasted three to Mickey's chest before he could get off a shot.

The wine and casserole went flying as Callan pushed over and ducked behind the table as Evie dove for cover behind the couch. Since she had a gun, the hitmen needed to kill her before they could get near the unarmed Irishman, so they separated and came at her from both sides. In a panic, she fired at the one closest to her, hitting him in the shoulder but the slug did not slow him down. Again, she fired, a gut shot that ignited a fury in his eyes as he continued toward her until a third shot dropped him right in front of her. Then two quick shots in the other direction went wide as the second hitman scrambled out of the line of fire, partially obscuring himself beside a bookcase. The entire shootout had taken less than five seconds, and now an eerie silence enveloped the room as Evie cautiously peeked out over the back of the couch and surveyed the aftermath. Mickey Feeney leaking blood all over the carpet while the remaining hitman eyed Callan's position like a lion drooling over a zebra sandwich. But first the girl.

Who was this girl, the hitman wondered? What could Callan have done to piss her off enough that she would want to kill him? Why didn't she take a powder when they gave her the chance, instead of making a mess of what should have been a nice clean job where he was now forced to eliminate her in order to get a clear path at the man he had been con-tracted to kill. A lot of guys in his line of work didn't like to kill women, but he loved it. Got off on it. Always felt a jolt of excitement shoot up his spine that he never got from putting down a man. A prison psychiatrist once told him that it had something to do with the thrill he had gotten from choking the life out of his mother when he was fourteen.

Evie knew that she would not get out of the apartment alive unless she became proactive. There was no trick to walking up behind a skinhead on a dark street or luring a horny drug dealer to a secluded area of a park, but how could she put a hole in a professional killer before he put a hole in her? Needed to take advantage of being behind the couch where he could not see her, and make her way to the other end where she would have a clean line of sight. But to accomplish this, Evie would be forced to crawl over the body of the dead

Gambino. Face to face with the dead man. The front of her body pressing against the front of his, blood smearing on her shirt as she slithered slowly over him toward the other end of the couch.

To aim and fire she would have to partially expose herself, but since her target probably assumed that she was still at the other end, would be able to get her shot off before he could make the adjustment. She readied herself, steadied her breathing and prepared to make her move. Then in a fluid motion, rose to her knees and squeezed the trigger just as the man who she thought was dead grabbed her by the collar and pulled her down. Grappling with Evie as his partner dashed across the room and stood over them with his gun inches from her head, but just as he fired, she managed to shield herself behind the man who would not die. Who finally did die, the bullet meant for Evie shattering his skull as she returned fire and shot the second Gambino dead, only to see Jimmy Callan racing toward her with a butcher knife in his hand. But he skidded to a halt as he faced her nine-millimeter.

Rock beats scissors. Paper beats rock. Gun beats knife. Evie laughed the laugh of a winner as it was finally over.

"Goodbye, Jimmy. This time for real."

She smiled as her finger squeezed the trigger.

CLICK.

Callan's eyes lit up. Bloodlust electrified as he stepped toward her, taunting her with the blade as she scrambled to her feet and backpedaled until she was against the bookcase with nowhere to run. All because she had lost count amid the chaos and tried to kill a psycho with an empty gun. She punched and kicked for all she was worth, but he was too powerful as his weight pinned her to the carpet. Still she continued to fight until he clocked her with a whack that knocked off her baseball cap. Laughed at her asymmetrical hairstyle and hacked off a fistful of brown locks to even it out, then with the tip of the razor-sharp blade he popped the top button off her shirt. Then the next and the next until there were none. He sliced off her bra and flicked the blade back and forth across her nipples. "I'm a very attentive lover, little mouse, so I guarantee there will be lots of foreplay."

Totally defenseless, Evie's brain struggled to suffocate the thought of being sexually violated with a butcher knife.

"I'll start with your fingers. One at a time. And this knife is so sharp it will slice through the knuckle joints so cleanly that you won't even feel it," he laughed as he pressed the cold steel blade flat against her cheek and slowly moved it upward until the razor-sharp point was a blink away from her eye. And as he held it there, explained to Evie in great detail exactly how he was going to dissect the rest of her. "And you know what the best thing about all this is? I'm going to cut you up while you're still alive, because I don't want you to miss one second of the fun."

Evie's eyes screamed in terror.

"You like the Rolling Stones?" Callan asked as he looked at the bookcase towering above them that also shelved dozens of LPs. "I think the singer's a queer, but my sister has all their records. She has lots of other stuff too. But it's your party, so tell me what kind of music you like."

Evie refused to give him the satisfaction of playing his sadistic game.

"Nothing to say? Not even one of your wiseass comments? Or maybe it's that you don't like music. Doesn't matter, the records were just to drown out your screams. But I suppose I can just as easily cut out your tongue." Then struck by inspiration, he said, "Hey, I got an idea. Maybe I'll reassemble you with the pieces in the wrong place like a Picasso painting. Then instead of being dumped in the drink off Ward's Island, you might end up in the Museum of Modern Art."

Finally, Evie had the answer to the question she had wondered about so many times when she had held a gun on someone. Finally understood what people thought about when they realized that they were about to die. She knew that she should be thinking of Tom, and she was, but her absolute final thought would be that she did not want to suffer. A silent plea that the end of her life would come quickly. That she would not have to endure the pain of being sexually tortured and cut into pieces. That somehow the sadistic Irishman would grant her a merciful exit by slitting her throat or driving the blade into her heart. But one look at the fire in that crazy motherfucker's eyes told her that she did not have a prayer. That any power of salvation resided within, so she summoned all of her remaining strength and jerked her body to the left, then to the right, then back and forth as hard and as fast as she could, trying to free herself from the lunatic who had her pinned to the floor. Igniting a resurgence of power as she thrashed wildly, wriggling her arms and legs in a way that kept her thrusting seemingly in both directions at the same time.

As Callan struggled to restrain her, Evie fought with all she had and was able to eventually free one arm and punch him in the face. Sending him into a rage where with both hands he raised the knife above his head then with all his strength thrust it downward, but Evie again jerked her body sideways just out of the way of the blade that sliced through the carpet and became deeply embedded in the wood floor beneath. As Callan strained to pull it out, Evie scrambled to her feet and yanked down the bookcase, crashing the heavy wooden shelves full of books and records on top of the crazed Irishman who let out a blood curdling roar as he attempted to free himself. On his knees grabbing for Evie, she kicked him in the face and knocked him out. Grabbed her purse and her gun and ran out of the apartment. Raced past the elevator, down the stairs and into the street. Holding her shirt closed with one hand as she flagged down a taxi with the other.

CHAPTER 46

Tom had settled into a comfortable living room chair with his new book of Bukowski poems, but before cracking it open he took a moment to enjoy the silence. Between falling in love and the non-stop responsibilities of running the task force, it had been several weeks since he had been allowed an evening to take a step back from the world and totally decompress. A personal indulgence he suddenly realized just how much he had missed.

Tom missed his girlfriend too, as even though he was with her pretty much every moment he was not working they were still at that early point in their relationship where they had not yet wafted down from the clouds to the reality of everyday life. *Out of sight, out of mind.* Tom figured that whoever coined that gem had never been in love, at least not the forever and always variety. *Absence makes the heart grow fonder.* Now there was a wordsmith who knew the score, and it made him think about the novel Evie was writing. Even if she would not tell him what the book was about, an author's superstition he supposed, he knew it would be good because she was a good writer. Something he had come to understand even before the piece in *Undercurrent*, from reading some of her other stories that had garnered rejection letters. He knew that rejection did not necessarily mean the work wasn't good, just that it was not a fit for that particular publisher at that particular time. He also knew that Evie was driven toward greatness, and that eventually her work would improve to the point where it would be impossible for publishers to ignore.

Tom enjoyed reading about the personal lives of great writers almost as much as the words they wrote, fascinated by the various facets of life that inspired their artistic direction. As for Charles Bukowski, there was something in particular about his lifestyle that held a certain attraction for Tom. Not that he wanted to spend his life guzzling rotgut and sleeping wherever he happened to pass out, but he admired a man who, even with less than sufficient means, was able to do pretty much whatever he wanted whenever he wanted. Which made him think about how amazing it would be to live an uncomplicated life with the woman he loved in the seclusion of a place like Blue Mountain Lake where their only responsibilities would be only to each other. But every time he thought about disappearing with Evie to a world all their own, Tom quickly realized that such an existence was an impossible dream as dedication to his job would never allow it. A job that consumed most every other aspect of his life as well, including his ability to step back from the world and decompress as he could not get the girl from the pawn shop out of his mind.

He placed the book of poetry on the coffee table and picked up the sketch, looking at the girl's face for the umpteenth time. Assessing each facial feature separately then in composite, not just sure that he had seen her somewhere, he was positive that he knew her or had at least spoken with her. But where and when he did not know, and it bothered him as he took a great deal of pride in being good with faces yet could not place her. A face that was fresh in his mind, or at least fairly fresh, and he thought of all the places he had recently been where he might have seen her or spoken with her. But who could remember everywhere they had been in the past couple days, let alone the past couple weeks or months. He might have given her his seat on the subway or maybe she was the waitress who served his lunch three weeks ago last Tuesday. Trying to remember seemed hopeless, but that just made it more of a challenge. He reread the personal information at the bottom of the sketch. Caucasian. Five-feet four. One hundred fifteen pounds. Blond hair. Blue eyes.

Eyes were windows to the soul when painted by masters whose work was exhibited in museums, but unfortunately not when sketched in charcoal by a police artist. Tom needed to capture what was behind those eyes, and dialed the number of Detective Ben Bassham and asked if there was a close-up image of the girl on the pawn shop security video. No dice, as he was told that the tapes were recorded over daily. That's when Tom realized there was no way that particular pawn shop had been the first place this girl had looked for Stoney's lighter. That logically, she would have started her search near where the old man had been killed and worked her way uptown. He made another call.

"Berto. First thing in the morning, I want you to collect the security tapes from the day of the Webb killing from every pawn shop in the city below 47th Street." He listened a moment. "That's right. And put as many men on it as you need so that we get those tapes before they're erased."

Tom looked again at the sketch, this time thinking that something wasn't quite right. Could the hair be different? With his hand, he covered the blond curls and tried to imagine her with a different style. Even though nothing clicked, he felt himself closing in on the answer. Cut a sheet of typing paper and placed it over the sketch to cover the hair. Took a pencil and drew a shag cut. Not her. He cut more paper and drew long straight hair. Nope. Drew an upsweep, drew pigtails, drew bangs. Nope. Nope. Wait a minute. He shaded the bangs thicker, then darker. It was her. An exact image of the girl who would lead him to the Houdini Killer. So close to the career-making arrest he could taste it, until frustration squeezed his brain even harder when he realized that he still could not place her. He looked at a framed citation for Meritorious Police Duty that hung on the wall above his stereo. An award he was particularly proud of because it had been earned using his mind and not his gun, but if he was so smart, why could he not identify this girl who had dark bangs when he met her? A girl whose picture he held in his hand. A girl he could remember but not place. He looked again at his award. Forcing himself to think. Award? Award! His mind jetted back several weeks to the bar where he had showed Evie and her friend the pool trophies he had won. A friend who demonstrated that she shot a pretty good stick herself by beating him at a game of eight ball.

"MANDA!" he yelled, calling out her name with the gusto of a prospector yelling *Eureka*. The girl in the police sketch was Evie's friend Manda.

Tom had only met her once but knew that she sold records at Bleecker Bob's, enough to be confident that he would have Manda in custody in no time flat. But what about Evie? The sweet girl with the crooked smile that, not twenty-four hours ago, he had felt guilty for even suspecting, and who now seemed to be in this up to her pretty neck. Or was she? Her connection was still circumstantial. Or so he tried to convince himself.

He got up and walked to the window holding the pair of high-powered binoculars he had used during the stakeout on West 26th Street. Aimed at Evie's apartment but with the lights off he could not see inside, so he took a peek into the lives of a few of her neighbors. Became interested in an elderly couple dancing the tango in their pajamas and a man shaking his fist at his television as he watched the news, quickly understanding how addicting it was to trespass into the lives of people who did not know that they were being watched. Not an invasion of privacy, but more the acceptance of an invitation because in New York City there was no privacy.

He went into the kitchen to get himself a beer, returned to the window and saw Evie's lights switch on. Through sharp focus he watched as his girlfriend locked the door and double-checked it, then noticed that her shirt was stained and hanging open. Watched as she passed through the apartment to her bedroom, where she stood on a chair and unscrewed the cover of the air vent above her closet. Then his voyeurism was interrupted by the beeping of his pager.

Tom put down the binoculars and checked the number on the display. Went to the phone and dialed. Then tensed as he listened.

"I'll be right there."

CHAPTER 47

"Jimmy Callan is not the Houdini Killer," said Tom, pacing in front of his boss' desk as they prepped for a news conference that was scheduled to take place shortly in the media room at City Hall.

"You're about to tell the world that he is."

"Based on what evidence? All we know for sure about the massacre last night is that Callan was in the murder apartment. His sister's apartment, which means that he had every right to be there."

"Callan's guilty, Tom." Leather creaking as the commissioner leaned back in his chair, very pleased with how the situation was playing out. "And even if he isn't, consider it justice for all the people he *has* killed."

Tom was not yet willing to share the fact that by the end of the day he would have the girl from the pawn shop in custody, and that the rest of the dominos would quickly fall. And that they would fall on his girlfriend. Love had blinded him into believing that Evie's connection to Manda, to Richard Hansen and to Stoney were nothing more than circumstantial, but the blood bath in the Callan apartment just one night after he had told her all about him was one coincidence too many. This sweet girl, whose naiveté from being raised in New Jersey had yet to completely wear off, had not only gunned down ten people on the streets of New York City, she possessed the mettle to survive a gun battle with two Mafia hitmen then escape the knife attack of a man more dangerous than either of them. The mountain of damning evidence could no longer be denied, and the time had come for Tom Vaught to accept the fact that Evie Eastway was the Houdini Killer. Leaving him to make the impossible choice between love and duty.

"I don't get it, Tom. Why are you defending a suspect that you yourself were building a case against?"

"It was just a theory with no evidence to support it. And now that Callan has been arrested, we still don't have any evidence."

"We have our man."

"A man we can't tie him to the Houdini gun because we don't *have* the Houdini gun. Which means that there will be enough holes in the indictment that any first-year night court attorney could drive a truck through them."

"That's the D.A.'s problem."

"No, Commissioner. That's our problem. Because the only thing worse than not being able to arrest the Houdini Killer would be if we were exposed for charging the wrong person. The public would crucify us."

"What the public needs is for Callan to go down for this."

"The Houdini Killer has become so popular that it might be difficult to seat a jury that would convict him."

"No matter what their bias, it will be very easy for the prosecutor to make them hate Jimmy Callan."

"And what if he can't? Prior bad acts are not admissible in court, and on the flimsy circumstantial evidence we have, there is no way he can be proven guilty beyond a reasonable doubt and he'll go free. Are you prepared for that, Commissioner?"

"I can assure you that it will never come to that, because Callan would not be the first man to prove his guilt by hanging himself in his cell. Which would provide the closure that this city and this department so desperately need."

"Have you considered that because we don't have the gun, the real Houdini Killer could knock off someone else while Callan is in custody? And if that happens, I wouldn't give two cents for either of our careers."

"I'm not saying that you are, but let's say for a second that you're right about all of this. He won't kill again because he'll have gotten away with it. The killings will stop and the city will once again be safe. Case closed."

"We can't prosecute an innocent man."

"Why are you continuing to be so damned obstinate? Do you know something that you're not telling me?"

"It's a simple issue of morality."

"Oh, for fuck sake, Tom. You know damn well that Jimmy Callan is an animal, and even though we may not have him for the right crimes, we sure as hell have him for the right reasons."

Tom thought of Busha. Finally understanding that the woman who had not set foot outside the East Village in sixty years was indeed wise to the ways of the world when she told him that if he wanted to have it both ways, he must be willing to go against what he believed in and do whatever it takes.

"He's killed a lot of people, Tom, and we are going to make sure that one way or another he finally pays the price. Give your conscience the day off and enjoy the fact that you're a hero," said the commissioner with a wide smile as he rose from his chair and straightened his tie. "Now let's get over to City Hall so you can tell the world how you captured the Houdini Killer. Then afterwards, I'll make you a captain."

"If I'm going to sacrifice every principle of integrity that I have ever believed in, it won't be for just a captaincy," Tom told his boss, throwing Callan under the bus by choosing both love and duty. "You're going to promote me to inspector."

CHAPTER 48

Two hot showers had done little to melt away the obscenity of being brutalized, and Evie cringed at the ghastly image she faced in the bathroom mirror. Yellowing bruises on her arms, cuts on her chest and hair that looked on one side as if it had been chewed off by a raccoon. No newspapers and no radio, as she did not want to relive the horror of walking into a nest of vipers with little more than a cocky attitude.

With no desire to face the outside world, Evie phoned one of the other bartenders to cover her shift at Jamesey's then sat on the couch with her book of Raymond Carver stories. But the words were little more than a blur, so she got up and turned on the television so that she would not be alone. Feeling pity for overly exuberant game show contestants competing to win a trip to Disneyland as they would never again experience a thrill such as they were realizing at that moment, which put into focus the fantastic life that she had to look forward to. With the Houdini Killer *finally* retired, there would be nothing to come between she and Tom and the endless possibilities of forever and always. Tom? Tom! All of a sudden, there he was on television, the game show having been pre-empted for a news conference at City Hall. Looking handsome in his pearl gray suit and the blue checked tie she had bought him one afternoon when they were browsing at Barney's as he stood at the podium beside the mayor and the police commissioner. She turned up the volume and stood in front of the television as Mayor Beame began to address the reporters.

> Good morning, ladies and gentlemen. I stand before you, proud to announce that through the tireless around the clock efforts of our fine New York City police department, the Houdini Killer has been arrested.

"WHAT?!" Evie screamed, watching as reporters shouted questions despite the mayor holding up his hands motioning for quiet.

It took a while for order to be restored, then hizzoner capitalized on the moment by goosing his reelection bid with a protracted spiel about how his administration had made the city safe again. After which he finally relinquished the microphone.

> Lieutenant Thomas Vaught, commander of the task force that brought the notorious Houdini Killer to justice, will fill you in on the details, then take your questions.

"Who the hell did you arrest?" she yelled at the television.

> James Callan, reputed leader of the west side criminal organization known as the Westies, has been arrested and is scheduled to be arraigned this afternoon on eleven counts of murder in the first degree, putting an end to the reign of terror that had become known as the Houdini killings. Mr. Callan was apprehended last night following a shootout in an apartment on West 49th Street that resulted in the death of his second in command Michael Feeney as well as Joseph Parilli and Marco Sodini, two members of the Gambino crime family. Right now, we are still processing evidence, and I hope to issue a statement with more information later this afternoon.

Evie was stunned. Her mouth literally hanging open as she watched her boyfriend field questions rapid-fired by a throng of reporters demanding details.

> Tell us, Lieutenant. Since Callan is the leader of the Westies, does that mean that all of the Houdini killings were gang related?

> The Gambino killings appear to be organized crime related, but beyond that, it's too early to know anything for certain.

> Have you recovered the nine-millimeter automatic that was used in the killings?

I'm not at liberty to share specifics of the case at this time. And as I said, I will be issuing a statement with further details later this afternoon.

As Evie watched Tom continue to tap dance around questions he could not satisfactorily answer, she could not understand why in the world he had made this arrest. Tom couldn't really believe that Callan was Houdini. Could he? Based upon what? His half-baked theory that Houdini was a hitman who had done a job for Callan? Because if that were true, Callan could not possibly be the Houdini Killer. Tom was too good a policeman to make this arrest, so why had he? The police didn't have the murder weapon or any other evidence of consequence, meaning that there was a very distinct possibility that Callan could beat the rap at trial. And if that happened, Tom would not be able to pick up the pieces of his shattered ambition even as a security guard at the White Castle under the subway tracks in Queens. So, Evie decided to make the case against Callan airtight by going back to the building on 49th Street and planting the gun somewhere the police would easily find it. But what if the cops were still lurking about or if she could not get into the building? Then she would simply hide it nearby and phone in an anonymous tip, which would guarantee the asshole Irishman lifetime accommodation at the gray bar hotel while she and Tom lived happily ever after.

Evie cracked a can of Fresca, newly invigorated as she sat at her writing table and looked out at the city as she planned her day. First stop would be an emergency salon drop-in to get her hair fixed, then over to Hell's Kitchen so she could plant the gun. From there a shopping odyssey to gather ingredients and exotic spices for Tom's favorite Indian meal. Maacher jhol was a Bengalese fish stew that she had hoped to someday have enough confidence in her culinary chops to make. And, tonight was the night that she would serve it to her man accompanied by a bottle of Taittinger pink champagne. Better yet, two bottles.

She would wear the yellow polka dot dress she had on that first night when Tom's gentle touch in the kitchen saved the scaloppini and later in the bedroom had rocketed her into outer space. But for chasing around town running errands she put on jeans and a tank top. Unscrewed the air vent cover and removed the nine-millimeter automatic from its hiding place, then out of habit began to reload. Closed up the vent then put the gun in her purse and walked out the door with a spring in her step.

On the way to a salon on First Avenue that she knew took walk-ins, Evie passed by the bodega and waved to Mr. Kim. He saw her but did not wave back which was curious, and as she walked in to see what was up, found that he was being robbed at gunpoint by a man so focused on the money that he did not notice as she entered then ducked into the back aisle. A robbery takes only a few seconds, but to Evie those seconds ticked away like minutes as she watched Mr. Kim hand over the money from the register. The robber's gun hand was shaking, probably a junkie she figured, meaning that he could not be counted upon to grab the money and scram like a normal stick up man. And he did not, instead demanding more cash. Mr. Kim pleaded with him to believe that he had no more, emptying his pockets on the counter to prove it. But the jittery gunman had convinced himself that there was money under the counter or in a safe, and he threatened to blow Mr. Kim's brains out if he did not come across.

As Evie peeked around a display of potato chips, she knew that she could not kill this guy with the Houdini gun when Tom had just gone on television to tell the world that he had arrested the Houdini Killer. But she had to help. Had to do something to save Mr. Kim, the seconds now ticking away like seconds as the jittery gunman had reached the end of his patience. No choice but to take the nine-millimeter from her purse. Aimed and fired, a ringing blast that decapitated a bottle of chocolate milk while scaring the would-be stick up man into the street, leaving the money on the counter and Mr. Kim to live another day.

"You saved me! Evie, you saved my life!" cried out Mr. Kim, who then picked up the phone.

"Wait," she said, all of a sudden realizing that even though she had not killed anyone, the cops would dig her warning shot out of the wall and match the bullet to the Houdini gun. Not right away, as with Jimmy Callan locked up they no longer had reason to rush any ballistics tests, but eventually they would match it.

"Why? I must call the police."

"Please put down the phone. I can't get involved."

"But you must. You are a hero."

"Please, Mr. Kim," Evie begged him, knowing that if he placed that call it would make happily ever after nothing more than another unfulfilled promise made to little girls in fairy tales. "Put the phone down."

"I do not understand. It is my duty to call so the police can arrest him before he tries to rob another store, where the owner might not be so lucky."

"We're friends, right Mr. Kim?"

"After saving my life, you are my best friend."

"Then please understand that I can't get involved, and that the police can never dig that bullet out of the wall. I can't tell you why, but I'm begging you to trust me."

"But why …"

"I'll pay you not to call the police. Name your price." She needed to wrap this up quickly, before he started blabbing to any customers who might walk in. "Use the money to buy a new car or start a college fund for your granddaughter."

"I do not want your money. You are not making sense."

"I saved your life. Don't you owe me something for that?"

"I owe you everything, Evie. That is why I must do the right thing and call the police."

"I'll go to jail if the police find that bullet."

"Do not be silly, Evie. You had every right to shoot at the robber."

"For the last time, Mr. Kim," she begged while keeping one eye on the door. "Please put down that phone."

"What you say does not make sense to me."

Evie knew there were other methods of trying to make the storekeeper understand, but there was no time.

"Evie, no!"

"I'm sorry, Mr. Kim."

"But why? You are my friend."

The bullet ripped through his neck, and Evie was out the door before he hit the floor. An innocent man murdered to keep him from identifying her to the police. A nice man. A man with a family. But also, a stupid man who had refused to put down the phone. A man who had been given every opportunity to live, but in obstinacy had chosen death, allowing her to dismiss the shooting as a necessary transaction. Her only problem now was how to get Tom out of the corner those two bullets had just painted him into.

CHAPTER 49

Retreating home to regroup, Evie plopped down on the couch and scratched her fingers back and forth through mutilated hair. Taking a moment to decompress as she came up with a slight variation of the original plan that would offer a somewhat plausible explanation of how the Houdini gun could have been used to kill Mr. Kim while Jimmy Callan was in jail. Satisfied that it would work, she was now ready to proceed with the day as originally planned. Salon, Hell's Kitchen, then shopping for exotic spices and pink champagne.

"I have a hard time believing that a girl who's scared to death of ants had the guts to murder eleven people."

Startled, Evie turned to see Tom walking out of the bedroom with her journal in his hand. Behind him the air vent cover was off and the box of ammunition and Stoney's lighter were on her bed. Unprepared for this moment because Evie had been positive that this moment would never come. Wishing that she had paid more attention all those times Stoney had told her to not be so cocky, though right now being cocky was her only play.

"How much did you read?"

"Every word."

"But you've known the truth for a while, haven't you Tommy? That's why to protect me you went against everything you ever believed in by standing in front of those TV cameras and announcing the arrest of somebody else."

"With a nudge from the commissioner, but yes."

"Which proves just how much you love me, Tommy," she said, then patted the cushion beside her, inviting him to sit. "You've had a hard day. Let me take off your shoes and put on some music so you can relax. I've got a few errands to run, then I'll come back and make your favorite Indian meal."

"Just like that? I'm supposed to kick back like none of this ever happened?" Tom gave her a curious look, then as he leaned closer and smelled the gun shot residue on her hand his expression sank. "Please, Evie. Please tell me you didn't kill somebody *after* I announced the arrest of Jimmy Callan."

"I didn't plan to. It just sort of happened."

"How the hell does murder just *sort of* happen?" He went to the kitchen and opened a beer, but was too angry to drink it. Then chugged half of it as he was too demoralized not to, as everything he had worked so hard for the past ten years was about to go down the toilet. "After making such a big show of locking up the wrong person, if I'm not fired, I'll end up walking a beat on Staten Island. And God forbid it ever comes out that the real Houdini Killer is my girlfriend, I'll be sitting in the cell next to yours. A decorated fourth generation New York City cop, the young hot shot who was going all the way to the top, arrested as an accessory to eleven murders."

"Mr. Kim makes an even dozen."

"You killed the man at the bodega because his coffee sucks?"

"Relax, Tommy. I can fix this."

"How the hell are you going to fix it? However this plays out I'll be ruined."

"I can make it all go away by planting the Houdini gun at the 596 Club and phoning in an anonymous tip, leading to the reasonable conclusion that whoever removed Callan's gun from the murder apartment used it in a robbery gone bad at the bodega before stashing it at the bar. A bar that's a known Westies hangout, which makes the scenario just believable enough to slap a guilty verdict on Jimmy Callan, the man police are already eager to railroad into eleven life sentences at the expense of the truth."

"Cover ups always backfire, Evie. Especially ones as flimsy as that."

"I'm giving you a way out, Tommy. It may not be the best plan, but right now it's all you've got."

"It's too big a stretch. Nobody's ever going to believe it."

"The commissioner will believe it. The mayor will believe it. With an election coming up, it's pretty obvious that right now they are both on the hook for this just as much as you are."

Tom knew she was right. But he also knew that if the Callan arrest blew up in their faces, the fat cats would save their own asses by hanging him out to dry as the person solely responsible.

"I guess I have no choice, Evie. If we do it your way at least I'll have a chance."

"I knew you'd see the light," she smiled, confident now that nothing stood in their way. "Do you remember how great it was up at Blue Mountain Lake? We can live in the Adirondacks or on a beach somewhere. We could go to New

Orleans and eat jambalaya every day. You told me that we were going to go everywhere. This is our chance."

"You expect me to quit my job and hit the road? Just like that?"

"Just like that." She tousled her butchered hair. "You haven't said anything about my new look."

"The rest of your hair is at the police lab, along with your fingerprints from Callan's sister's apartment."

"Which they can't connect to me because I've never been fingerprinted."

"If they expose the cover up they'll come looking for us, and they'll find us no matter where we are."

"To expose the cover up they would have to suspect a cover up, which they won't because once they're pointed in the right direction they will come to the necessary conclusion on their own and the case will be closed." She hit him with the same sparkling smile that captured his heart at the Blue Mountain Lake. "You can take early retirement as the hero who captured the Houdini Killer, then we can leave town without ever having to look over our shoulders. All that's left to do is decide where we're going to go."

"My life is in New York."

"I'm your life now."

"What about Busha?"

"When real love turns your life upside down you have no choice but to roll with it."

"So, you're saying that the only way we can be together is if I quit my job and leave everything behind?"

"That's right."

"Then I'll say that the only way we can be together is if you stop killing people."

"I will, Tommy."

"We both know that's a promise you can't keep."

"I *will* stop."

"I read the journal, Evie. You wrote in very glowing terms how you're addicted to murder. The thrill you get watching the light go out of your victims' eyes."

"That's not all I wrote."

Evie picked up the journal and flipped through the pages until she found the passages she was looking for. A heartfelt sweetness in her voice as she began to read.

"I have received closure after all. Not only for losing Stoney but for the spectacular, yet short lived, career of the Houdini Killer …. Finally, it's time to begin writing my novel, while devoting the remaining hours of every day to pleasing a man who is both charming and handsome. Virile, urbane and can always be counted upon to do the impossible ….. The combination of sex and love I get from Tommy sends me further into orbit than a dozen Millcrosses or Black Widows ever could. And I'm going to spend every minute I'm not sitting at my Smith Corona making my man as happy as he makes me." She dropped the journal on the table and kissed Tom like she had never kissed him before. "I've kicked the habit. You have to believe me when I tell you that the only thing I'm addicted to now is you."

So much so quickly and Tom did not know what to think. Opened a window, lungs filling with urban scuz that hung heavy in the air even though he was eleven floors above the hustle and flow. As if for the first time noticing the garbage and the grime to which a lifetime in New York had made him immune. Defenseless against a cacophony of traffic, sirens and the general din of a city bursting at the seams. Where was the peace? Where was the serenity that allowed a person's thoughts to nurture and blossom? That's when he turned to Evie and said, "I might be able to get used to the idea of living on a beach."

"OH, TOMMY!" She sprang from the couch and threw her arms around him, squeezing as hard as she could.

"Or maybe be the sheriff of some sleepy little town."

"Like Mayberry?"

"Why not?"

"Where I can write books, and have your dinner on the table promptly at seven."

"Or maybe eight, so we can prepare it together."

"Are you sure, Tommy? Reinventing ourselves in a place where we can enjoy a life of just being together sounds like a dream, but there would be no turning back. Are you sure you could walk away from your job and the future you've planned for so long?"

"For a while I've been disillusioned with both the commissioner and department politics. And after what's happened the past few weeks, I'm not sure that I want to be part of it anymore."

"You wouldn't miss it?"

"The reason I became a policeman in the first place was so that I could make a positive difference in peoples' lives, but working out of an office at One PP, I don't see how that's ever going to happen. But in a small town I could actually get to know the people and dedicate myself to serving them on an individual basis."

"In a small town, there's no chance for advancement."

Evie watched closely as he considered what she had said, and saw that a bit of the enthusiasm had gone from his eyes.

Tom finished his beer then went into the kitchen for another. When he came back, Evie's gun was pointed at him.

"We've been kidding ourselves, Tommy. I love you with all my heart, but it's a dream that can't possibly come true. Not for long anyway, because you're too dedicated to your work here. You might not realize it at this moment, but you would rather change what's wrong with the department than turn your back on it. Being a New York City cop is in your blood, just like you told me on our first date at that Indian restaurant on 6th Street. And, no matter what the consequences, we both know that eventually your conscience would demand that you arrest me."

"I would never turn against you."

"Maybe not. But you would definitely come to resent me for making you give up your career."

"I've thought a lot lately about how amazing it would be to leave the city and start a new life with you, someplace quiet and uncomplicated where our only responsibilities would be to each other."

"Then why is this the first time I'm hearing about it?"

"Because then it was an impossible dream that my job wouldn't allow."

"It wasn't your job, Tommy. It was your ambition."

"I have never been more certain of anything, Evie, so believe me when I tell you that right now all I want is to leave this city behind and create a new life with you."

"I want to believe you, Tommy, but this is a life-changing decision and you made it too quickly. A few minutes ago, you were worried about losing your job and now you're ready to chuck it and walk away? We wouldn't get ten miles out of town before you would turn around and come back."

"You were right when you said that when real love turns your life upside down you have no choice but to roll with it. I'm willing to do whatever it takes for us to be together."

"Even though killing is in *my* blood? Vowing to give it up was a life-changing decision that *I* made too quickly, and one day I'll resent you for making me try. And that would put us right back in the same situation we're in right now." She smiled. It was a sad smile. "Besides, how many Indian restaurants are there in Mayberry?"

"One minute you tell me that you're my life now and the next minute you're ready to turn your back on our future? I don't get it, Evie. You either love me or you don't. Which is it?"

"I love you with all my heart, Tommy. Do you remember the first time we had sex together?"

He smiled.

"And do you also remember the joke you told me afterward?"

"I do."

"Tell me again."

"How many Polacks does it take to screw in a lightbulb?"

"I don't know," she smiled. "But I do know how many handsome Polish policemen it takes to screw Evie Eastway."

The bullet went straight through his heart.

No orgasm. Not even a ripple of physical pleasure as Evie stood over her dead lover. Her only satisfaction was knowing that his final thought had been a happy thought.

Evie packed a duffle bag with the bare essentials needed to begin a new life. A few clothes and toiletries. Gun, ammo, journal and Jimmy Callan's $25,000. Also, the found wallet that she had figured would probably come in handy one day. She liked the name Carol Caldwell.

CHAPTER 50

The police always worked harder to catch a killer when the victim was one of their own, and as her bus chugged across the George Washington Bridge toward New Jersey, Evie was preparing for the challenge. Confident that she had plenty of time to put distance between herself and her pursuers as Tom's body, locked inside her apartment, would probably not be found for at least a day or two.

Her purse and duffle bag on the seat beside her, she plotted a zig-zagging trail of misdirection that would first lead the police south to Philadelphia where she would use her own name to check into a hotel. She would mail Stoney's lighter to Nanette, get her hair cut then take a bus up to Newark, chatting with the driver to make sure he remembered her. A taxi to the train station where she would make sure to call attention to herself while purchasing a one-way ticket north to Buffalo, where police would assume that she had crossed the border and disappeared into Canada. Meanwhile, Carol Caldwell will have dyed her hair red, paid cash for a car and aimed it toward the beaches of sunny California. But first she had a stop to make.

"Evie!"

"Sorry I didn't call first, Mom, but it's been a crazy day."

"Don't be silly. Come in," said Maxine as she welcomed her daughter, then noticed the duffle bag. "Are you going somewhere or did you bring me your dirty laundry?"

"No laundry, Mom." Evie felt a bit light headed as she set the bag on the floor in the entryway, suddenly realizing that she had not eaten all day. "But would you mind making me a sandwich?"

"Turkey, Swiss cheese and cranberry sauce on toast. Just like I used to make for you after school," Maxine smiled as she led her daughter into the kitchen. "What would you like to drink?"

"How about a cold glass of milk, just like after school." Evie sat down and hung her purse on the back of the chair. Glad that she had stopped at home. One of the first places the police would look, but feeling that she had a big enough head start that it was worth the risk to see her mother who she loved so much.

Mother and daughter chatted at the kitchen table for the better part of an hour. What a shame it was about Elvis, the new fall TV season and the Star Wars movie that neither of them had seen yet. Maxine updating her about Cousin Sue's peanut allergy and how Uncle Joe's Corvette had landed him a girlfriend, while Evie put off telling her mother that this would be goodbye. Forever? She hoped not. But at least for now.

Maxine looked at the clock, then got up and began to rush around the kitchen. "It's been so nice having you here that I lost track of the time. I have to get dinner started."

"It's Thursday. That must mean meatloaf."

"With mashed potatoes and gravy. Will you stay for dinner? Please say you'll stay."

"Whose bag is this?" boomed Marv's voice from the living room.

"It's Evie's," Maxine called back.

"She better not think that she's moving back home," he groused as he entered the kitchen, then looked at his daughter. "You made the decision to waste a good education on that bartending job. You can damn well live with the consequences."

"Nice to see you too, Dad."

"I don't smell meatloaf."

"Dinner's going to be a little late, dear. You see, Evie and I got to talking and ..."

"When I come home from work I expect my dinner to be on the table, not to hear your excuses."

"She's not your slave," Evie snapped at him. "She's your wife. Start treating her with respect."

"What did you just say to me?"

"I said that you've treated her like shit ever since I can remember, and it's finally time that you stop."

"Who the hell are you to come into my house and talk to me like that?"

"I'm your daughter."

"Which does not give you the right to disrespect me."

"Would you say that if I was your son?"

"A son wouldn't be so ungrateful," Marv shot back, not knowing whether to smack her or just throw her out. "Where's this attitude coming from? I've done everything for you."

"And *to* me."

"What's that supposed to mean?"

"Are you really going to make me say it?"

"What the hell are you talking about?"

"Was rape part of my punishment for not being born a boy?"

"Evie!" yelled Maxine. "How can you say such a horrible thing?"

"I don't hear him denying it. Well, Dad? What about it? Do you have the balls to admit that you raped me when I was seven years old?"

"Get me a beer, Maxine."

"Stop ordering her around!"

"Or what, Evie?"

Evie took the nine-millimeter Smith & Wesson automatic from her purse and aimed it at her father.

"EVIE!" screamed Maxine.

"Tell me, Dad. How's your pal Dean Martin? Has Sinatra stopped by the house lately to play a few hands of gin rummy?"

"Where do you get off insulting my business? The business that fed you and clothed you and paid for the braces that straightened your teeth."

"The same business where you forged the autographs on the wall to make yourself look like a big shot to all the housewives who bring in their husbands' shirts." She looked at him disgustedly. "Yet you make Mom wash *your* shirts."

Marv was afraid of the gun but did his best not to show it. Refused to beg for his life. Not in *his* house. The house where he was always in charge and exercised complete control over everyone in it. He just stood defiantly as his daughter continued to unleash a lifetime of pent up hostility.

"I guess it makes sense that instead of having his suits cleaned in Hollywood, Robert Redford would drop them off at Marv Eastway's Star Cleaners in Clifton, New Jersey. Don't you think your hunting buddies know that the number of celebrities who have ever set foot in Clifton is almost zero? But they don't say anything about your bullshit stories because they enjoy watching you make an ass of yourself, then laugh at you behind your back."

"Maxine. I told you to get me a beer."

"Don't do it, Mom." Evie then looked at her father. "I didn't come here to kill you for raping me. In fact, I didn't come here to kill you at all. Just to see the look on your face when you found out that your daughter is the biggest celebrity, the *only* celebrity, to have ever set foot inside Marv Eastway's Star Cleaners. That your daughter is the famous Houdini Killer."

"The Houdini Killer is in jail. Or haven't you heard?"

"Jimmy Callan will be released soon, then the real story of your daughter the Houdini Killer will be all over the news."

"Even if that's true, do you expect me to be proud of the fact that you're a murderer? That just makes you even more of a disappointment to me."

"Doesn't it matter to you that I protect the public by dispensing justice where the courts won't?"

"I gave you every advantage, and you turned out to be nothing but a disgrace."

"There are bumper stickers on cars all over New York City that call me a hero."

"Delusional is what you are."

"You need help, Evie," said Maxine. "A nice rest, maybe in that private hospital over in Passaic."

"*I'm* not paying for it," asserted Marv.

"You know, Dad. I pictured your face on every person that I killed. Every bullet that blew out a man's brains was really meant for you. A fitting payback for how you abused me and continue to abuse my mother." Evie's eyes opened wide as she assumed the stance. The stance her father had taught her that day at the gun range in one of his failed attempts to turn his teenage daughter into a son. "And now I get to kill you for real."

"Put down the gun, Evie."

"No, Mom."

"I mean it, Evie." Maxine's voice deadly serious. "Put down the gun."

"He raped me."

"No, he didn't."

"How can you keep closing your eyes to his abuse? Why do you keep sticking up for him?"

That's when Evie saw that her mother was holding Marv's prized Ithaca shotgun, and that it was aimed directly at her.

"Put down the gun, Evie."

"Stop protecting him," she demanded, the nine-millimeter still pointed at her father. "You know what he did to me. You may not have actually seen him do it, but you cleaned me up afterwards. Held me in your arms for days until I finally stopped crying."

"Your father never touched you, Evie."

"Remember my Barbie? The one with the stewardess uniform?"

"Stop it, Evie."

"He raped me with it! This animal you're married to jammed that doll inside me again and again and again! His helpless seven-year-old daughter!"

"No, he didn't."

"For God sake, Mom. How much more do you have to hear until you finally accept the truth?"

"Complications from giving birth to you prevented me from ever having another child. Prevented me from giving your father a son."

"You make it sound like that was my fault."

"It was your fault, Evie."

"That's insane."

"And because I couldn't give him a son, your father never touched me again."

"As twisted as that logic is, do you really believe it excuses the fact that he raped me?"

"You ruined my marriage, Evie. And for that you had to be punished."

"It was *you*? *You* raped me with my Barbie!" Evie was as horrified as she was confused. "But we were so close. What about all of those mother and daughter trips to the city?"

"When a mother punishes a child, she doesn't stop loving that child."

"You didn't punish me, you *destroyed* me!"

"How does it feel to know that all those men you pictured with my face died for nothing?" Marv laughed, enjoying the moment as he continued to mock her. "Which means that you became a serial killer for nothing. And none of it ever would have happened if you had been born a boy."

A lifetime of belittlement and being treated as if she was incomplete had not destroyed Evie's self-respect, as what had never been allowed to develop could not be destroyed. But a killing spree with vigilante purpose had allowed her to earn that self-respect. Meaning that she had *not* killed for nothing. She took a good look at the man upon whom she would exact her revenge, this time not needing to imagine his face. Her focus on her father crystal clear as she steadied herself and aimed the gun.

The roar of the blast exploded through the kitchen. Buckshot from the Ithaca leaving only a grotesque stump where Evie's head used to be, as her body crashed against the table before dropping to the floor. No chance for a final thought as she never saw it coming.

Maxine put down the shotgun and looked at her daughter's headless corpse sprawled on the cold linoleum, a smile on her face as all she saw was a sweet little girl in white socks and patent leather shoes standing in front of the Palm Court at the Plaza Hotel.

"Hurry up with that beer," Marv ordered his wife.

"Right away, dear."

"And get that meatloaf in the oven, then call the police."

CHAPTER 51

"Will you be in the courtroom later this morning when your wife is expected to plead not guilty by reason of insanity to the charge of murdering your daughter?"

"I will not," Marv told Tom Brokaw on the set of the *Today* show, his first interview of an all-day New York City media blitz. "No father and daughter were ever closer than me and my Evie, and because of what Maxine did I will never see her sweet smile again."

"What do you say about evidence pointing to the fact that Evie murdered all those people so that she could write about the experience?"

"That's a load of baloney. Evie was always inspired by the beauty she found in books, that's why I sent her to Montclair State to study literature. And even after she moved to Manhattan, I continued to encourage my daughter by telling her to quit the bookstore where she worked and take the bartending job at Jamesey's because, as a writer, I felt she would find inspiration interacting with all of the interesting people who patronize the place."

"Yet according to her journal, she instead found that inspiration by killing people on the street."

"The people of New York City called my Evie a hero."

"Can you explain why a hero would murder a New York City police lieutenant in cold blood?"

"That can never be proven. Nothing can ever be proven because Evie never had her day in court."

"Would you have attended her trial?"

"Absolutely. And she never would have been convicted because the public loved her. That's why I'm auctioning all of her possessions, including the journal and even her childhood toys, with a portion of the proceeds going to the general scholarship fund of Montclair State College."

And so it went for the rest of the day. Sodomizing the truth on WABC, WPIX and the local talk shows as Marv Eastway touted the sale of his daughter's belongings, while neglecting to mention that the portion of the proceeds earmarked for Montclair State would be one percent. Then just about the time he was wrapping up his long day of self-promotion on the WNBC news, a few blocks west Jimmy Callan murdered yet another rabbit-eared RCA as Reggie Jackson blasted his third home run of the game to lead the New York Yankees to victory in the World Series.

THE END

ACKNOWLEDGMENTS

Thanks to Sue Campbell for much more than another great book design. To Jim Hogenson, Harry Fagel and Andy Walsh for spot-on technical advice. To Allan Carter for always stepping up. To Scott Dickensheets for aiding and abetting justifiable homicide of the Oxford comma. To Velvet who will always have a special place on the pages I write. To Dirk Vermin—I implore you to get off your ass and finish that book you started. Many thanks to Chantelle Aimee Osman. To Holly West, Travis Richardson, Stephen Buehler, Ginger Bruner, Drew Cohen, Scott Seeley, Amy Prenner, Lance Corralez, Chris Andrasfay, Steve Fahlsing, Louie Thomas and Ally Carter. To James, Staci and Third. To the Bradshaws, the Yorkshire mob, Davey Klubs, Mark T. Zeilman, Bamboo Ben, Geoff Carter, Dayvid Figler, Andrew Kiraly, Jenn O. Cide, Hossy Von Bloodcock, Arpington K. Sampson, Donald Frazer, Porkpie, Rob Gelardi, Richie Rock and Reverend Timmy Bloodcock. I will be grateful always for the leg up given me by Carolyn Uber and Geoff Schumacher. And, last but never least, much love to the irrepressible Tom Vaught who will live forever.

ABOUT THE AUTHOR

PMoss is an author whose books and short stories offer a twisted view of life away from the spotlight. He is a musician and songwriter whose band Bloodcocks UK, the only American band never to play in America, recently returned from a seventh sold out tour of Japan. A bar honcho in Las Vegas and NYC, he is also a film noir and pulp fiction enthusiast. Find out more at **pMoss.com**